THE ORO VERDE

AJ BAILEY ADVENTURE SERIES - BOOK 14

NICHOLAS HARVEY

HarveyBooks LLC

Printed in the United States of America

First Printing, 2023

ISBN-13: 978-1-959627-19-7

Cover design by Wicked Good Book Covers

Cover photographs by Lisa Collins at Capture Cayman

Author photograph by Lift Your Eyes Photography

This is a work of fiction. Names, characters, businesses, places, events and incidents are either the products of the author's imagination or used in a fictitious manner unless noted otherwise. Any resemblance to actual persons, living or dead, or actual events is purely coincidental. Several characters in the story generously gave permission to use their names in a fictional manner.

This book is dedicated to Bob and Suzy Soto.

My wife Cheryl and I have shared a passion for scuba diving which was born from our first underwater adventure together in the Cayman Islands. The father of diving in the Caymans was the late Bob Soto, truly a pioneer and a man I wish I could have met in person.
His effervescent wife, Suzy, was incredibly enthusiastic, patient, and helpful with me as I pestered her for information about her husband, the Oro Verde, and life in the Cayman Islands in the late 70s and early 80s. Thank you, Suzy!

You can find her wonderful book about Bob, called Extraordinary Adventures, from all credible book retailers.

PREFACE

Lord Byron famously wrote "*...for truth is always strange, stranger than fiction.*" And of course he was right. So when an author comes across a story, laced with a handful of truths, then wrapped in rumour and tall tales, the temptation to embellish is irresistible. The *Oro Verde* is indeed a ship, sunk as an artificial reef off the coast of Grand Cayman through the efforts of Bob Soto, as mentioned in this novel. Many of the events and circumstances describing the fate of the OV and her journey to the bottom of the Caribbean Sea are fact, and some are pulled from suspicions, conclusions, and unsupported sea stories told to me by Cayman Island locals, a few of whom were present when the events took place.

The rest is a tale stitched together from my own imagination, following the misfortunes of Raymond Butterworth, a fictional captain of the *Oro Verde*. The *Silvia Azul* is made up. The Seaview Hotel was a very real place, but the resident mentioned in the story is of my own invention, although... some are adamant that an alphabet agency kept rooms at the Seaview for many years.

And that's how this novel came together. Spawned from a comment shared with me by Chris Alpers of Indigo Divers while we bobbed on the water during a surface interval off the west side of Grand Cayman, my research turned up a fact here, a rumour there, with plenty of room for my muse to fill in the gaps. I hope you enjoy the result!

1

Miami - 1976

Despite the early hour, Butty was in a good mood. Unburdening his hold of cargo always felt like progress, and as he piloted the 179-foot freighter, the *Oro Verde,* to the north side of Pier C at the Miami City Docks, he hummed a Pink Floyd tune with a half-smoked Marlboro hanging from his lips.

The OV, as Butty and his crew referred to the old tub, was a former US Army Transportation Corps ship, turned Navy environmental research vessel, now private cargo ship. Bananas from Ecuador to Miami were their bread and butter, and whatever fitted in her hold and needed delivering to the Cristóbal port in Colón, Panama was a return trip bonus. It was a short jaunt from the Banana Supply Company dock on the river to the City Docks in Biscayne Bay, and Butty had the twin 500hp GM Cleveland Division six-cylinder diesel engines just above idle, their low throb rumbling through the steel ship.

He watched several of his ten-man crew scurry along the deck to ready the lines as he slowed, approaching the dock. Ships lined the berths and large cranes were already busy swinging back and forth with bulky crates dangling from sturdy chains. Ten minutes later, with the OV secured to the mooring bollard, and a fresh cigarette pinched between his fingers, Butty trotted down the steps to the deck and waited for Rolando and the first mate, Pepe, to secure the gangway. He chatted to them in Spanish and the three shared a laugh about Felix, the youngest member of the crew, who was still in his bunk after an overindulgent night.

One of the dockmasters strode towards Butty as the Englishman stepped to the concrete dock and extended a hand.

"How's your luck, Santiago?" Butty asked in Spanish.

"I'm quitting jai alai forever, amigo," he replied in heavily accented English, shaking his head. "I'm going back to the ponies."

Butty laughed. "Last month you were quitting the ponies, mate, and jai alai was the only game for you."

Santiago shrugged his shoulders. "I'm not a lucky man, Butty," he said with a crooked grin. "If you saw my wife, you'd know I tell the truth."

Butty laughed again and Santiago crossed himself then touched his fingers to his lips.

"What have you got for me today, mate?" Butty asked.

Santiago shuffled through wads of forms attached to his clip-board as beads of sweat formed on his forehead. It was still early, but the balmy South Florida heat was already rising.

"I got a shipment of tools earmarked for you," Santiago mumbled, searching the manifests. "Here," he declared, pulling several sheets from the stack and somehow gathering up others which flew on the breeze.

"Like spanners and what have you?" Butty asked.

Santiago frowned at him. "Like what the hell did you just say?"

"Wrenches," Butty translated into US English and then repeated it again in Spanish. "You giving me a hold full of wrenches? That's gotta weigh more than the OV itself, mate."

Santiago shook his head. "Nah, you're good, man. A bunch of it is tool chests, and they're big, but not so heavy."

Butty lowered his voice. "They filled with anything I need to know about?"

Santiago paused for a moment and double-checked the company name on the paperwork. "Nah, you're good. But that's a good point. They'd make nice containers for… other stuff."

Butty scoffed. "I don't have the stomach for it, mate," he said, then lowered his voice again. "Least not for both trips."

Santiago laughed and handed the captain his paperwork. "I'll get you loaded here shortly, so don't let your boys wander too far."

"Cheers, mate," Butty replied, and squinted as he stared at the tall crane on the dock.

The operator, waiting for his next instructions, looked down from his cab at the side of the OV, which was held away from the dockside by thick rubber bumpers. Butty was about to walk to the edge to see what had got the crane operator's attention when Pepe called out.

"What we getting, Captain?"

Butty turned his attention to his crew, several of whom leaned against the gunwale, looking his way.

"Crates of tools and tool chests," he shouted back, then scanned through the pages of the manifest. "Need to make sure the heavy crates get loaded first or we'll be swaying like Pepe's mother on Cinco de Mayo."

Butty grinned at his first mate, who shook his head as the other guys laughed and ribbed their co-worker. As the Englishman re-boarded the ship, he threw a glance over his shoulder at the crane operator, but the man was now deep in conversation with Santiago, who was pointing to a large wooden crate being dropped on the dock by forklift. Butty continued onto the deck and climbed the steps to the wheelhouse, pausing at the door.

"Pepe!" he called down, and his first mate looked up. "Send someone to kick Felix out of bed. He can bring us all some coffee, yeah?"

Pepe nodded, and without another word, one of the men went below to rouse the kid.

For Butty and Pepe it had been a long night, short on sleep, but for different reasons than the rest of the crew. The men had enjoyed their last hurrah in port and deprived themselves of sleep in exchange for a good time. The captain and his first mate had been at the Banana Supply Company dock at midnight, overseeing the unloading of their cargo. Butty kept the number of people involved down to a minimum. Once the pallets packed with boxes of bananas were in the trucks and down the road, the company men disappeared into the warehouse, herded away by their foreman whose wallet was a little fatter than it had been earlier. Pepe worked the crane, and Butty guided three more identical-looking pallets into the back of an unmarked lorry. Their extra cargo, which didn't appear on any manifest.

Felix looked like death warmed up. "Get some good greasy bacon inside yer, lad," Butty told him when the youngster handed him a steaming mug of coffee, and the kid bolted from the wheel-house, hoping he'd make the gunwale before he threw up for the umpteenth time.

The captain chuckled. It wasn't that long ago he'd have been hung over with the rest of them - heck, he'd have been the one keeping them out till dawn - but it was funny how times change. A one night stand with a gorgeous Cuban girl left him wishing he could see her again. Three months later, she tracked *him* down... with a very angry father in tow. Now, six weeks before the kid was due, he was married to a woman he barely knew and only saw for a few days between trips. Butty wasn't sure how she felt about him, and had a hard time understanding his own feelings about his new wife, beyond the fact he found Lucia physically irresistible. But they seemed to have one thing in common; they were both excited about the baby.

Two years out of the British Navy, Butty hadn't given a fleeting thought towards marriage or a family. He was a man of the seas, and a girl in every port had suited his lifestyle perfectly, right up until he'd been told he was soon to be a father. His own dad had been a labourer in London, and a fine example of how not to be a parent. His mother had died from complications in the birth of the family's second child, who didn't survive either, which Butty counted as a blessing for many years.

After his wife's passing, Graham Butterworth began a series of dysfunctional relationships with an array of down-on-their-luck women who'd begrudgingly kept an eye on his son, while he drank himself into a stupor at the local pub. Throughout his early life, little Raymond was passed along the ever-changing parade of girl-friends, live-ins, and two stepmothers until he was old enough to fend for himself around age eleven. The Royal Navy took him at age sixteen with his father's consent - which he forged on the paperwork - and he never looked back. His aunt — his mother's sister — wrote to him several years later to inform Raymond, or Butty as everyone had taken to calling him as a teenager, that his father had passed away, and the tiny terraced house in London was now his.

Butty had never gone home. His aunt found tenants to rent the house in exchange for a percentage of the lease, and after leaving the Navy Butty had signed on as crew with a freighter heading for America. Now, he was captain of his own vessel, working for an Englishman he'd never met, with a ship registered in Panama and a Hispanic crew from all over the place.

Butty realised the crane, which had been steadily loading crates into the OV's hold, had now paused, with the next piece of cargo dangling over the dock. The operator was standing by the water's edge, talking to Santiago, and pointing at the hull of the ship. Butty stepped outside the wheelhouse.

"What's the matter?" he yelled down.

Santiago looked up and waved him their way. Butty hurried down the steps and across the gangway.

"What's up, mate?" he asked as he approached the two men.

Santiago pointed down at the four-foot space between the dock and the *Oro Verde*'s hull, held apart by the bulky rubber bumpers.

"What's that, amigo?" Santiago asked. "Horace noticed it."

The crane operator leaned over the edge. "I kept looking at it, man, and it don't look like something that's supposed to be there."

Butty squatted down and stared into the deep turquoise water. An object a bit smaller than a cereal box was stuck to the hull with a bubble floating next to it, attached by what appeared to be – he lay on his stomach to get a better look – electrical wires. He jumped to his feet.

"Pepe!" he yelled and shielded his eyes from the bright mid-morning sun.

"Captain?" his first mate replied, leaning over the gunwale.

"Get everyone off the ship. Now!" Butty ordered, and turned to Santiago. "You'd better call the Coast Guard, mate."

"What the hell is it?" Santiago asked, staring down.

"Looks like a bomb to me," Butty replied.

All three men took a few steps back.

2

Grand Cayman - Present Day

AJ Bailey glanced up at the hulls of the Department of Environment and Joint Marine Unit police boats 60 feet above. She couldn't imagine doing this kind of diving work in her native England, where there would be freezing cold water, visibility next to nothing, and a mucky seabed instead of pristine sand. Her dive buddy, Reg Moore, gave her a nudge on the arm and pointed to the 38-foot motor yacht sitting upright on the sea floor before them. AJ gave him a two-finger salute in return and glared at him through her mask.

Most of the time, AJ and Reg ran their dive boat operations from a dock at the north end of Seven Mile Beach in the township of West Bay, but occasionally the Royal Cayman Islands Police Service had need of expert divers. Like when a 1998 Cruisers motor yacht sinks and the owners go missing. Their job was to see if the boat was leaking harmful diesel and oil, report on the immediate hazard to the neighbouring coral reef, and see if the missing couple were still inside.

The dead people inside part was the cause of her hesitation. They'd flipped a coin before splashing in, and she'd lost. The authorities assumed the boat had sunk overnight as no one had reported it in distress or witnessed it going down. A pair of divers, hunting lionfish away from the marked dive sites that morning, had stumbled across the *Tickled Pink* and called the police after surfacing. The registered owners, George and Meredith Pink, hadn't answered the number on file for them, weren't home, and as yet hadn't called the authorities to report their boat missing.

Reg nudged her again, and she could tell he was grinning behind his regulator and shaggy beard. AJ finned forward, crossing the raised cockpit above the railing, careful not to snag her tank on the hard top. Ahead at eye level, the fly-bridge was a mess, with seat cushions caught in the Bimini top's framework and the fabric torn and wafting in the light current.

At the back of the cockpit, left of the starboard side moulded steps to the fly-bridge, the salon hatch was open. AJ turned on her underwater torch and held her breath, hoping she wouldn't be illuminating a corpse. Inside, more cushions, furnishings, and assorted junk floated around obscuring much of her view, and she knew there was no other option but to go inside. Using the salon steps to ease herself forward, she tentatively pulled and dropped down into the salon. On the left was a sofa, and to the right a door leading aft to a stateroom. Ahead, steps dropped to a dinette on the starboard side and the compact galley to port. If she stayed above the height of the dinette table, there was just enough room for her to rotate inside, providing she bent her knees to keep her fin tips from catching the curtains.

Everywhere AJ shone her light, flotsam floated past, casting dancing shadows on the surfaces beyond. Reg was at the doorway, and he set his torch down so it spread a beam of light along the floor, which for AJ was better than it swinging about creating more ghost images and moving spectres. A door towards the bow was closed, and so was a second door on the starboard side. Passing through either would take away her ability to turn around, so she hoped a quick peek would be sufficient. Turning the handle, she opened the door on her right and aimed her torch inside.

Something rushed her and AJ yelped into her regulator, waiting for the weight of the body to hit her, but instead she felt fabric against her cheek and swiped it away with her hand. It was a thin towel, pulled from the head by the motion of opening the door. A quick check revealed the loo was clear of anything more sinister, so she gently closed the door. Taking a few deep breaths, she turned her attention to what she guessed to be the bow stateroom.

The door opened into the cramped sleeping quarters, and this time AJ prepared herself for an onslaught of linens, so she wasn't surprised when a sheet moved across the bed and a stuffed teddy bear floated by her torch beam as it fell from the berth. Panning the light around the room once again revealed no bodies, so AJ used her arms to carefully shove herself backwards into the salon. She was getting used to the debris bumping into her, so she didn't flinch when a cushion hit her face as she attempted to spin herself around. The words 'I'm retired, you can find me on my boat' were stitched on the cushion which AJ swatted out of the way, and she hoped the Pinks weren't currently correct about that.

The last place to check was the aft stateroom, and once AJ had turned herself to face the stern, she focused on the door next to the salon steps. Reg pointed his torch beam into the back corner so he didn't blind her, and she used the dinette seat to pull herself towards the stern and take hold of the door handle. The door once more swung into the berth, and AJ pointed her torch inside. Everything in the tiny stateroom was positioned at odd angles, where the designer had skilfully maximised every inch of space. Combined with the darkness and bedclothes askew, it was strangely disorientating, so AJ paused for a moment before moving inside. The en suite head was on the port side, so she had no choice but to enter the stateroom, although she could just keep her fins outside in the salon and still reach the door handle of the head.

Slowly pulling the door open, having learnt her lesson earlier, a quick scan let her breathe easily. She found no one inside. Unless they'd packed themselves in the engine room, which she doubted could house two fully assembled humans, the boat was deserted. Using her finned feet, she tried levering herself in reverse out of the stateroom, but all she managed to do was swing herself around and face the stern. AJ reached out and pushed against the stern wall, but now her left fin caught on something inside the salon. She grunted into her regulator, feeling a little unnerved at being stuck inside the motor yacht at 60 feet down.

AJ grunted sharply again when she felt something around her ankles, then realised it was Reg's hands. At least she hoped they were Reg's. He gently eased her backwards until her shoulders exited the stateroom, then released his grip so she could wriggle the rest of the way herself. She paused for a moment, letting him extract his big frame from the salon, then pushed herself clear of the berth and finned her way out to the cockpit.

Away from the wreck, AJ checked her Shearwater Teric wrist-mounted dive computer and noted she had plenty of air remaining, so they made a final inspection lap around the Cruisers before slowly ascending. After three minutes to 'off-gas' at 15 feet, they surfaced at the stern of the DoE boat.

"Find any Pinks?" Casey Keller asked, peering over the stern.

"Nope," Reg replied, in his booming deep voice with a London accent. "Pulled a floundering flippered mermaid from the aft cabin though."

AJ, who was halfway up the ladder, swung her fins at him, but he was strategically positioned out of reach, laughing. She clambered aboard and slipped out of her buoyancy control device, or BCD, lowering the vest-like apparatus holding the scuba tank to the deck. Using a tag line on the back zipper, she wriggled her arms free of her wetsuit and let it fall to her waist, revealing her artistically tattooed arms. Casey helped Reg over the transom, then handed them both towels.

"Not sure how they'll get straps underneath her," AJ said, as a tall, broad-shouldered, dark-skinned man joined them from the wheelhouse.

Ben Crooks wore the uniform of the Royal Cayman Islands Police Service Joint Marine Unit. "It's still upright, though, correct?" he asked in the local accent of the islanders.

"It is, and you'll get the bow no problem," Reg said. "But it's one of them motor yachts with a high cockpit over a stateroom, so it'll be a hell of job getting one under the stern. Can't say I saw any obvious lift points, but it has a swim step. Could try under that, but it'll pull it off I reckon."

"Might be alright if you go slow," AJ added. "Let the lift bags do all the work. The salon hatch is one of those wrap-over jobs, so it's going to be a bugger to pump air into it."

Ben scratched his chin and looked at the water. AJ guessed he was visualising the boat in his mind. They had pictures of sister vessels from an online search.

"I'd put a lift bag or two inside the salon and fill them," Reg suggested. "That'll displace enough water to move her off the bottom I suspect. Get her up top then pump out the rest."

"Couldn't say why she went down though," AJ said, putting on a Mermaid Divers logoed sun-shirt. "I didn't see any damage inside or out."

"Insurance job," Reg responded. "Bet you'll find the bilge is rigged or something similar."

"What makes you say dat?" Ben asked.

Reg looked at AJ. "You see anything personal inside there?"

"There's all kinds of rubbish floating about inside."

"Sure, but did you see anything personal in there?" he persisted. "A wallet, phone, keys, photos, computer or one of those reading tablet things."

AJ thought for a moment. "No, I don't suppose I did. Plenty of towels and bedclothes. Had a teddy bear staring at me. That could be considered personal."

Reg shook his head. "Mark my words. The Pinks'll show up right as rain, saying someone pinched their precious boat. Insurance job."

"Why wouldn't they drop it over the wall?" Casey asked. "Be better if it wasn't salvageable at all, wouldn't it?"

"But that would take forever, right?" AJ answered. "There'd be a search to find it, and who knows if we ever would. Wouldn't even know where to start."

"Bingo," Reg agreed. "This way, takes a day or three, and someone stumbles across it. I'm surprised more of the flotsam hadn't found its way out and given the location away."

"Pull a hose off the raw water cooling system and she'll go down in a hurry," Casey said, shaking her head.

"Oh bugger, that's right," AJ reacted, stifling a laugh. "You had a dive boat go down that way, yeah?"

"Yes! And stop laughing!"

"Those engines will be sealed cooling systems," Reg pointed out. "But a hose off the heat exchanger would do the same thing. They bring raw water in and pump it through a heat exchanger instead of the engine itself, then out the exhaust system. Pull or cut a hose on the inlet side and it'll fill the boat up."

"Well, thank you both," Ben said. "We'll get da salvage guys out here to start working on it. I'll make sure we check da bilge wiring and heat exchanger once we have it out of da water. I'm glad there was no one inside."

AJ scoffed. "Me too."

Reg grinned. "You jumped a bloody mile when that towel attacked you."

"Hush up, you old goat," she replied. "But thanks for the help getting me out of the aft stateroom. I was a bit stuck."

"No problem," he said in a more serious tone. "It's already past my lunchtime so I wasn't waiting around for you to faff about too long."

He burst into deep guffaws, with his shoulders shaking and water sprinkling from his mop of salt and pepper hair.

Casey shook her head. "If you knuckleheads get the ladder, I'll take you in. I'm ready for some lunch too."

3

1976

Butty looked around the dock. It appeared people were more interested in looking at the device than worried about being blown up.

"This is turning into a right dog's dinner," he mumbled, and Pepe looked at him sideways.

His first mate had become used to odd phrases and sayings coming from the captain. If it was important, he'd say it in Spanish, but either way, Pepe got the gist of his complaint. Three men from the Coast Guard stood discussing the situation, occasionally waving the growing crowd away. They'd immediately called the sheriff's office and were currently waiting for someone to show up. Santiago had other dock business to attend to and had left, but Horace, the crane operator, waited with the uniformed officers.

Butty had about had enough of the delay. The smile he'd worn at sunrise was a thing of the past, and all he wanted was to finish loading and head out to sea. He'd feel safer on the water.

"Sod this," he growled, flicking his cigarette aside, "I'm going in."

He was about to kick his shoes off when Pepe nudged his arm and nodded to where the Coasties stood. A man in the brown uniform of the Sheriff's Department had joined them. Butty walked over.

"This your vessel?" the man asked. "I'm Captain Tom Brodie with the Sheriff's Office bomb squad."

Butty shook his offered hand. "Captain Butterworth. What do you think it is?"

Brodie shrugged his shoulders. "Has all the makings of a home-made bomb, but Horace here says he noticed it first thing this morning, which as I understand it, was right after you docked."

Butty nodded his agreement.

"Where did you come from?"

"Up the river," Butty replied. "Unloaded overnight, then motored here to take on the new cargo."

Brodie scratched his chin. "My guess is someone stuck this thing on there last night then. Should have gone off by now."

Butty felt like taking a few steps back, but despite his words, the bomb expert didn't show any signs of concern, so the Englishman nervously stayed put. *Maybe it was a good thing he hadn't jumped in the water*, he decided.

"What makes you say that?" Butty asked.

"See the little balloon?"

"Sure. Looks like a johnny."

Brodie frowned. "I've no idea what you just said, but it's actually a condom."

"That's what I just said," Butty responded.

"Oh. Well, anyway, I believe it's a crude fuse. An acid pellet triggering device. If I'm right, the bomb-maker did something wrong, as those fuses are designed to go off within an hour or two."

"Bloody hell," Butty mumbled.

"Who would want to blow up your ship, Captain?" Brodie

asked, and the Coast Guard men joined him in looking expectantly at Butty.

"I've got no bloody clue, mate. I carry bananas across the Caribbean. No idea why anyone would want to waste their time with us. Probably just a nutter with a soldering iron and too much time on his hands."

The officials appeared appeased to Butty's relief. He did in fact have an idea who might want to screw with the *Oro Verde*, or more accurately, with the extra cargo she carried into Miami, but these guys were the last people who needed to know that.

"So what's the plan?" he asked.

Brodie kicked off his shoes and began unbuttoning his shirt.

"Blimey, mate," Butty said, "Shouldn't you have protective gear? Or some other blokes here?"

Brodie shrugged his shoulders. "I'm just taking a peek. If it goes bang, it won't matter how many people I have as back-up, and we don't have any gear we can take in the water, so I'd best get on with it."

Butty didn't have a good argument to persuade him otherwise or a good reason to stop the man. He needed the device off his hull so he could get en route and out of further harm's way.

"Be careful then," he said.

"Can you get me a dinghy in the water?" he asked the Coasties, and one of them left to arrange it.

Without wasting any more time, Brodie stepped off the concrete dock, and splashed into the water six feet below them.

The two remaining Coast Guard men took a few steps back and made more of an effort to clear onlookers out of what they guessed to be the blast radius. Butty couldn't help but look over the side, curiosity getting the better of him. Brodie stayed at arm's length away from the device, studying it through the water. He didn't have a mask or goggles, so ducking under would reveal the bomb as nothing more than a fuzzy blob. Butty sucked in a sharp intake of breath and watched in horror as the bomb squad expert pulled the device from the hull and held it above the bay.

"Cigar box!" he yelled up in amusement. "Cubans too."

"I'm betting they didn't leave us any in there, mate," Butty shouted back, wincing in anticipation of an explosion.

Brodie laughed and pulled a wire from the balloon-like prophylactic. Butty's brain told him to leap clear, but his feet didn't move in anything near the time frame his inner alarm bells instructed. Instead, he stood frozen in place, staring down at Brodie, who simply grinned up at him.

"Disarmed," the man said. "Tell those pussies to get their dinghy over here."

The two Coast Guard officers leaned over the side and nodded at Brodie. "On its way," the senior officer replied. "And for the record… you're nuts."

Twenty minutes later, Butty stood next to the bomb squad expert under a lean-to at the edge of the dock. Brodie cut the silicone sealer around the seam of the cigar box and flipped the lid open. Inside, two square-profile sticks of explosive were secured in place with what Butty assumed was the primer in between.

"Pentolite," Brodie announced, merrily dismantling a few more parts. "Don't see it that often, but some of the Cuban militant types like to use it."

Butty stiffened and was glad Brodie was too immersed in the device to notice.

"And you're sure there aren't any more of these down there, right?" Butty asked.

"This was it," Brodie replied absentmindedly.

"So, can I give Santiago the green light to finish loading, mate?"

Brodie didn't look up. "Sure, sure. Go ahead."

Butty quickly stepped away and looked along the dock for Santiago or Horace. He spotted the crane operator leaning against his cab and made a circle gesture in the air with his finger.

"Back in business, lads. Let's finish loading."

Horace nodded and flicked his cigarette away as he climbed into the cab.

"Pepe?!" Butty shouted up to his ship. "We can finish up," he added when his first mate peered over the gunwale.

Relieved to be back in action and closer to leaving port, Butty took a deep breath and shook a Marlboro loose from the pack he pulled from the chest pocket of his shirt. The dock had cleared of onlookers, but a few workers and other boat crews still pointed and talked in hush tones. Several officers from the Sheriff's Department were making their way along the dock questioning anyone who may have seen anything suspicious, along with inspecting the other ships. But they wouldn't find anything. Butty knew Brodie was right. The device had been placed upriver at the Banana Supply Company.

Letting out a stream of smoke to the breeze, Butty noticed a familiar face walking his way and groaned. Sal Herrera was a stern-looking man at the best of times, but now his chubby face was knitted into creases. The man was neither tall nor athletic, but he scared the hell out of Butty, especially when he brought along his two bodyguards who trailed a few steps behind. They were brawny and mean as hell looking.

Although Sal didn't appear the least concerned about the law enforcement presence, Butty still met him off to the side under the shade of a shipping container.

"Tell me what happened," the Cuban growled in Spanish.

Butty ran through his morning for the man, struggling over a few words but getting the point across. When he finished, Sal's cheeks were flushed red and the man ground his teeth, making Butty cringe inside.

"Pérez?" Butty finally asked.

"Of course it's Pérez," Sal snapped, before running off a string of obscenities under his breath. "He hoped to bring the authorities to the ship before it was unloaded. Screw with my supply chain. But the idiot screwed it up."

Butty doubted it was Pérez himself who'd got the delayed

igniter system wrong, but he pitied the man who did. Or he would have if the bloke hadn't stuck the device to his ship. As it stood, he hoped the unsuccessful bomber's body was being dumped in the Everglades, although it wouldn't matter. The top Cuban drug dealers in Miami seemed to have an endless supply of young men trying to lift themselves out of the barrio at any cost.

He also sensed Sal's glee at the error was focused solely on the Cuban's own good fortune rather than concern for the ship or its crew. A pang of guilt twisted Butty's stomach into a knot. Only he and Pepe knew about their illicit cargo. The rest of his men were completely innocent. That wasn't to say they didn't know something fishy was going on, but so far they'd been smart enough not to ask questions or interfere.

"What do you want me to do?" Butty asked.

Sal waved a hand. "Get me another shipment from Panama, man. What else?"

"Do you think he'll try again?"

The Cuban laughed. "Of course he'll try again, but he doesn't know what hell I'm about to rain down on him, that fat piece of shit."

In another situation, Butty might have laughed at the chubby drug dealer calling his equally chubby rival fat, but he was more curious how Sal planned on raining anything down on his far more powerful and established countryman. Alfonso Pérez had owned the marijuana supply into Miami for over a decade, and it was only his distraction with his even more profitable cocaine imports over the past few years which had let Sal Herrera grab a piece of the pie. In Butty's opinion, if Pérez was behind the cigar box bomb it signalled he was done playing around. He wouldn't be surprised to return from the next trip to find Herrera had been fed to the alligators, and Pérez waiting for the shipment.

"Don't worry about that bastard Pérez; I'll handle him," Sal promised. He was about to turn away when he paused and planted a stubby finger in Butty's chest. "Unless you know something you're not telling me?"

Both bodyguards edged forward and glared menacingly at Butty, waiting for the boss's order.

"I sure as hell wouldn't have sailed down the river to here if I'd known a bomb was along for the ride, would I?" Butty said. "How would I know anything about it?"

Sal tapped the Englishman's chest one more time. "You know why. Make me regret the trust I have in you, and it won't just be you who'll suffer a painful death, my friend. Your father-in-law can be sure of that."

"He's not my father-in-law," Butty said, but the Cuban had already turned away and was leaving. His two goons sneered at Butty before following. "He's her uncle by marriage," Butty added, but he was speaking to the receding backs of the three men.

He shook his head. How he'd managed to marry a relative of one drug lord while his ship owner had thrust him into business with another was beyond his comprehension, but it certainly complicated matters.

4

Present Day

Casey dropped Reg and AJ off at their dock a little after 11:00am. They unloaded their dive gear and tanks before saying goodbye and watching Casey carefully pull away in the DoE boat, idling across the shallows so the props didn't stir up the sea floor.

"How'd it go?" came a woman's voice with a London accent, and AJ turned to see Reg's wife, Pearl, walking towards them.

A pretty woman in her fifties with a curvy figure and wavy blonde hair, she wore capri leggings and a V-neck blouse which fluttered in the breeze. Reg leaned down and gave her a kiss. He was a foot taller than his wife. Their dog Coop ran past Reg and furiously wagged his tail for AJ. She leaned down and made a fuss of him.

"Insurance job, I reckon," Reg said, continuing up the dock. "But we'll see when they fish it out the water."

"At least no one was still in there," Pearl responded.

"Just a couple of guard towels and cushions that leapt out at her ladyship," Reg replied, trying not to laugh.

Pearl gave him a slap on the arm and AJ rolled her eyes. They dropped their gear outside the tiny, blue-painted hut which served as an office, storeroom, and bathroom, and AJ turned on a fresh-water hose to rinse their BCDs and regulators.

"What's for lunch, love?" Reg asked. "I'm bloody starving."

"Tupperware inside," she replied, pointing at the hut. "Vegetable soup."

"Vegetable?" Reg grumbled, opening the door. "Why do I have to suffer 'cos she's a bloody vegetarian?"

"I'm a pescatarian," AJ shouted from outside. "And it'll do you good to eat a salad or two."

Pearl patted Reg's stomach as he plucked the lid off his lunch. The man was in remarkable shape for his age, but he had gained a few pounds around the middle in the past couple of years.

"That's reserves, love," he said with a grin. "In case we have a food shortage."

Pearl smiled at her husband. "Makes you even more cuddly."

"He's cuddly all right," AJ said, reaching in the hut and grabbing a Tupperware of soup. "That's why he sent me inside. He was worried he'd get stuck in the doorway like Father Christmas in a chimney."

"Oi," he rebutted. "Who had to come inside and pluck you out of the aft berth, then? I fit through the hatch just fine, I'll have you know."

"Bet you had to tilt at an angle?" she fired back, scooping a spoonful of soup to her mouth.

"A bit," he admitted, grinning behind his beard.

Setting up three beach chairs, they attempted to catch the shade from the hut, but the midday sun denied them. They settled for the ocean breeze and tucked into their lunch, chatting about the dive.

They all looked up as a 36-foot Newton with a Mermaid Divers logo on the hull approached the dock. A dark-skinned young man beamed and waved from the fly-bridge before easing the custom dive boat alongside the pier. AJ put her soup down, trotted down the dock, and caught a line thrown to her by a second crew member at the bow. He was a tall, lean man with a close-trimmed beard and long hair held back in a ponytail.

"How was it?" she asked her boyfriend, Jackson, as she tied the bow line to a dock cleat.

"All good," he replied in his soft Californian accent.

They both moved towards the stern and repeated the process with a second line. Thomas, AJ's only full-time employee, shut the engines off and climbed down the ladder from the fly-bridge.

"Check dis out, Boss," he said playfully. "Everybody even came back wit us."

AJ grinned at him and the customers laughed as they gathered their gear. She helped everyone step to the dock and eagerly chatted with them, listening to their stories from their two morning dives. Once all their clients had left, AJ unravelled a hose and was about to start washing down the boat.

"Hey!" Pearl called out. "You didn't finish your lunch!"

Thomas took the hose from her. "We got dis, Boss. Finish your food."

"You haven't eaten yet either," she pointed out.

"But mine ain't getting cold," he said.

Jackson was pulling rental gear off scuba tanks at the stern, so AJ took Thomas's arm and pulled him closer. "Did you lead both dives?"

Thomas nodded.

"I noticed Jackson's hair was dry," she whispered. "Everything okay?"

Thomas nodded again. "Ain't no big deal, Boss. He said he had phone calls to make, and asked if I didn't mind. We don't have an afternoon trip, so 'twas fine wit me."

"Thanks," AJ replied with a smile.

She walked up the dock and wondered what could have been so urgent to keep Jackson on the phone most of the morning. She hoped his family were fine. He had grandparents who were getting older but in good health as best she knew. Sitting down, she picked up her soup and watched Reg's boats begin to arrive.

"How many you have going out this afternoon?" she asked.

"Two, I think," Reg answered, looking at his wife, who handled the bookings.

"Yeah, two. Could've put them all on one, but we have students finishing their open water certs, so we'll take them separately."

"They can go to Chain Reef over here," Reg said, nodding his head towards the dive site just to the north of the dock.

He was about to say something else, when his mobile rang, and he pulled it from his pocket.

"This is Reg," he said, then listened for a moment. "Hold on, Casey, I'm putting you on speakerphone. AJ and Pearl are with me."

"Hi, Pearl," came Casey's voice in a cheery tone.

"Hello, love. These two didn't give you any trouble, did they?"

Casey laughed. "Of course they did, but they're like relatives' kids. I get to hand them back."

AJ grinned.

"Alright, alright," Reg jumped in. "Tell them what you were telling me."

"The Pinks called 911 a bit earlier to report their boat stolen," Casey explained, sounding slightly amused. "Apparently, they said it was moored in the canal outside their house last night, then gone when they looked outside this morning."

"Sounds like their morning starts a bit later than yours and mine," Reg said.

"Said they didn't look out back until they returned from a late breakfast," Casey added. "Their phones were at home which is why they didn't answer."

"I hope the police are looking for the tender," Reg said. "They had to get ashore somehow, right?"

"Ben said they are," Casey replied. "Pinks told them they had an eight-foot dinghy with an outboard."

"Bet they only find the Pinks' fingerprints on the tender," Reg said.

"I suspect you're right," Casey replied. "Gotta go. Salvage boys are here. I told them what you said and they're gearing up to take a couple of lift bags down now."

"Thanks for the update, love. Talk to you later," Reg said, and ended the call.

"You really think they'd be stupid enough to reverse wire the bilge and think no one would figure that out?" AJ asked, setting down her empty Tupperware.

"But the bilges pump out above the waterline," Pearl pointed out. "Wouldn't reversing them just pump air in."

"Stick a hose in the outlet and dip it in the water until the boat gets low enough, then pull the hose out and leave," AJ explained.

"Blimey. That's devious, innit?" Pearl grinned.

"Problem with that," AJ continued, "is that there's no visible reason for the boat to sink. It's one thing to pull that off in rough seas, but not bobbing around out here on a lovely night. If they float her and there's no hole in the bottom, but a bilge wired backwards, it's a straight-up giveaway."

Reg scratched his beard and thought for a moment. "People don't always do the smartest things when they're desperate. And I'm guessing that regular folks like I'm assuming the Pinks are must be desperate to deliberately sink their own boat for the insurance money."

"I've never done that of course," AJ said thoughtfully. "But I'm guessing it would take a while to sink a boat from a single bilge pump."

"It would," Reg countered. "Some also have check valves, so I'd say Casey was right. They'll find a hose off the heat exchanger. That wouldn't take long. Pumps a lot more water than a bilge, and it'd be tough to prove it was deliberately loosened rather than worked itself free."

"Won't have to prove anything if they stick to their stolen boat story," AJ rebutted. "The thieves pulled the hose and left the engine running to sink the boat and hide the evidence."

"You two both have terrifyingly sneaky minds," Pearl said with a grin. "You're not master jewel thieves on the side, are you?"

AJ laughed. "If we are, I bet you're wondering where all the jewels got to. When was the last time old stingy here gave you something sparkly?"

"Oi," Reg said, getting up from his seat. "I'll have you know I gave my love something silver just the other week." He leaned down and kissed Pearl's forehead before walking towards his docking boats.

"He did?" AJ asked.

"Yeah," Pearl replied with a broad smile. "He bought us a new dishwasher 'cos the old one bloody died. It's silver coloured."

AJ chuckled all the way down the dock as she joined Thomas and Jackson, who were nearly finished cleaning the boat. She dragged the air fill lines from the dock and stepped aboard *Hazel's Odyssey* with them.

"Tanks, Boss," Thomas said, trying to take the manifold from her.

"I've got this, mate. Finish up what you were doing."

"I was about to get da lines and fill da tanks," he said, still holding out his hands.

"Well too bad. I stole your job then," she rebutted and began slipping the yokes over the tanks in the racks behind the benches lining the deck.

Thomas followed behind her, tightening the yokes onto the tank valves. The two of them worked seamlessly together, as they had done for many years now. When all the connections were secure, AJ stood on the bench and put a fist on the top of her head; an okay sign used at the surface in diver sign language. Pearl returned the same signal and opened a valve at the hut, releasing high pressure air into the fixed plumbing running down the pier. AJ and Thomas spun the tank valves open and a chorus of rushing gas was met by the rumble of compressors starting behind the hut.

AJ turned around and looked for Jackson, about to ask him what he had planned for the afternoon. At first she didn't see him, but then saw through the cabin windows he was standing at the bow, texting on his phone. They weren't a couple who needed to be fawning over each other all the time, but it seemed like he'd been strangely distant and distracted since the boat had docked. He turned and looked her way. His face broke into a smile, but it wasn't with the carefree manner that accompanied his easy-going character. Something was definitely up, she was sure of it.

5

1976 - 21 days later

Leaving room for the extra cargo was always a pain in the arse, but after multiple trips, and having tried a variation of methods, Butty and Pepe had their system figured out. By lifting two crates of bananas from the top of the stack in the hold, they revealed the hole they'd carefully left and lowered the bonus shipment in place. Once the bananas were returned to their spot on top, everything appeared the same and on they went, leaving Panama for the return journey through the Caribbean.

For over a year, the process had been the same. Drop the outbound cargo in Colón, Panama, motor through the canal, travel 1,000 miles south to the port city of Guayaquil, Ecuador, fill the hold with bananas, then return to the port at Balboa outside Panama City. They'd stay the shortest possible time, loading the additional crates at night, before heading north. No customs officials ever showed up at the dock. Military guards ignored the *Oro Verde*'s presence, and Butty dealt with one man every time. Díaz was a tall, skinny Panamanian with unruly dark hair and a friendly disposition. Until this trip.

Right away, Butty could tell something was different. Díaz had lost his ready smile and was chain smoking his hand-rolled cigarettes. Usually, he had two or three men with him who drove the flatbed lorry, operated the crane, and helped out, but this time there were at least six more, uniformed and all armed.

"What's going on, mate?" Butty asked Díaz in Spanish. "Why all the extra security?"

The man nervously looked around for the umpteenth time. "The boss is coming to see you," he replied, taking another long draw from his cigarette. "Just act like everything is okay."

Butty was taken aback. "I thought it was."

"Yes, yes. Of course," Díaz agreed, patting the Englishman on the shoulder. "Everything is fine. But he wants to meet you."

Butty instinctively knew why, but if pretending like everything was normal was the game, he was more than keen to play along. "Why now? And who is your boss anyway?"

Díaz fidgeted, flicking the stub of his cigarette away in a shower of tiny sparks. "I don't know why. My boss told me he's coming, that's all."

"So this bloke isn't your boss?"

"Yes, yes. He's my boss, but he's everyone's boss, you know? The *big* boss."

Butty really didn't know. He had no clue who he'd been dealing with for the past year. Díaz was his point of contact in a world where asking questions was frowned upon. The English owner of the *Oro Verde* had told Butty via telephone to meet with Sal Herrera in Miami, who in turn had given him instructions which included meeting Díaz at the dock in Panama. That's what he'd been doing for the past year and a bit.

"Wait," Butty said, looking at the lorry. "There's an extra crate."

He counted again. He'd watched two being loaded, yet two still remained on the flatbed.

"There's an extra crate?" he repeated.

"Yes, yes, my friend. I should have said. We were told to increase the shipment."

"First I've bloody heard of it," Butty complained. "We left room for three like usual."

Díaz waved a hand towards the ship. "Just move something around."

"That's not the way it works, mate," Butty replied, running a hand through his clammy, salty hair. "We plan for every crate. The load has to be packed perfectly, else it'll move in rough seas. I didn't leave room for the extra crate. I can't take it."

The crane picked the next wooden crate from the lorry and the long arm slowly swung over the cargo hold. Díaz stiffened even more and dropped the paper and tobacco he'd been attempting to roll. Two soldiers with M16 rifles slung across their chests preceded a stocky man dressed in a beige uniform shirt. He had an almost square face with prominent features and a pockmarked complexion. The three marched across the dock and stopped before Butty and Díaz.

"Hold out your arms," one of the armed guards ordered, and Butty did so.

The man patted him down while the second soldier stood poised with his M16 at the ready. Once the guard was sure Butty wasn't carrying any weapons, the two soldiers stepped aside, and the man Butty assumed was the *big boss* took a step forward.

"Why a problem, Miami?" he asked in heavily accented English.

"Someone tried to blow up the ship," Butty replied in Spanish and the man looked surprised. Butty wasn't sure whether it was his ability to speak Spanish or the fact that an explosive device had been attached to the ship that made him raise an eyebrow, but Butty continued. "We disarmed it."

"Who did this?" the man asked, now switching to his native tongue.

"I don't know for sure."

The man ran his tongue across his teeth. "You and Herrera need to take care of this."

"I'm just the captain of this ship, sir," Butty said. "I do the ocean part of the process and leave the rest to you fellows."

Butty sensed Díaz tense even more, but the expression of the man he was talking to didn't change. "You were captain when someone attached a bomb to your ship, no?"

"I was," Butty reluctantly conceded.

"Sounds like a problem you *should* be concerned with."

"Concerned, yes," Butty responded, wishing he could be back at sea where all he had to worry about was the weather and a compass. "But it's not something I can do anything about, sir."

The man leaned towards Butty. "As captain, it's your job to make sure my cargo reaches its destination in perfect condition. It's important you understand this."

Butty had spent enough time in the Navy to know what an officer expected of a subordinate, and he was clearly a subordinate to whoever this guy was. At least in the Panamanian's eyes.

"Yes, sir," he said, ready to move on.

The man nodded. "This time you have thirty-three percent more product. Next time will be more again."

He didn't phrase it as a question or request, but at least Butty knew what to expect when he came back. If he came back. He was already thinking about what options he had to move on to new employment. Somehow, his easy-going nature and the extra money he'd welcomed for his new family had led him down a path he'd never intended visiting. Butty didn't feel bad shipping weed - he didn't see the difference between smoking dope and having a few drinks - but he wasn't interested in the drug lords and scary military blokes he now faced.

"I'll make it work," he said, and the man nodded.

Next to them, Díaz finally relaxed enough to roll himself another cigarette, no doubt relieved Butty had decided to play along. The uniformed man took a final look at the *Oro Verde* over Butty's shoulder, before his eyes settled on the captain again.

"Take care of my cargo. I'll see you next month."

With that, he turned, and the two armed guards flanked him as he left. Díaz breathed out a long stream of smoke and his shoulders slumped as though the weight of the world had fallen away. Butty looked at the crane, which was lifting the fourth crate in the air.

"Captain?" Pepe called down from the deck.

"I know," Butty shouted back, "I'll be right there."

He left Díaz on the dock and hurried across the gangway to the OV, glancing at his watch. They'd sent the crew away for a last meal on dry land before leaving for Miami, but they'd be back soon. It was one thing asking the men to ignore what they didn't see, but that became tougher when it took place right in front of their eyes. Besides, several men had quit after the bomb incident, right before they'd left the Miami docks. Pepe had scrambled to find two Cuban men as replacements, and Butty had wished they'd sailed short handed. One of them fitted in just fine, but he didn't trust the other new recruit who'd been slow to work and quick to stick his nose into everyone else's business.

"We have no choice," Butty said, reaching Pepe, who stood next to the open hold. "Drop this last one in the final space and we'll tie the crate of bananas to the deck near the bow."

Pepe looked as concerned as Butty felt, but the first mate didn't say anything more, and went about directing the crane operator as instructed. Fifteen minutes later, with the cargo secure, the crew returned and they readied to leave. On his way to say goodbye to Díaz, Butty spotted the nosey Cuban standing over the hold, looking at the rearranged cargo. The captain paused, and instead of going across the gangway, walked over to the man.

"You can help with the lines. We're about to leave."

The man sneered at Butty. "What did you take aboard?"

"How's that any of your concern?" Butty replied.

The man shrugged his shoulders. "We're all on this ship together, Captain. Pepe told me it was all a misunderstanding with the bomb in Miami, but maybe it had something to do with what you're up to here."

Butty considered his options for a moment. He didn't like or trust this man.

"I'll have Pepe pay you for the trip down. There's plenty of ships heading north. You'll find another one in the morning."

"No, no, no!" the Cuban said, waving his arms. "I'll help with the lines, man. We can part ways when we get home, but let me stay on until then."

Butty sighed. "What's your name?" he asked, trying to remember what Pepe had told him.

"Jorge," he said, having lost the sneer and the smart-arse attitude. "I'll work hard for you. I promise, Captain."

Butty nodded and the man scurried away before the captain could change his mind. He lit a Marlboro and walked over the gangway to where Díaz stood near the crane. The extra armed security had already left, leaving two guys Butty recognised from prior trips. Díaz was back to his smiling ways and shook Butty's hand.

"Safe travels, my friend."

"Thanks," Butty replied. "I'll be much happier when I'm on the open sea."

"Rather you than me, man," Díaz replied. "I get seasick."

Butty grinned. "See you next month, mate, and feel free not to invite the *big boss* along. He makes me nervous."

Díaz shook his head, and his smile faded. "He does as he pleases I'm afraid, my friend. I can't promise he won't show up again."

"Fair enough," Butty said, slapping Díaz on the shoulder. "But I thought you were going to have a heart attack, me ol' fruit. Never seen you that wound up."

Díaz scoffed. "You know who that was, right?"

Butty shrugged his shoulders. "Not a clue."

Díaz looked stunned. "That's Manuel Noriega," he said in a low voice.

"And I'm supposed to know who that is?"

Díaz nodded slowly. "Yes. If you have business with Panama, you should know who that is."

6

AJ had errands to run on a rare afternoon without customers, so it was almost five o'clock when she finally made it home to her little cottage in the grounds of a large home on Seven Mile Beach. The amount she paid was pittance compared to the ever-increasing rent prices on the island, but her landlords had never raised the number, happy to have a trustworthy person keeping an eye on their holiday home. They also enjoyed diving with her for free when they were in town, which wasn't that often.

Parking her fifteen-passenger van near the end of Boggy Sand Road, AJ opened the gate in the tall wooden fence and strolled towards her little home. Well placed away from the main house, the guest cottage angled towards the beach so neither dwelling looked directly into the other. Beside the small building, AJ's motorcycle sat under its cover, and she wished she'd been able to spend the afternoon riding the Ducati instead of driving the van. But dive gear and five-gallon water jugs didn't fit too well on the Multistrada.

Opening the front door, she was greeted by The Eagles playing from the Bluetooth speaker on the coffee table.

"Hey," she said, seeing Jackson sitting at the two-person dining table.

He looked up from his laptop computer and smiled. "Hey, you," he greeted her, but she caught the same tension in his face she'd seen earlier. *Or was she imagining things?*

She walked towards the kitchen, which was no more than four paces away, but he stood and intercepted her with a kiss. AJ set the shopping bag on the dining table and kissed him back.

"How come you didn't lead a dive this morning?" she asked, and mentally kicked herself for not having more patience.

Sometimes people needed time and space to share what was on their minds, and AJ knew this, but issues and conflicts had a way of kidnapping her mind and rendering her unable to think about anything else.

"Let me pour us both a glass of wine, and I'll answer your question," he said, kissing her forehead before moving away, taking the grocery bag with him.

Her brain went into instant panic mode. His response hadn't been, *I had to sort out some rubbish which needed sorting out.* Or *My grandmother's not doing very well* - which AJ certainly hoped wasn't the case - but anything would have felt better in that moment than *We'll need wine to get us through this.*

AJ scurried to the bathroom and closed the door behind her, sitting on the loo although she didn't need to pee. Alone inside a shipwreck a hundred feet underwater she could handle, or providing advice and support for a friend in crisis was a strength she possessed, but her own personal drama was a different story. One of the things which made her relationship with Jackson so perfect was his even-keeled approach that made her feel more relaxed, confident, and grounded. They never had relationship problems, they never argued, and after living together for several years, he was as much a part of her life as the ocean and the air she breathed.

Leaning her head back, AJ took several long, deep inhalations, and tried her best to calm down. In all likelihood, there was going to be a simple and understandable explanation for why he was acting strangely. Everything had seemed normal first thing that morning, although she was not a morning person and could have been oblivious to any oddities in his behaviour. Until the sun rose and she had coffee inside her, it was possible for the apocalypse to be commencing and she might not notice.

It dawned on her that the explanation could well be that he was dealing with something important and needed her support and understanding. There she was, thinking only about herself, and Jackson had been protecting her from whatever difficulty he faced. Her shoulders slumped as the idea of how selfish she was being took hold. He'd proven time and again that he always put her first, and yet here she was thinking of no one *but* herself.

After several more minutes of coaching and telling herself to stop being an idiot, AJ splashed water on her face, towelled herself dry, and left the sanctuary of the bathroom to find out what was going on. Jackson sat at the table by his laptop with two glasses of white wine before him. He slid one across the table and closed his laptop lid, pushing the computer aside.

AJ put her arms around him, gave him a kiss, then took her chair on the opposite side of the little table. Outside, the late afternoon sun blazed from above the palms which divided the garden from the beach, so she reached over and tilted the blinds. Jackson took a sip of wine and she tried to read his expression. His eyes met hers and the familiar warmth in the way he always looked at her made her breath catch.

"Tell me what's wrong," she said softly.

He took a long, steady breath as though he was preparing himself for a freedive, then spoke in his typical calm and collected manner.

"A few weeks ago, I received a call from a friend of mine in the Sea Sentry office. He said a position was probably coming available, and asked if I'd be interested."

AJ's world fell from its axis. In one sentence, everything she knew to be true about their relationship imploded, sucking her lungs dry of oxygen. Something had been happening over weeks, and she'd been oblivious. More to the point, he hadn't said anything to her about it. Sea Sentry, the ocean environmental group he'd been volunteering for when they'd met - the life he'd given up to live with her on the island - had come calling once more, and she knew what he was about to say. Her lips quivered and her hands began to shake as she stared into his hazel eyes.

"Today, they formally offered me the position of captain for the *Sword of the Sentry*, the boat I used to crew on. It's a paid position with benefits."

"You're leaving me," she blurted.

He reached a hand across the table, but she pulled hers away.

"Hon, what happens next is up to the both of us."

"You haven't given them your answer?" she asked, her voice sounding firmer than the life-crumbling dread consuming her.

Jackson paused, wrapping his fingers around his wine glass. "I've accepted the position."

"Then it's not up to *us*, is it?" AJ snapped. "You decided without asking me. You *are* leaving me!"

He shook his head. "I don't want to leave you, I want us..."

"Then why are you?" she countered, interrupting him.

"I was hoping we'd stay together," he said. "I'll just be gone more."

AJ scoffed. She felt like bawling her eyes out, but she loathed crying, and all her emotional energy was quickly becoming anger.

"Like when we dated? You were always gone. I saw you every three or four months when your ship would stop by. We spoke once a week when you had internet that worked. That's what you want to go back to?"

"I don't want to lose you," he said softly.

His calm was now having the opposite effect on AJ. It was making her even more livid. *How could he sit there and tell her he was throwing away the past five years as though they were deciding on take-out for dinner?*

"Then don't leave me!"

"That's what I'm saying," he tried to explain. "I'm not leaving you. I'm taking a job which means I'll be travelling a lot. This will still be my home, and you'll still be the love of my life. People make this work all the time. We did before and we can again."

The *love of my life* phrase left AJ in danger of falling apart. She believed the sincerity in his words and the look on his face, but how could he choose to live apart from the *love of his life*? Clearly, Jackson had thought this through at length and come to the conclusion his plan was workable and acceptable. All without saying a word to her. Until now. After the decision had been made.

He got up from his chair and moved towards her, but she held out a hand.

"No," she grunted, barely managing to utter the word.

"You know I love you," he said, respecting her space. "This isn't something I've taken lightly. It's been a really hard decision."

"But you made a decision about us, without involving me," she replied, the anger rising once more, pushing out the words. "You're dictating your terms to me, and that's not how a relationship is supposed to work."

"I knew you'd be upset," he said defensively. "It's been just talk until today, and then they needed an answer quickly. I wanted to discuss it with you but I knew it would freak you out."

"So you decided dropping the bomb and giving me the choice to take it or leave it was the right move?" she rebutted, rage now beginning to consume her. "I don't know what's worse. You leaving, or not having enough faith in us to talk to me about it."

"Come on, AJ, you know it's not like that. If they'd come back and the job wasn't available after all, we would have gone through two weeks of turmoil for nothing."

"Until the next job offer comes along!" AJ responded with gritted teeth. "You're obviously not happy here, or this wouldn't even be a conversation."

"I'm happy with us and I love Cayman, but I feel useless here," he replied, his voice finally rising. "You have the life you've built for yourself, but I don't. My life used to have purpose, and now I'm just existing alongside your world."

AJ shoved her chair back and got to her feet. Thoughts and words flew around her head but she bottled them in. She marched across the room to the dresser by their bed and began pulling workout clothes from drawers.

"What are you doing?" he asked, his voice soft and calm once more. "We can work this out, AJ. We just need to talk it through."

Stepping into the bathroom, she closed the door behind her, and changed into yoga shorts, a sports bra, and a tank top. She laced her trainers with fury before shoving the door open and snatching up her earbuds and phone.

"AJ, please," Jackson said, watching her from across the room.

Without a word, she left the cottage and jogged across the garden to the gate in the low fence to the beach. Her feet stomped the hard-packed sand near the ocean, and with the gentle ebbing of the water up and down the shore, her mind began to settle despite her heart rate climbing from the exertion.

The feeling that her life would never be the same, never be this good again, hung like a storm cloud over her head, but something worse ate away at her soul as her mind slowly stepped back and looked at what was happening. He was right. Jackson had given up his life to be with her. She'd robbed him of the environmental work he was so passionate about. He'd volunteered for all kinds of things on the island, but none of it compared to the front line work he'd been involved in with Sea Sentry. His work visa allowing him to stay in the Cayman Islands was sponsored by Mermaid Divers, so he couldn't work anywhere else unless they hired him full time.

He'd become a satellite around her planet, and she had no right to hold him here.

7

The *Oro Verde*'s route took them 300 miles north-north-west from Colón on the Caribbean coast of Panama, between the two Columbian-owned islands of San Andres and Providencia, then another 600 miles to the western tip of Cuba. From there, they'd go north-east along the Straits of Florida, picking up the Gulf Stream as they passed below the Florida Keys, before following the coast-line north into Biscayne Bay and Miami.

Butty settled in at the helm having relieved Pepe at sunrise, and enjoyed a steaming hot mug of coffee. He'd have preferred tea, but getting a decent pot brewed by anyone on the ship besides himself had proved fruitless, and by now he was starting to like the strong Cuban coffee. Surprised, he turned to see Pepe standing in the port side doorway. His first mate was supposed to be getting a bite to eat and then some shuteye.

"We got a problem, Captain."

Butty noted his friend's face was wrinkled with worry. More so than usual, which was concerning as the man took his job seriously and fussed over the smallest of details.

"What's wrong?" Butty asked, scanning the gauges for the twin diesel engines, wondering if his keen ear had missed an issue.

"It's the crew," Pepe said in a firm but quiet tone. "That bastard Jorge has them all stirred up."

"Bloody hell," Butty muttered to himself, wishing he'd left Jorge in Panama after all. He silently berated himself for being too nice. It wasn't the first time he'd assumed someone would be true to their word, only to regret it. "What are they saying?"

"Rolando cornered me at breakfast," Pepe explained. "And you know if he says something, the others must be really mad. Rolando never complains." Pepe shifted uncomfortably, leaning against the door to the wheelhouse. "They're worried about what we're carrying and want to know why it's a big secret."

Butty scoffed. "Worried, my arse. Jorge wants more money, and he's figured the best way to get it is if the whole crew kicks up a stink. He's more transparent than Farrah Fawcett's nightie."

Pepe gave him a slightly confused look.

Butty thought about explaining, but he was too aggravated to think about how to rephrase his meaning in Spanish. "We can stop by Grand Cayman," he said instead. "Take us a few hours out of our way but it'll be worth it to get rid of the bugger."

"Here looks good to me," Pepe offered in return, looking at the vast ocean around them.

Butty laughed, but he sensed his first mate was at least partly serious. "Tempting, I must say, but we don't need that on our conscience."

Pepe shrugged his shoulders. "I'd sleep just fine."

Butty unfolded a map onto the table behind the helm station, and Pepe stepped inside, taking the wheel.

"Would have been easier to kick him off at Providencia, but I'm not doubling back now," Butty said. "We'll make Grand Cayman by noon tomorrow. Give me a few minutes to figure it out and I'll adjust our heading."

Pepe stared out of the window at the gently rolling swells filling his view of the horizon. There was no land in sight in front or to either side of them.

"Grand Cayman is not so big, Captain. It'll be easy to miss. Maybe we lock the bastard in a berth until we reach Miami."

"Have some faith, mate," Butty replied, busy plotting their new course. "If we lock him up, it'll create more of a fuss with the lads. Best we kick him off and get everyone together for a quick meeting. Throw a few pennies their way and I'm sure they'll settle down."

Pepe didn't look convinced. "We can try that."

"Don't see we have a lot of choice," Butty added. "This whole extra cargo bollocks has got out of control." He paused from the map and looked at his first mate. "Just so you know, I'm done after this trip. I was fine sliding a bit of dope under the radar, but this has all got too crazy for me. I'm calling the boss once we dock."

Pepe looked over his shoulder at the captain and nodded. "Yeah. Better to get out while we still can. This shit has a way of pulling you in so you can never be free of it again."

"Short career, I reckon," Butty agreed, and went back to his map.

After telling Pepe to get some rest, Butty made his course change and spent the next four hours sipping coffee, humming tunes, and watching the ocean pass under the keel. One of the crew showed up for his watch at the helm, but Butty sent him away, telling him he was fine to double up. The man was a quiet fellow, so it didn't seem odd when he left without a word. To avoid more drama, Butty had decided not to tell anyone he'd adjusted his course until they showed up at Grand Cayman and he could handle the situation.

The rest of the day rolled by without incident, as far as he knew, Butty staying in the wheelhouse and trading turns at the helm with Pepe. The cook brought them lunch, then dinner, and apart from bathroom breaks, the two whiled away the hours telling stories and avoiding the crew. It was a long night. Each man rested as best he could while the other took watch, and when cook brought them breakfast and coffee in the morning, they were both exhausted and ready to reach the island.

When lunchtime arrived, they could make out the low island in the distance, and Butty left Pepe at the helm while he went below to gauge the men's mood for himself. He figured he'd eat with them, then announce that they would be anchoring near Grand Cayman and Jorge would be leaving. But when he walked into the mess, right away he could tell the men were all on edge.

Cook, who would usually be whistling a tune or joking with someone, went about his business in silence, and no one would look Butty in the eye.

"Let's hear it," he finally said, tired of the uncomfortable mumblings around the table. "Say whatever it is you have to say."

The group looked at each other, all hoping someone else would lead. Cook quietly retreated to the galley, and the kid, Felix, scurried after him, leaving seven men at the table, plus the captain.

"The men want to know what's in the extra crates," Jorge said. "Everyone's concerned."

Butty stared at the man who'd promised to work hard until port. "That's funny. We've been running this route and doing just fine until you showed up. Now, all of a sudden, *everyone* is concerned?" He looked around the table at each man in turn. None of them would face his glare. "Seems like you're the one stirring up shit and causing trouble, mate."

Jorge sneered. "They've all been worried since that bomb in Miami. I'm just the first one to speak up. It ain't fair risking their lives while you're smuggling dope, man."

Butty began seething inside, but he fought to keep calm, or at least appear calm. "What do you know about the bomb?" he asked, as a thought crossed his mind.

Jorge shrugged his shoulders. "It ain't no secret, man. They all been talking about it," he said, pointing around the table. "You're asking them to take the risk and you're pocketing all the money. That's bullshit."

"You work for Pérez, don't you?" Butty said, sliding his chair back and standing.

"I don't know what you're talking about, man," Jorge replied. "I don't know no Pérez."

Damn, Butty thought to himself, annoyed he hadn't realised it before. Alfonso Pérez planted a guy on his ship to do exactly what Jorge had successfully done. Cause a shitstorm.

"Did you plant the bomb on my ship?" he demanded, pointing at the Cuban.

"You're crazy," Jorge replied, rising to his feet. "You're just saying all this bullshit so you don't have to explain to these guys what you're up to."

Butty knew he'd been right; Jorge was a spy. The Cuban had a brief look of panic on his face when he'd been accused. The man had recovered quickly, but Butty had seen it. That was it; he'd throw Jorge overboard as soon as they reached Grand Cayman. The guy didn't even deserve a ride to shore. The captain took his first step around the long dining table when he heard someone slam the metal top. He halted and looked at Rolando, whose face was blossoming red and his fist shook with rage on the table.

"I signed up to ship bananas from Ecuador to Miami. Not this other thing you're doing," he hissed. "My family can't eat if I'm in jail, or dead. It's not right you never told us what's going on."

The wind went out of Butty's sails, and he sighed. Rolando was right. The boss had told Butty to pick up extra cargo in Panama, and that's what he'd done. It had taken two or three trips before Butty and Pepe had figured out what they were transporting, and by then it was running smoothly. No one said anything more and time passed by, until he hadn't thought about it again. Until the bomb. All this time, the rest of the crew had played along, but as screwed up as Jorge's motives were, he was right in the fact that Butty and his boss had taken advantage of the crew.

"I'm sorry, Rolando, you're right," Butty said, looking around the table. "I apologise to each of you. I should have told you what we were doing and made sure the boss gave you something extra."

Faces softened, and several men nodded. Except Jorge.

"Saying that now don't make it right, man," he said. "You owe these guys."

"How about you stay out of this," Butty snapped. He knew he should have kept his cool, but the man was pushing his buttons. "You're not helping the situation."

"I'm not helping *your* situation, you mean," Jorge rebutted. "These men deserve better."

"I agree, they do," Butty said, trying to force his attention back to the crew he'd known for over a year. "And I'm saying I'll make things right."

"By putting them in the middle of a drug war in Miami?" Jorge continued. "How's that doing right by them? You'll get them killed."

"I want no more of this," Rolando shouted, and several of the men muttered their approval. "Let's get rid of the extra cargo before we get home. We want no part of it."

Butty threw his hands up. "Do you even know what you're saying? That's the last thing we should do. That'll have everyone mad at us."

"Mad at *you*," Jorge pointed out, his accusatory finger aimed at Butty.

"You're off this ship!" Butty yelled and stomped towards Jorge. "We're arriving at Grand Cayman now. That's as far as you're going."

Before Butty could reach the Cuban, several of the crew grabbed his arms and stopped him.

"He spoke up for us and now you want him gone," Rolando protested. "He stays, or we all go!"

Several of the other men cheered in agreement. It wasn't unanimous support, but Butty knew he was in big trouble. He shook the men from his arms and backed away.

"Don't listen to him, fellas. I'm telling you he's working for Alfonso Pérez, who wants nothing more than to see us at each other's throats. Let's finish this run; I'll get you more money to make it worth your while, then we'll all go our separate ways and let some other suckers run their drugs for them."

The crew looked at each other and for a second, Butty thought he'd won them back. Then he looked at Jorge, who pushed his shirt aside to reveal a gun in his waistband.

"Shit," Butty groaned, and ran for the steps.

"Hey," Rolando said, as Jorge rushed past him in pursuit. "We don't want any of that."

His words echoed around the mess as Butty flew up two flights of steps to reach the wheelhouse.

"Pepe!" he yelled. "Jorge's going nuts, mate, he's got a bloody gun!"

Butty threw a glance out of the window and saw they were near to the north side of the island, which was far less inhabited. Not that the place was big to start with, but all he could see was iron-shore coast, mangroves, and a dangerous-looking reef protecting a large sound. He scrambled to the back of the wheelhouse where he kept a shotgun in a cabinet, but he'd barely touched the handle when Jorge burst in.

"No!" Butty screamed as Pepe lunged at the gunman.

The shot was oddly muffled by Pepe's body as he wrapped himself over Jorge and shoved them both out of the door into the railing. Butty left the cabinet and rushed to help his friend. Jorge's eyes were wide, and Pepe's lifeless body slumped to the metal walkway, bringing Butty up short. The two men stared at each other. Jorge's expression soon shifted from shock to anger, and his right arm rose. Butty didn't wait to ask after his intentions. He raced across the wheelhouse and swung out the port side door as a deafening blast followed him and a bullet ricocheted off the door jamb.

Butty flew down the steps to the main deck, leaping down the last three, and continuing towards the bow. Wood chips flying in the air to his right told him not to stop or look back, so he took the only option which came to mind in the moment. Veering left, and sailing through the air, it felt like he'd plummeted a hundred feet before hitting the ocean below with a bone-crushing splash.

8

After her run, AJ had called Pearl to come and pick her up, and texted Jackson, saying she'd see him the next day. She hadn't touched the glass of wine he'd poured her at the cottage, but she put a dent in a bottle of Chardonnay at Reg and Pearl's house, then crashed in their spare room with Coop for company. The dog thought the sleepover was the best thing ever, which almost coaxed a smile out of AJ. Somewhere around 2:00am, she finally couldn't stop the tears from coming. Thirty minutes later, exhausted and cried out, she fell asleep.

With a lot of coffee, and Thomas's ever-present smile, she made it through the next morning without falling apart in front of her customers. She led the deep dive, and as usual, being in her 'happy place' underwater was the best therapy, but hanging out alone on the boat while Thomas led the second dive on a shallower reef reversed the effect. Jackson texted her once, but she hadn't replied.

His decision had hit her so hard, AJ needed to keep the problem at arm's length, allowing herself breathing room to cope with it in pieces rather than face the enormity of how her life was about to change. Jackson was leaving. That much was fact, and no amount of discussion would change it, or, she'd decided, should change it.

The only remaining decision was how many bags he'd be packing when he left. Everything he owned, or just what he needed to be at sea for several months.

With the boat cleaned and the rental gear stowed away, Thomas idled *Hazel's Odyssey* out to the overnight mooring, and AJ wandered up to the hut. Pearl handed her a sandwich and another cup of coffee.

"I need a nap," she grumbled, but knowing she couldn't avoid going home and facing Jackson.

"Heard anything more about the *Tickled Pink*?" Pearl asked, although AJ knew she was just being motherly and making conversation to avoid the uncomfortable silence that tended to hang over anyone going through troubled times.

"I texted a bit with Casey," Reg said, with one eye on his crews turning his boats around for the afternoon trips. "They raised her and towed her around to the Yacht Club marina, so I assume she didn't have a gaping hole in the hull we couldn't see. Casey said she'd let me know once the boat had been inspected."

"Do we have to give statements, or fill out a report?" AJ asked, hoping the answer would be no.

"I expect so," Reg replied. "How in-depth that will need to be will probably depend on what they find."

"Insurance companies are going to be involved," AJ grumbled. "So it won't matter if the sinking was accidental or not; they'll want reams of paperwork just to delay them writing a cheque."

"Maybe so," Reg replied, and they all turned to look as a white car pulled into the sloped car park.

It was too early for afternoon customers as the boats wouldn't leave for another hour. A young man in beige shorts and a grey golf shirt got out of what AJ guessed to be a hire car. He looked their way.

"Oh," Pearl blurted, nudging her husband. "Forgot to tell you. A fella called and wanted to meet you."

"Me?" Reg questioned.

"Yeah. Says you might have known his grandfather."

"Who's his grandfather?"

"He said a name, but I can't remember," Pearl replied. "I was driving when he called so I couldn't write it down."

"Hello," the young man said in an English accent as he walked towards them. In his hand he carried a folder. "I'm Andy. Are you Pearl Moore? Do I have the right place?"

"Yes dear," Pearl greeted him and shook his hand. "This is our friend, AJ, and my husband Reg."

Everyone shook hands and the young man looked at Reg. "It's good to meet you, sir."

"Reg'll do nicely, mate. Sir is for officers and old men. I'm still pretending not to be an old man."

AJ managed a chuckle and Andy nervously smiled.

"Your wife probably explained. I'm hoping you're the Reg Moore who served with my grandfather. Here, I have a photograph."

He pulled a picture from the folder, carefully guarding other papers from flying away in the stiff ocean breeze. Reg took it from him and studied the faded photograph.

"Blimey. That's going back a few years, mate," he said.

Half a dozen men casually posed for the shot by the gunwale of a Royal Navy ship. Around them sat an assortment of commercial-style diving equipment and helmets. Reg looked at a much younger version of himself, then stared at each sailor in turn.

"Recognise any of the others?" Andy asked.

Reg nodded. "I remember them all. This must have been early seventies."

"1973, I believe," the young man confirmed.

"Who's your grandfather then?" Reg asked.

"Far left. So I'm told."

Reg looked up. "Right," he muttered. "You couldn't have met him."

"My father never knew him either," the young man said. "He was raised in Florida by his mother, my grandmother, until she died. He was only a lad. An aunt in London took him in after that.

My mother and father were never married, and he was killed in a car crash when I was only four, so I really don't remember much about him. They had an on-again, off-again sort of relationship. Mainly off, from what I could gather."

"Your family's had a rough go of things," AJ said, and Reg and Pearl both nodded in agreement.

"Where'd you get the picture?" Pearl asked.

"It was one of the few things of my father's my mum ended up with. She said he didn't have any other family after his aunt passed away, so she had to go through his stuff. Mum kept a box of things in the attic which I never knew about. A few years back I was asking her about my dad, and she brought the box down. I've been researching ever since, trying to find out more about him and my grandfather. This picture and a few others either came with my father from America or from his auntie in the UK. My grandfather owned a small terraced house in London, which then became my dad's, and after a few years in probate with us trying to figure out if he had other relatives, finally came to me. My mum and I have lived there ever since."

"So you came all this way to see our Reg and show him the picture?" Pearl asked.

Reg laughed before Andy could answer. "Dare say the lad wants to go diving too, don't you?"

"I would," he replied. "But I'd also like to know anything you can tell me about my grandfather. The only family I've ever known is my mum, and her side of course, but she's an only child so it's only my maternal grandparents."

"Let's sit and talk," AJ said, bringing a pair of folding beach chairs from the hut.

Reg fetched two more and while the hut didn't offer much in the way of shade from the midday sun, they were at least able to feel the breeze on their faces. AJ quickly devoured her sandwich, Pearl handed out water to everyone, and once they were settled, all eyes turned to Reg.

"He was a character, your grandad," he began. "Always up to

something. Why he got into the military, I've got no idea, 'cos he was never much for rules and discipline. If there was a curfew, he'd figure out a way to sneak in after hours, just to know he did it. Never bragged about nothing, but he'd get this wily grin on his face, and you knew he'd pulled something off."

"How long did you serve together?" Andy asked.

"Couple of years, I suppose," Reg replied, thinking it over. "Maybe three years. He was older than me. I met him after basic training. He'd already been in a while. Your grandad was a diver, like me."

"Was he a nice man?" Andy asked. "Loud? Quiet? Sad? Happy? I'd love to know anything you could tell me."

"He was a super bloke," Reg said, looking at the picture again. "Once he decided I was alright, he looked after me proper, you know? He was like that. If you were cocky or full of crap, he wouldn't have any time for you, but if he thought you were one of the good ones, he'd go to the ends of the earth for you."

Reg pointed out two other men in the picture. "Those two were Daniel and Freddie." He paused and rubbed his chin.

"Were?" AJ urged.

Reg nodded. "Lost them both in the Falklands. Unexploded ordnance in a flooded compartment. They were the two divers next up on rotation. We never knew what actually happened, but they'd just gone inside the hull breach, and bang, that was it."

"Bloody hell," AJ mumbled. "Poor buggers."

Reg shrugged his shoulders and Pearl squeezed his burly arm. "Wouldn't have known too much about it, so that's good." He pointed to another man in the photograph. "We called him Short Straw. If that bloke fell in a barrel of boobs, he'd come out sucking his thumb."

Pearl gave him a cuff on the arm this time, but Andy and AJ laughed.

"We thought he was the unluckiest sailor in the whole Navy, but things turned out alright for him in the end. By the time I retired, he'd made lieutenant commander."

"How long did you serve?" Andy asked.

"Thirty years," Reg replied. "I did the full stint."

"So who's the last one in the picture?" AJ asked, setting her empty Tupperware down and giving Pearl a thumbs-up in thanks.

"That's Riggs," Reg replied. "He did his three and got out, if I recall. He wasn't cut out for the Navy life. He'd seen a Jacques Cousteau documentary and thought diving would be fun. You know, all pretty fishies and colourful coral reefs. Then they put him in a hard hat and dropped him in a muddy harbour with freezing cold water silted out so bad you couldn't see your hand in front of your face. He said no thanks, so they trained him for topside support. Once his time was up, he couldn't leave fast enough."

AJ chuckled. She'd learnt to dive in the waters off the southern coast of England where some days it wasn't much better than what Reg had described. But others were better, and she'd still become hooked.

"So, are you here to dive and took the opportunity to say hi to Reg?" AJ asked. "Or the other way around?"

"They're hand in hand, really," Andy answered. "I got my certification a year ago with plans to come down here and dive the wreck, and this is the week I booked. Then I received an email yesterday from the Royal Navy's records department with a list of shipmates my grandfather served with, so I spent the flight over searching the names on the in-flight internet. That's how I found Reg."

"Blimey," AJ blurted. "Which wreck are you wanting to dive?"

Andy and Reg both looked at her as though she was a bit slow.

"The *Oro Verde*," Reg said. "His grandad was Raymond 'Butty' Butterworth. He was the captain of the OV."

9

Butty felt like he'd crashed through a plate glass window instead of water. He'd made an attempt at a dive, but his leap over the side had him off balance and twisted so the impact knocked all the wind from his lungs. Spluttering and coughing, he clawed for the surface, gulping for air. He spun around, expecting to see Jorge, but the *Oro Verde* had motored on, towering over him like a mountain-side gliding by. Realising his bigger problem was the thrashing propellers, he turned and swam as hard as he could, desperate to get away from the ship's drag.

He'd always been a decent swimmer, but Butty felt like a floundering fool as he splashed and pulled against the tug of his own ship's wake. Gasping for breath and taking in as much seawater as air, he was forced to stop swimming just to keep his head above the surface. Bracing for the inevitable pull from the ship, he turned and watched the stern leave him behind.

Leaning his head back, Butty took advantage of the smooth water left by the hull, and steadied his beating heart. He prayed Pepe had survived the gunshot wound, but from the way his friend had dropped to the deck, he knew he hadn't. The man had reacted in the way few people would have done; he ran straight at the source of the danger. Butty was riddled with guilt. He had run *away* from the shooter and led Jorge to the wheelhouse, where he'd killed Pepe. He slapped at the ocean in anger and screamed into the wind. What a series of errors he'd made which had led them all to their current dilemma.

He watched as the *Oro Verde*, now several hundred yards away, slowed and began a turn to port. Butty looked to shore as a swell lifted him up. At a guess, he figured it was half a mile to what appeared to be a point of land on the north-east corner of the sound. His clothes and canvas shoes were weighing him down, but he feared he'd need them if he reached the beach, so he struck out, trying to find a steady rhythm. The salt water stung his eyes, which he closed as he dipped his head, taking a breath every third stroke. Occasionally, the timing would allow him to see the *Oro Verde* but between his blurry vision and the spray from his own arms, he couldn't make out whether it was still moving or not.

Sighting the land was also difficult, and with the waves rolling in from the north-west, he was constantly being rotated, requiring corrections to his direction of travel. Finding a pace which allowed him to manage his heart rate and breathing, Butty's mind shifted back to his ship and the crew. *What would they do now?* He'd been worried Jorge would come after him and try to shoot him in the water, but the grey hulk in the distance didn't appear to be getting larger. Surely the men wouldn't side with Jorge after he'd killed Pepe? He knew that was true, but then he realised he had no way of knowing what story Alfonso Pérez's man was spinning. He could be telling them Butty had shot Pepe after taking the gun off Jorge. He groaned at the idea and pressed on towards shore.

Exhausted and mentally drained, Butty perked up when he noticed the water colour changing. He couldn't see anything clearly, but he knew the brighter tone below him was sand, which meant he'd cleared Grand Cayman's famed drop-off, and was now over the shallow finger reef. The swells soon settled and before him he noticed the waves breaking over coral which reached the surface in places. He stopped swimming and treaded water for a moment, getting a better view. The point of land was ahead to his left, still at least 500 yards away. But to reach it, he had to clear the protective reef which met the surface. Not looking forward to dealing with the sharp coral, he put his head down and continued swimming.

Glad he'd kept his shoes on, Butty stood on the old, dead coral near the surface, called ironshore, and tried to pick his way across without losing his balance. The waves, although small, continued crashing over the rocks and he struggled not to have his feet swept from under him. On the far side, a sandy bottom extended all the way to shore, where he now spotted a rickety-looking jetty with several fishing boats tied alongside. With a bold leap, he cleared the rest of the reef and splashed into the calm, clear, coastal waters, where he found he could easily stand.

For a while, Butty found it easier to swim rather than walk as the sand was soft under foot and the water still came to his chest. As he closed on the dock, he finally stood and with the water reaching his thighs, he shuffled the rest of the way.

"Dat your boat?" a voice came from one of the fishing vessels.

Butty turned and looked at the *Oro Verde*, resting dead in the water.

"Yeah," he admitted, but decided he didn't ought to say too much. He still had no idea what story would be coming from Jorge and the crew. "Had a bit of trouble, so I volunteered to swim ashore."

"Could have radioed, yer know," the man said in his musical island accent, peering over the gunwale from where he was cleaning fish. "Woulda come picked yer up."

"Next time, then," Butty replied, hoping there would never be a repeat of the circumstances he'd found himself in. "Would you happen to have some water, mate?"

The local man handed him an old, dented canteen and Butty took a long swig. The water wasn't cold, but it was salt free and tasted like heaven. He'd been cooled by the ocean but now, standing near the shore, Butty realised how intense the sun was. He lived in Florida, and his pale English skin had tanned over time, but he could feel the flesh on the back of his neck cringing in the heat.

"Thank you," he said, handing the canteen back, but the local waved him away.

"Finish dat – you'll need it. I got more."

"Thank you again," Butty responded, and gladly drained the canteen down his throat. "What town is this?"

The local man chuckled, and they both looked towards the low-lying sandy shore where one thatched roof structure was in view and a handful of taller metal roofs protruding through the casuarina trees. Town was probably a generous term.

"Dis Rum Point," the man said. "North Side's east of here aways. Dey have a store. Most everyting over da udder side of da island."

"Airport?" Butty asked.

"Yes, sir. We got one."

"Other side of the island?"

"Yes, sir."

Butty realised, having left the *Oro Verde* in a hurry, he didn't have his wallet, passport, or anything except his sopping wet clothes.

"Dat's da Wreck Bar over dere," the man said, pointing to the thatched roof building in the shade. "Maybe someone in dere from George Town, but can't be sure."

"You've been more than kind," Butty responded, handing the man the empty canteen. "I'll check at the bar."

Taking the canteen, the local man returned to cleaning his fish as Butty splashed his way out of the water and across the sand towards the rickety-looking bar. The place had a concrete knee wall with mosquito netting filling the gap to the ceiling instead of windows. Sturdy branches acted as pillars supporting the frame under the thatch-work of tightly woven fronds. The words 'Wreck Bar' were hand painted on a white piece of wood above the door, which was constructed from branches bound together. Butty pushed his way inside with sand making its way down the sides of his soaked canvas shoes, grating his skin like sandpaper.

"Hello," he said, seeing three men seated at the bar once his eyes adjusted to the dim light.

Two of them were dark-skinned local men who nodded a greeting, and the third was a Caucasian in pale blue linen trousers, a white button-down short-sleeved shirt, and a straw trilby with a dark blue band. Butty had the man pegged as American before he'd spoken a word.

"Could have saved you a swim if you called on the radio," the man said, his New York accent confirming Butty's guess.

"So I was told," Butty responded, walking between a handful of chairs and tables.

The bar appeared to be made from driftwood, and the furniture a mixture of whatever someone had been giving away. Several creaky ceiling fans whirred above them, combining with a gentle ocean breeze to push the balmy tropical air through the place, offering a relief from the blazing sun.

One of the local men slid from his stool and stepped behind the bar. "What'll it be?" he asked.

Butty noticed the men had cold beers in front of them, so somewhere was power for the fans and a cooler of sorts, but he reminded himself he was penniless.

"I left my wallet on the ship, I'm afraid," he replied, the phantom taste of a cold beer teasing his senses. "But I'd take a ride into town if anyone's heading that way."

The man in the trilby hat nodded to the barman, who reached into a cooler behind the bar and produced a Miller, popped the top, and handed it to Butty.

"You're a good man, sir," Butty said, holding up the bottle before draining half of it in one gulp.

"What brings you to Rum Point, if you don't mind me asking?" the American queried.

Butty considered his answer for a few moments. *What should he say?* There were now four men who knew he'd swum ashore from the *Oro Verde*, where the body of his friend lay in a pool of his own blood. *Would the others come ashore too? Should he go to the local authorities and tell them exactly what happened?* Butty felt overwhelmed, confused, and exhausted.

"I need to go to the local police as soon as possible," he said, and relief seemed to flood through him.

"Are you the captain of the ship?" the man in the trilby asked.

Butty nodded.

The American finished his beer, threw some money on the bar top, and slipped from his stool. "I think I can help you out. Come with me," he said, walking for the door.

Butty nodded his thanks to the two other men and followed, his feet feeling like they were being scrubbed with a wire brush. Around the front of the little bar sat a dust-covered green Jeep Wagoneer with a wood grain trim down the sides and a white roof.

"I'm still wet, mate," Butty said as the man opened the driver's door.

"I have a towel in the back," he replied, moving to the tailgate and swinging it open. "Here," he said, passing Butty a blue and white striped beach towel. "Sit on the back and shake some of that sand off your shoes."

Butty did so and let out a sigh of relief when he slipped the canvas shoes from his feet. "I appreciate you helping me out. It's best I get the police out here as soon as I can."

"What's your name?" the man asked.

"Raymond Butterworth. Everyone calls me Butty."

"I'm Gene Gould," the man responded, extending a hand. "And in the forty-five minutes it'll take me to drive you to the police station in George Town, I'm gonna give you an alternative on how to proceed."

Butty let go of the man's hand and looked at him curiously. "An alternative? But you don't even know what's happened on that ship."

Gould shrugged his shoulders. "Maybe I know more than you think. Give me forty-five minutes, then decide."

Butty wasn't sure what to say, so he finished brushing off his feet, walked to the front, and placed the towel on the passenger side of the bench seat before getting in.

"You bought me a beer and are about to give me a ride. Least I can do is listen to what you have to say."

"That's the spirit, Butty, old boy," Gould said, and started the Jeep.

10

The Fox and Hare pub was AJ's favourite hangout, which she frequented at least once a week. A couple of times a month it was mandatory, as Pearl played and sang on their little stage in the corner. Those Friday nights were always a packed house, with a mixture of expats and Caymanians enjoying her gritty rock 'n' roll voice. The pub itself was a plain-looking building on the inland side of North West Point Road, but once inside, the decor was the dark wood of a traditional English alehouse, with football and rugby on the television screens and dartboards in the back.

AJ was in no mood for socialising, but after spending the afternoon going around in circles with Jackson, she didn't want to be home either. His second bombshell had been that he was leaving the next day, meeting the *Sword of the Sentry* in Miami before leaving for several months at sea. On that note, she'd gone for another run, briefly stopped back by the cottage to grab clean clothes, then driven to Reg and Pearl's to shower.

"Stop looking at me like I'm made of china and about to break into pieces at any moment," she announced to her friends at the table. "I'll be fine."

"Of course you will, love," Pearl agreed, squeezing her arm.

"You don't look fine," her young Norwegian friend Nora said, in her flat tone with a hint of a Scandinavian accent. "You look like shit."

"Thanks," AJ responded, but couldn't hold back a grin.

Nora kept her words to a minimum, but the ones she did use were always to the point without a hint of sugar coating.

"Nora," Pearl admonished, scowling at the tall, slender blonde. "She just needs a little support right now."

"Sorry," Nora replied, not sounding the least bit apologetic. "But she says she's fine when she doesn't look fine, so I'm saying I think she's not. But she doesn't look Chinese either."

"China, like ceramic, not the bloody country," AJ explained.

Nora's English was almost perfect, but occasionally there were phrases or idioms she didn't understand, especially the English terms with multiple meanings. She still appeared puzzled.

"Jugs and dinner plates and whatnot," Pearl said.

"You think you look like a dinner plate?" Nora asked.

"No!" AJ replied, rolling her eyes. "I was saying everyone was looking at me like I was made of the stuff plates and jugs and coffee cups are made of. You know, because that stuff breaks easily."

Nora nodded. "So that's why you say I'm like a bull in a china shop, because I break things. I always thought you meant I was like a bull in a shop owned by a Chinese person, which I never understood. Makes more sense now."

"Glad that's cleared up," Reg said unenthusiastically. "Who needs another drink? It's my shout."

With nods from everyone, Reg stood and made his way through the crowd to the bar.

"Did you say he's leaving tomorrow?" Thomas asked.

AJ nodded. "Yeah. The Miami flight after lunch."

"I can arrest him in the morning if you like," Nora offered.

AJ chuckled. "Tempting, I must say. But I don't think that's appropriate use of your authority as a police constable. He's decided to leave, so I need to let him leave."

"Dat's too bad," Thomas said sympathetically. "I really like da dude."

"Good gracious me," Pearl said, shaking her head. "You two are bloody awful at cheering her up!"

"I'm sorry!" Thomas blurted. "I mean, I feel bad for you and all. I was just sayin'…" With a look from Pearl, he trailed off and gave up.

"Yeah," Pearl said. "I think it's better you stop trying to help." She stood. "It's time for me to play something." She put a hand on AJ's shoulder. "Got a special request, love?"

AJ shrugged her shoulders. "Nah. You know I like everything you sing."

Pearl turned to leave.

"Actually I do have one!" AJ said and Pearl paused. "'Tears of a Clown' seems appropriate."

AJ laughed and Pearl waved her off with a shake of the head, continuing towards the stage.

"Break a leg, love," Reg called after his wife as he placed drinks on the table. "Look who I found at the bar," he added, and AJ turned to see Andy Butterworth standing next to the big man.

"Hi Andy," she greeted him. "Grab a chair. This is Thomas, who you may have seen at the dock today. We work together. And this is our friend Nora."

Everyone shook hands and said hello, shuffling chairs to make room at the table.

"Reg mentioned you'd all be here tonight," Andy said. "I had nothing else to do so I hope you don't mind me crashing your group?"

"More the merrier," AJ replied, although she was feeling the least merry of anyone. "Ready for tomorrow?"

Andy smiled. "I'm excited. I know the wreck is almost unrecognisable now, but it'll still be a great experience for me."

He'd originally booked with another dive operator, but had called them and explained his story after talking with Reg and AJ. The other dive op had graciously cancelled his booking so he could go out with Reg. Reg then decided he'd dive too and they'd go on AJ's boat as she only had four customers for Saturday.

From the stage, Pearl's voice came over the speakers, and the house music died down.

"Who's ready for a little reggae to get the evening started?"

The crowd cheered and Reg looked at AJ.

"She don't usually do much reggae."

AJ laughed. "I think that's my fault."

Pearl launched into The Beat's ska version of 'Tears of a Clown', which got AJ to her feet, dancing along with the rest of the crowd.

Twenty minutes later, Pearl wrapped up her first set with a cover of 'Daniel' by Elton John, then returned to the table with the house music resuming and conversation restarting all around them. After reluctantly dragging herself along to the pub, AJ was now glad she'd come. Escape is what she needed, and for a short while at least, her friends pulled her out of her melancholy funk.

"You're amazing," Andy said as Pearl took her seat.

"Just an old woman squawking out a few tunes," she replied.

Reg shook his head and kissed her cheek. "Young man knows talent when he hears it."

"How's your mum doing over all this, Andy?" AJ asked. "She encourage you to find out more about your dad and grandad?"

Andy thought for a moment before replying. "She's been tolerant. That's probably the best way to describe it. I wouldn't say she's encouraged me, but she hasn't tried to discourage me either."

"Probably a bit awkward for her, yeah?"

"A little, I think," he agreed. "Mum's never said as much, but I get the impression she was in love with my father, and wished their relationship had been much more than it was. She used his surname on my birth certificate, which I think was wishful thinking of what might have been. She never married, and has never dated much that I recall."

"Do you have a girlfriend?" Nora asked, and her abruptness clearly startled the young Englishman.

"Ummm... no. Well, I..." he took a moment to gather his thoughts while the beautiful Norwegian stared at him impatiently. "I mean, I did have a girlfriend, but I don't think I do now."

"You don't think you do?" Nora responded. "I think you should know this." She looked at AJ. "Although there seems to be a lot of confusion lately about this sort of thing."

AJ stuck her tongue out at her friend before turning to Andy. "Pay no attention to her. She has the social graces of a chainsaw."

"I prefer bull in a Chinaman's shop," Nora said, and grinned.

A woman pushed through the crowd and approached the table, smiling at the group. She had the polished appearance of a professional despite her casual attire and light use of make-up, a toned figure, and perfect dark skin which belied her real age of forty-three.

"Hello, Sally," Pearl greeted her.

Reg nodded and AJ managed a smile. She liked Sally Regis, but the Fox and Hare wasn't the reporter from the *Cayman Islands Daily News'* usual haunt, so she guessed there was a reason for her appearance.

"Lovely set, Pearl, thank you," Sally replied. "Hi Reg, AJ," she continued, acknowledging them both. "I was hoping to bump into you two."

"Writing an article about the friendliest dive ops on the island?" Reg replied with a sparkle in his eyes.

"I think we already did that a few years back," Sally replied. "I was actually curious about the boat that sank, the *Tickled Pink*. I believe you two were the first to dive it?"

"We were not," Reg said.

"Oh. I was told you two dived from the DoE boat yesterday morning to evaluate the wreck."

Pearl nudged her husband.

"Yeah, we did that. But the first to dive it were the two blokes who stumbled across it that morning," Reg said, frowning at his wife.

Sally laughed. "Right. Good point. Well, Reg, as the second divers to the site, and the first official eyes on the wreck, what could you tell me about it?" She looked back and forth between Reg and AJ.

"Sitting in the sand, away from the reef, which was good. Hadn't started leaking diesel to any large degree," Reg replied. "Looked to be pretty straightforward to salvage, which I believe they did in the afternoon. We weren't there for that part."

Sally nodded. "I see, thank you. And why did it sink?"

"Somehow, they let the sea get on the wrong side of the hull."

AJ stifled a chuckle as best she could and Sally rolled her eyes at Reg.

"Honestly, love, we don't know," he said, shrugging his shoulders. "Could have been a bloody great big hole in the bottom, but we couldn't see while it was sitting in the sand. I don't know if they've completed their inspection yet, but you'd need to talk to the RCIPS about that."

Sally's eyes flicked to Nora, who frowned in return.

"Not my department," the constable said quickly.

"My apologies," Sally said, looking at Thomas. "I don't think we've officially met, but I've seen you with AJ."

Thomas rose from his seat and extended a hand. "Thomas Bodden, miss."

"I'm Sally Regis. Nice to meet you," she said in return before turning to Andy.

"Andy Butterworth," he said, introducing himself and standing to shake her hand. "I'm just visiting for a week."

Sally held his hand a moment longer. "Butterworth? That name sounds familiar. Have you been to the island before? Family here, perhaps?"

"I haven't," he replied. "But apparently my grandfather spent a little time here."

AJ watched the woman's eyes brighten. She smelled a story.

"When would that have been?" she persisted, finally releasing the young man's hand.

"1976," Andy replied. "But I'm here to try and find out more about him."

"Really?" Sally said, looking around for a chair she could use.

"Here," AJ said, getting up. "It's my shout anyhow. Get you something, Sally?"

"A gin and tonic, please," the reporter replied, sliding quickly into AJ's vacated chair.

11

They headed east along the coastline, passing a few scattered homes near the water on their left. The road was nothing more than a marl trail, barely wide enough for two vehicles to pass, but that didn't appear to be an issue as Butty hadn't seen another car yet.

"Beautiful part of the island up here," Gould said, pointing to the beachfront land. "Slice of paradise, don't you think?"

"I dare say I could get by living here," Butty replied, admiring the tropical coastline, although his thoughts were still elsewhere. "Isn't George Town south of here?" he asked, recalling the marine chart he'd used to navigate.

Gould nodded. "It is. In fact, it's south-west of here, but between us and town is the North Sound and acres of low-lying wetlands. We have to go east, then south, before backtracking all the way west."

"Sounds like a boat is the best way to get to Rum Point," Butty commented, bouncing on the seat as Gould tried his best to miss the worst potholes.

"It is," the man agreed.

"So what brought you out there?" Butty asked, his curiosity running wild.

"The *Oro Verde,*" Gould replied nonchalantly.

Butty spun in his seat. "How did you know we'd be there? I didn't know we were coming to Cayman until a day ago."

"I told you, I know more than you'd think." Gould turned his head and threw Butty a mischievous grin. "I saw you in the distance from my hotel this morning. Took a guess you'd end up on the north side."

"Why the interest in a small private freighter carrying bananas?" Butty asked.

Sure, the man could have seen the name of the boat through a pair of binoculars, but he seemed far too interested for it just to be a coincidence. Butty began to shift uncomfortably in his seat. A few more homes appeared on either side of the road, and Gould made a right turn into a small township before answering.

"Tell you what, Captain. You seem like a good guy, so I'll talk straight with you. How's that sound?"

"Best way to be," Butty agreed, although he was becoming more unnerved by the stranger.

"You're not just carrying bananas on board, are you?"

Butty's heart froze for a moment. His day was going from awful to unimaginably bad.

"What do you mean?" he said, but he knew his words held no conviction.

Gould laughed. "The four crates of marijuana in your hold, my friend."

"Who the hell are you?" Butty responded, unsure whether he should be running from the man or hearing him out. He was leaning towards jumping from the Jeep, but the landing looked vicious on the limestone trail.

"Settle down, Captain, I'm on your side, man," Gould assured him. "Tell me what went wrong aboard your ship."

Butty still wasn't ready to admit to anything as he had no idea who he was talking to. Getting justice for Pepe was foremost on his mind, and getting to a police station still felt like his safest option.

"Who are you working for?" Butty asked.

"I doubt you'd believe me if I told you," Gould replied.

"Try me."

Gould reached into his trouser pocket and for a second, Butty wondered if he was about to have a gun pulled on him for the second time that day. Instead, the man flipped open a wallet to reveal a gold badge with an eagle across the top and the words 'CIA' in raised letters against a blue background.

"Bloody hell," Butty muttered, figuring he was now completely screwed.

The guy was playing friendly, but he already knew about the drugs, and pretty soon, he'd surely know about Pepe.

"Were you here already?" Butty asked. "Or did you fly here because of the *Oro Verde*?"

"I'm based here," the man replied. "A lot of money passes through the island, and I represent the CIA's interests in some of those transactions."

"So it's coincidental that I redirected the ship here?"

"Essentially," Gould agreed. "But regardless, you would have been coming by here next time through. And I'd say it's fortuitous, seeing as I can help you through this little mess. So tell me what happened."

Butty sighed. At this point, he couldn't think of a good reason not to be honest with the guy, but he was still wary. "There's a guy aboard the *Oro Verde* called Jorge. I have his full name in the paperwork in my berth. He shot my first mate, Pepe, this morning."

Gould didn't flinch. In fact Butty couldn't detect any reaction at all from the man. Not even a change in his casual expression.

"Okay," he said calmly. "Who's this Jorge guy, and why did he shoot your first mate?"

"I think he's a plant," Butty said, before he could filter himself.

He was too tired and devastated by his friend's death to play games anymore.

"If you know about the drugs, I'm guessing you know who's involved?"

Gould shrugged his shoulders. "If you're talking about Sal Herrera, then yes."

"Do you know who Alfonso Pérez is?"

"Of course," Gould replied. "*He* planted the Jorge guy?"

"I'm pretty sure. He was trouble from the start. Stirred up all the crew, turning them against me and Pepe. He was after me when Pepe tried to stop him and got himself killed instead of me."

"I doubt Jorge intended on killing you," Gould said, which took Butty aback once more.

"He was chasing me through the ship with a bloody gun, mate," Butty protested.

"Sure, but Pérez wants Herrera put out of business in Florida, not the middle of the Caribbean. The bomb wasn't big enough to sink the ship, but it would have had the authorities swarming if it had gone off before you unloaded the cargo."

Butty shook his head. "You knew Pérez planted that bomb, yet you let me sail along with it strapped to the hull? That's bloody brilliant. I'm not feeling too much like trusting you."

Gould held up a hand. "We didn't know until the sheriff's bomb squad pulled it off. But who else would be interested in blowing a hole in the *Oro Verde*?"

Butty took a few deep breaths. The man was right and he knew it. But why wasn't he seizing the *Oro Verde* right now? He could make a drug bust, catch a murderer, and maybe even link Jorge to Pérez. The CIA could take out two Miami drug lords in one bust.

"You don't have any jurisdiction here, do you?" Butty asked, connecting the dots.

They'd reached a T-junction, and Gould turned right along another, slightly wider, packed limestone road. The dust swirled around the Jeep and came in through the open windows. Butty guessed he must have the Wagoneer detailed just about every time he drove it.

"I have influence," Gould replied, resting an arm out of the window. "But if you're wondering why I don't storm out there and grab your ship and its cargo, you're right, I don't have the authority in the Cayman Islands to do that."

"But there's more to it than that, right?" Butty suggested, sensing the man was in no hurry to rush out on the water, regardless of the jurisdiction issue.

Gould's expression turned serious for the first time, and he looked over at Butty, sizing him up. "There's a lot more going on behind the scenes than you're aware of. You're not a US citizen, correct?"

Butty shook his head. "British. I work out of Miami but for an English owner on a boat registered in Panama. In theory I'm paid in the UK, so it's legal."

"Well, no matter," Gould responded. "Probably better for what lays ahead that you're not an American citizen. But you know there is a US presidential election coming up in November, right?"

"Sure. I read the newspapers. Sometimes," Butty replied, although he usually sought out any English newspaper he could find, just to see the sports scores from back home.

"Okay, so everyone who hasn't lived under a rock for the past few years knows about Nixon and his Watergate mess."

"Sure," Butty said again, more curious about the man's comment regarding what lay ahead.

"So here's the thing," Gould began. "I told you I'd be honest with you, so I will be. But what I'm about to tell you is top secret, and I'll deny I ever said a word of it if a situation ever arose. Understand?"

"All sounds a bit James Bond, but okay," Butty replied.

Gould shrugged his shoulders. "I'm CIA, what do you expect? So here's the deal. We had some things in play under that idiot Nixon, which Gerald Ford got cold feet over, and now he's about to lose the election to the peanut farmer. If Reagan had won over Ford in the primary we'd have had a chance, but now Carter will sure as shit back out of everything that don't smell of roses. Are you following me?"

Butty recognised all the names involved, but had even less

interest in American politics than he did in elections back home. "Sure," he said, just to keep things moving.

"All right. Now, South America is a shitshow, as you've seen, having had a few dealings down there. We got revolutions, communists, dictators, and every other jumped-up rebel group trying to take over this government and that. What this also gives us is opportunity. We're the land of the free, right? And we support democracy wherever we can lend a hand. At the CIA, we're charged with facilitating some of that support."

Gould paused and looked over at Butty.

"Okay," the Englishman said, completely baffled how any of this had anything to do with him or the *Oro Verde*.

"So right now, under that wimp, Ford, we're what you might call treading water for a while. When Carter wins in November, we'll be put on a tight leash, then in four more years' time, we'll get a Republican back in the White House, this time one with a decent pair, and we'll be back in business, stamping out commies."

"Because Vietnam went so well for you..." Butty found himself saying.

Gould laughed. "Fair point, Butty, fair point. Let's assume that some of us learned a thing or two from that disaster and are using those lessons this time around."

Butty thought for a moment before speaking. "I still don't see how I, or the *Oro Verde*, have anything to do with all this, Gene."

"You really don't know much about what you've got yourself into, do you?"

"I guess not," Butty admitted. "But you talked about what lies ahead. How about you tell me what that is?"

Gould grinned. "I understand," he said, as they finally joined a paved road on the edge of a town which was clearly larger than anything else Butty had seen. Which wasn't to say it was big, just more than a few scattered homes.

"The people you work for also work for us," Gould said.

Butty's mouth opened, but nothing came out. He had no idea

what to say. "The owner of the *Oro Verde* works for the CIA?" he finally managed.

"No," Gould replied, laughing again. "Sal Herrera is working with the CIA."

"He's a drug dealer!" Butty blurted, as the Jeep slowed and he noticed a police station sign ahead.

Gould shrugged his shoulders. "America smokes weed, man, who cares? The Bible punchers and politicians get on their high horse about it, but the bottom line is, no one really gives a shit, and everyone's taking a toke. Herrera's doing nothing different than a rum importer, except he's having to do it under the table."

Gould brought the Jeep to a stop outside the police station, put it in park and sat back, looking at Butty.

"You walk in there and lead the locals out to your ship, you're going to jail in the UK for drug smuggling. If you tell me you'll continue helping out Herrera as captain of whatever ship is in play, then I'll make all that go away, and you'll be a free man."

Butty wished Gould had got to the point a little sooner so he had more time to think about everything he'd just learned. A lot of it was still baffling to him.

"What about Pepe?" he asked.

"I can't make him undead, I'm afraid," Gould replied. "But if you say this Jorge guy killed him, I'll make sure Pérez's man is locked up, or takes a one-way trip to the deep blue. Your choice."

Butty flinched at the ease in which the CIA agent had put such power in his hands. He'd wanted Jorge arrested and sentenced for killing Pepe, but he was now offered the opportunity for instant justice, and the idea was terrifying.

"We can handle all that later," Gould continued. "Right now, I need to know whether you're on board, or not. Those guys won't sit around for too long on the *Oro Verde*, wondering whether you're coming back. Someone's gonna start steaming for Miami."

Butty let out a long breath. Sitting in an English jail didn't hold any appeal for a man of the seas. He didn't much care for the drug trade, but Gould made a persuasive point. Who cared about a little weed.

"I guess I'm in," he said quietly.

Gould slapped him on the shoulder. "Good man, Butty Boy, I knew you'd see sense."

"I have one more question," Butty said, although he really had a hundred queries racing around in his mind. "What does the CIA get out of shipping weed into America?"

Gould laughed. "Not a goddamned thing, Butty. But you know that guy you just met in Panama?"

"Noriega?"

"Yeah, Manuel Noriega. Well he works for us, too. And he's the fella putting guns in the hands of the good guys down there. That's what the weed is paying for."

"Bloody hell," Butty muttered, as Gould pulled away from the police station.

12

Metallica echoed around the little cottage and AJ slowly stirred awake. Perhaps if she chose a different song by a different band it would jolt her into consciousness, but her brain was used to hearing the same guitar chords every morning, so despite the boisterous sound, she eased into wakefulness. For a few seconds, her world was as it should be. Annoyed to be awoken so early, as she felt every working day at 6:00am, yet buoyed by an underlying feeling of contentment. After all, she was living out her dream in paradise.

But as she reached over to turn off the alarm on her mobile, the reality of current events engulfed her like a fisherman's net, dragging her back to one of the worst days in her life. For a moment AJ couldn't breathe. Next to her, Jackson moved, and she sensed he was awake. She turned off the alarm. The words 'don't go' hung on the edge of her lips, but that wasn't what she said.

"Flight's at two?" she asked, knowing full well that it was.

"Yeah," he said softly. "Let's not leave things like this, AJ," he continued, sitting up. "This doesn't have to be the end. We're too good together."

AJ swung her legs out of bed. Her feet only just reached the floor, and she wondered if her legs would give way if she tried to walk. Her words and actions in the next few moments would define her future, and his. She felt paralysed, knowing her only choices were misery or more misery. The part of her life she'd considered to be set, etched in stone, was now suddenly adrift. She was losing her anchor in a raging sea encircled by brutal rocks.

"I can't make you stay. I know it wouldn't be fair," she said, her voice on the brink of deserting her. "But I can't go back to missing you constantly and only seeing you for a few days every three months. After having the past few years, we can't take that step backwards and imagine it will work. When we were apart before, there was always the hope of a future together."

"I'm not pretending it'll be easy," Jackson replied, resting a gentle hand against her shoulder. "But we can still have a future."

"How?" she rebutted. "I carry on waiting until maybe, one day, you decide you're done saving the world and can be with me? Hardly a future."

"So I should stay here and ignore my passion and calling?" he responded. "You're living with a part of me. I'm not whole living like this. In the same way I could stay, you could come with me."

He moved closer and she stood, slipping from his touch.

"You moved here," she snapped. "You said you were done with Sea Sentry and ready to live with me. You did all that, and said all that, and now it's you whose decided that's not enough. I'm not enough. You've decided to leave and you're asking me to sit and wait for something that may never come."

"You'd rather I stay and feel like I'm wasting my life away?"

"I'm sorry you feel that living with me is wasting your life."

Jackson groaned. "You know that's not what I meant, AJ. You're the only woman I've truly loved, and I can't imagine ever feeling this way about anyone else."

She walked in the dark to the bathroom and closed the door. There was so much more she wanted to say, but there seemed no point. She couldn't win. The past thirty-six hours couldn't be erased. There was no reset button. No do-over. If there could have been a compromise solution where Jackson worked remotely for an ocean conservation effort, whether that was Sea Sentry or someone else, it didn't matter now. Maybe he'd fully pursued that avenue or maybe he hadn't, she didn't know for sure, but he had booked a flight at 2:00pm that day to leave the island, and leave her behind. That much she knew.

"So this is it?" Jackson said from behind the door she was now leaning back against, her face in her hands. "You're saying we're done?"

She wanted to scream. Pummelling the man she loved with all her heart was also an option. In the end she did neither.

"It's bullshit. You created this whole mess. You're the one breaking my heart, and you're the one leaving. But yes, if that's what you need to hear. We're done. Now just leave, Jackson."

She felt a hand thump on the door. "It's not what I want. I don't want us to be over."

"Too bad," she snapped back. "We are. Now take a walk somewhere until I leave. I don't want to see you."

AJ held her breath, listening for sounds of movement. After what felt like forever, she heard footsteps on the hardwood floor and dresser drawers opening and closing. Finally, the front door creaked open, and she slid to the floor and sobbed.

Thomas had *Hazel's Odyssey* alongside the dock with the customer gear already attached to tanks by the time AJ arrived.

"Morning, Boss," he said in a slightly more subdued manner than usual.

She dropped the bags of ice she'd bought at Foster's market by the cooler, and handed Thomas a brown paper bag.

"Hey," she managed.

Thomas took out the pastry she'd bought and moaned in delight when he sank his teeth into it.

"Tanks, Boss. I set up gear for Mr Andy. I guessed him at a medium for the BCD."

AJ nodded and sipped from her stainless-steel travel mug. Setting it down, she opened the bags of ice and tipped them into the cooler. Thomas had already filled the reusable drinks bottles they supplied for their customers to use, negating the need for one-time-use plastic bottles on the boat. Tap water was safe to drink on the island as it all came from a desalination plant.

Thomas sensed she needed space, so he sat on one of the benches and began scrolling on his mobile. With one man leaving her life, her crazy brain tossed out the thought of Thomas leaving. It would simply be too much. The two had worked together for seven years now. She couldn't imagine working with anyone else for that long. He was the perfect balance on the other side of the scales. She loved him like a brother. Her whole morning had felt like she was trying to breathe at 20,000 feet above sea level, each inhalation falling short of the air she needed. The concept of running her business without Thomas was now like a gut punch when she was already winded. *Why was her mind doing this to her?*

"Are you happy, Thomas?" she asked.

He looked up from his mobile as surprised as she'd been by the idea falling from the sky.

"Of course," he answered. "Why?"

"Because you're as big a part of Mermaid Divers as I am," she said, unsure where her confused thoughts and emotions were taking her. "I don't know that..."

Her voice trailed off as a lump formed in her throat.

"You're da mermaid, Boss," he said, his usual sparkle replaced by concern in his eyes. "You're da only ting irreplaceable in dis deal. Me, boats, dock, all of it, we're just decoration around what you do. And I'm happy to be dat, Boss. I love workin' wit you."

AJ couldn't look at her friend. She didn't want him to see the tears rolling down her face. She wasn't as uncomfortable with sappy discussions as some of her countrymen, but she had a limit to the emotions she was willing to share in public. And crying simply made her mad. Her throat had closed up so there was no chance she could say anything anyway.

"Hey," he said brightly, letting her off the hook. "Dat lady, Miss Regis, she run an article on Mr Andy in da *Cayman Islands Daily News* dis morning. It's online."

AJ wiped her face and spun around. "I felt bad we couldn't really warn him. That woman can get anyone to start blabbering when she tries."

"Maybe dis will help him find out more about his grandpappy," Thomas offered. "Could be a good ting."

"Could be, I suppose," she agreed, sitting on the bench beside him. "Blimey, she banged out a story pretty sharpish, eh? Even found a picture of him and one of the *Oro Verde* before they turned her into a submarine."

"I bet she was a pretty good dive before da hurricanes tore her apart," Thomas commented, looking at a very grainy black and white picture of the ship from her military days.

AJ peeked up and noticed Coop trotting down the pier, which meant his dad wouldn't be far behind. "Of course," AJ began in a loud voice. "That was back so long ago that even ancient dive operators like Reg weren't running boats yet."

"Ha bloody ha," Reg said, standing on the dock with Coop sitting next to him.

The dog was staring at AJ with his lower lip quivering in anticipation.

"Permission to board," AJ said, and the Cayman brown hound vaulted onto the deck and skidded to a stop at her feet.

She made a big fuss over him while Reg stepped aboard at a more leisurely pace and set his gear by a tank towards the stern.

"Sally didn't waste much time, did she?" he said, plonking himself down on the opposite bench.

"We was just readin' da article," Thomas replied. "Not much to it."

Reg laughed. "No, but she's a sly one. You wait. She'll have a follow-up article every day this week until Andy leaves. Everyone who knew Butty, or thought they knew him, will be ringing her bell with stories."

"She'll be after you then," AJ said.

"She tried last night when she was done with Andy," Reg replied. "Told her I couldn't remember much and I'd have to talk to Andy before I said anything. Respect the family's privacy and all that."

"I bet she'll be standing on the dock when we come back in," AJ said, grinning at her friend and mentor.

"You might be right," he admitted. "We'll cross that bridge when we come to it. Besides, I meant what I said about talking to Andy. Figured we'd chat this morning. There's an awful lot of rumour and tall tales surrounding the *Oro Verde*. Enough that I'd say some of them hold a bit of truth. Might be best for ol' Butty's sake, and his good name, to let sleeping dogs lie."

"I think Andy's too curious for that," AJ said, getting up and retrieving her travel mug of coffee, much to Coop's disappointment.

"Might be right again," Reg said, lifting a tatty and faded base-ball cap off his head and scratching his scalp. "That's twice this morning. That's more times than you're usually right in a week. Probably need a nap."

AJ stuck up two fingers at him then quickly dropped her hand as two customers approached.

"Good morning," she said, as brightly as her lousy mood would allow.

13

The Seaview Hotel was exactly as the name suggested. Built along the shoreline south of George Town, the place looked more like a collection of white cottages with a main building behind a pool, all with a magnificent view of the Caribbean Sea. Oddly, parking was between the buildings and the sea wall along the ironshore coast, but the room Butty was guided to was elevated enough to look over the vehicles to the turquoise water beyond.

His clothes had dried on his body and now itched from the remaining salt, but he stood staring out the window at the ocean, thinking about Pepe. More than anything, Butty wanted to lie down on the queen-sized bed and sleep for a day, but the vision of his dead friend on the *Oro Verde* drove him to the shower. Gene Gould had left him with a change of clothes he'd purchased from the gift shop and the promise he'd arrange a boat for them to return to the ship to find Jorge and get the situation with the crew squared away. Butty scrubbed himself clean, keeping the water cool in an attempt to wake himself up.

Gould was waiting in the lobby when Butty made it down, and the two walked to the Wagoneer.

"I have a boat lined up," Gene explained on the way. "Local guy who won't ask questions. I've used him before."

Turning left out of the Seaview, Gould headed into George Town before cutting through a series of back roads avoiding the little downtown area. In no time Butty had lost his bearings until he saw a sign for the airport.

"We're not driving back out to Rum Point?" he asked.

Gould shook his head. "Like you said, it's quicker to take a boat across the North Sound. The captains all know the cuts through the outer reef."

After a few more minutes they arrived at a small marina, parked, and Gould led Butty to a wooden skiff with a grubby-looking outboard hung off the stern. A dark-skinned local man looked up as they approached. Without a word, Gould stepped aboard, so Butty followed. The man, who appeared to be in his sixties, pulled the cord on the motor, and on the third try, it burbled to life. Gould cast off the bow line and the man shoved the skiff away from the dock, twisting the throttle on the tiller to motor away.

For twenty minutes they stayed in silence, smoking and looking across the vivid aquamarine water of the sandy-bottomed sound. The local raised a hand to another fisherman making his way to shore; otherwise he sat still, making fine adjustments to the tiller as the reef grew closer and the *Oro Verde* was clear to see. Occasionally, stingrays would dart away from the oncoming boat like large grey underwater frisbees.

"Damn it," Butty muttered, unsure whether his eyes were playing tricks on him or not. "She looks beached."

Gould stared at the horizon, squinting. "You sure?"

"No," Butty admitted, wishing he could stand up to see better, but figured he'd upset the boat too badly.

"It on da reef, no doubt," the local man said from behind them.

Both men turned and looked at him. The old man shrugged his shoulders.

"Ain't rockin' none, and da bow up," he said in way of explanation.

Butty's heart sank. He was captain of the *Oro Verde* so she was his responsibility, no matter how events had unfolded. He'd left her adrift and assumed the crew would keep her safe while he was gone. Truth be told, he half expected the ship to be gone when they came out to look, Jorge at the helm having convinced the crew their best course of action was to sail for Miami and deliver the cargo. Except he'd be delivering the extra goods to Pérez instead of Herrera. It had never crossed his mind that his ship would end up on the reef.

It took a frustratingly long ten minutes to run through the break in the reef and cut east to where the *Oro Verde* could now clearly be seen beached on the reef. Butty directed the local man to the stern where small steps were welded into the hull allowing boarding to an open passageway.

"One of the lifeboats is gone," Butty noted aloud. "Someone left."

"Hey," Gould called out as Butty began climbing aboard once they were alongside. "Let's slow down, Lone Ranger. We don't know what's happened since you've been gone."

Butty paused for only a moment, too eager to save his ship. He hopped through the opening to the passageway and waited for Gould to come aboard. The CIA man pulled a handgun from a chest holster Butty hadn't noticed.

"Go ahead, slowly and carefully," Gould instructed.

Below them, the steel hull screeched and groaned as the swells ground the ship onto the coral reef, gouging grooves, destroying thousands of living colonies of polyps with every movement. Butty moved forward, listening for signs of human life as he tried his best to tread lightly. Moving up to the cargo deck, he paused and stole a glance across the open space. Slumped over the raised cargo doors lay a body. At first, Butty wondered if it was Pepe. Perhaps the crew had brought him down from the pilothouse, but he realised the shirt colour wasn't right.

"There's another man lying on the deck," Butty whispered. "Let's go up. We'll be able to see more from the helm."

A tap on the shoulder told him the CIA man agreed, and he quickly moved across the deck to the metal steps leading up the side of the superstructure. Glancing up through the steel grating, he immediately saw Pepe's body exactly where he'd last seen him. He scanned the cargo deck as he stayed close to the cabin wall and scaled the last flight of steps, arriving at his friend's corpse. Butty paused and listened once again, expecting someone to be in the pilothouse. The ocean breeze whistled through the structure and the waves slapped against the hull, but no sound came from inside.

He quickly looked inside the open door, his eyes struggling to adjust to the darker room. All appeared as he'd left it. Stepping over Pepe, he knelt down and checked in vain for the man's pulse. His first mate's skin felt cool to the touch. Gould stepped past them and double checked the pilothouse. Standing by the front window, he surveyed the rest of the ship as it shuddered and yawed a little.

"Recognise the other man from up here?" Gould asked, and Butty stood and looked down to the deck.

"I think it's Jorge, the guy who caused all the trouble, but I need to go down and check."

But instead of heading out of the door, Butty stayed in the pilot-house and began attempting to start the engines.

"What are you doing?" Gould asked.

"Getting her off the reef if I can," Butty replied, wondering how he could accomplish the feat without anyone in the engine room.

"I think we have bigger fish to fry first," Gould responded, looking down at Pepe's body. "We need to make this mess go away before the local police show up."

Butty was relieved to see the electrical system was still active, and he picked up the mic for the ship-wide tannoy.

"Hold up, Butty," Gould hissed. "Don't go off all half-cocked on me."

"There's the killer," Butty said, pointing out of the window.

"And there's the victim," he added, nodding towards Pepe. "The locals can write it up however they see fit."

"Oh yeah? So who killed the Jorge guy?" Gould jabbed. "We're missing a second killer, and so far the only other person associated with this ship is you."

Butty took a half step back and pondered the man's words.

"This ain't Miami, my man," Gould continued. "Up there they don't give a shit about a couple of Cubans killing each other. Know how many murders we get here on the island?"

Butty shook his head.

"None. That's how many. Maybe one every five to ten years. A double homicide will turn this little paradise on its head."

Butty realised Gould was right. The captain would have a lot to explain, starting with two dead bodies and a cargo hold full of weed.

"I told you I can make all this go away, and I still think I can, but we have to do this my way," Gould insisted.

Butty nodded. "Yeah. I suppose you're right. But surely, having the ship off the reef is going to keep the officials off our arse a bit longer?"

Gould holstered his weapon and scratched his head. "Maybe. I really need to speak with Mr Rosewater."

"Who the bloody hell is Rosewater?" Butty asked, anxious to move the ship while he still thought he could.

He's my boss," Gould replied. "He *manages* affairs in the Caribbean."

"Sounds like a codename," Butty said, holding up the mic once more.

"We're the CIA. Of course it's a codename," Gould replied, and this time he didn't stop the Englishman from speaking over the ship-wide tannoy.

"This is your captain speaking. If anyone is still aboard, please make your presence known."

His voice echoed throughout the ship and the two men waited for anyone to respond. No one did. Butty repeated the announcement in Spanish. They waited for what felt like a minute, but still no one appeared or radioed the bridge.

"Okay," Gould began. "Here's what we'll do. Let's get the ship off the reef. Then we'll lose these bodies and mop up. After that, we need to get the hell out of here. I thought we'd figure this out so you could carry on to Miami, or I'd at least have more time to take care of the cargo, but now we gotta scramble."

"Lose the bodies?" Butty questioned with a frown.

"Yeah," Gould replied. "This ain't no time to get all soft on me, Butty. Your buddy's dead, and I'm sorry about that, but it don't matter to him anymore whether we put him in the ground or put him in the ocean. Now show me what you need to get these engines started so we can move the damn ship."

Butty nodded, although the man's words didn't sit well with him. The idea of tossing Pepe overboard with a weight around his ankle made him shiver, although he didn't have the same reservation about Jorge. If indeed it was Jorge on the deck. Pushing his feelings aside, he led Gould below to the engine room and rather than walk him through the procedure, he simply did it himself. Once both diesels were running, Butty had to yell above the ruckus to explain how the engine order telegraph worked and what Gould should do based on the command sent down from the helm. Leaving the CIA agent below, Butty returned to the pilothouse and quickly lit a cigarette before scanning the water all around. The man who'd brought them out had motored clear, no doubt once the engines started, and the rest of the ocean appeared clear of boat traffic.

Butty moved the telegraph to slow astern and a few moments later he felt the ship move with a slight jerk. What it didn't do is free itself of the reef, which was evident by the continued scraping sound coming through the hull. Butty moved the telegraph to half astern, and after a short while of holding his breath, the *Oro Verde* began moving away from the reef. The horrible noise of the ship dragging on limestone ceased, and the bow dropped into the water as they motored backwards. Shifting the telegraph to slow astern, Butty swung the wheel to point the stern directly out to sea from the angle it had been shoved by the incoming swells.

He let out a long sigh of relief, and now hoped the reef hadn't punched a hole in the hull, or they'd have a short-lived reprieve. Butty left the wheel and stepped to the doorway, looking down at the water below. He could see sandy patches and the coral heads below, which soon gave way to more solid reef which faded into deep blue as he reached what he presumed was a drop-off down to a deeper ocean floor. Going back inside he checked the depth, which now registered 600 feet. He moved the telegraph to stand by and waited for Gould to make his way up top.

They wouldn't have too long before the ocean pushed them back towards the shallow reef, but they shouldn't need much time. Resigned to the fact he needed to do what the CIA agent said, Butty picked up Pepe's body underneath his dead friend's arms and began dragging his corpse down the steps to the main deck. Gould arrived just as Butty reached the second body and confirmed it was Jorge.

"We'll need something to weight them, and a rope or chain," Gould said and took over dragging Pepe.

"Two lines and two weights," Butty said firmly.

"It'll save time if we do one," Gould pointed out.

"I draw the line at sending Pepe down there tied to that wanker. My first mate deserves better."

Gould nodded, and Butty ran to the machine room, knowing exactly where to find what they needed. Five minutes later, they stood by the gunwale, out of breath, with chains tied to both men's ankles, each connected to pieces of steel stock.

"One last thing we need to do," Gould said, as he wiped his brow then pulled a folding knife from his pocket. "This'll vent the gases and stop the bodies trying to float if the sharks don't take care of them for us."

Butty looked away as Gould thrust the blade into Jorge's stomach and cut a two-inch slice before moving on and doing the same to Pepe's body. Butty wasn't sure if he could keep his breakfast in check, and looked out to sea for a moment.

"I kinda need a hand here," Gould said, sounding completely unbothered by what they were doing.

Butty took a deep breath and helped the man throw the two bodies over the side, dragging the ballast behind them and hitting the water with a big splash.

"If I had a crew, I could still take the *Oro Verde* to Miami," Butty said, trying to think of anything except what just took place.

"Looks like they've left you," Gould replied, wiping his bloody hands on his undershirt. "Besides, we don't know if the ship's damaged, right? And we sure don't have time to round up a scuba diver to check it out."

"So what's the plan?" Butty asked, as he followed Gould across the deck, noting a trail of blood where they'd dragged the bodies.

"First thing is to get a couple of buckets and mops," Gould responded. "We need to make this look like nothing bad happened here." He stopped and searched the North Sound.

Butty looked as well. All he could see were a few fishing boats.

"Then we'll drop anchor out here and let the authorities come find her," Gould finished. "By the time they figure out she's abandoned with a hold full of bananas, Mr Rosewater will have made plans for the extra cargo."

The word *abandoned* stung like a whip, but it was true. The crew had apparently abandoned her after taking their displeasure out on Jorge. They may have been angry at Pepe, but he'd still been one of them, and Jorge had gone too far. But the captain was abandoning her too, and that was worse. *But what choice did he have?* Reluctantly, Butty followed along, and hoped this Rosewater guy knew what the hell he was doing.

14

Thomas motored out to deeper water then turned south, as AJ gathered her customers together to discuss their choice of dive sites. The two couples had been on the boat all week so they knew each other and appeared to get along well. She'd overheard them talking about shore diving together the night before.

"This is Andy," she began. "He's the grandson of the captain of the *Oro Verde*, the wreck I'm sure you've all been to before."

The couples introduced themselves to Andy, who AJ was glad to see appeared relaxed. He was a newer diver, so she hadn't been sure what to expect, but he didn't seem overly nervous or distracted, which was a good start.

"Our plan is to dive the OV second, but where would you like to go first?" AJ asked. "We could do Eagle's Nest which we haven't been to this week."

Her four customers all looked at each other and shrugged their shoulders. Cris, a friendly man in his fifties, spoke up.

"I don't think we'd mind at all if you want to double-dip the OV."

He and AJ both looked to the others, who all nodded and smiled.

"There's always loads to see amongst the wreckage, and the nearby reef is great," he continued. "It's not often you get to dive with a relative of the captain from a ship."

"Brilliant," AJ enthused. "Thank you for being flexible."

"This is really kind of you," Andy added. "As you can imagine, I've been looking forward to this for a while."

AJ stepped up the ladder to tell Thomas and Reg, leaving Andy to fend off a barrage of questions from the other divers. Two of them had really nice underwater camera set-ups, so along with her own GoPro, he should come away with a nice visual record of the experience.

"That worked out," Reg said as AJ joined them.

Thomas moved *Hazel's Odyssey* outside the wall dive sites and opened up the throttles a little more, finding a comfortable cruising speed around 16 knots. AJ leaned against the waist-high sides of the fly-bridge, enjoying the shade of the hardtop and the wind rushing through her hair.

"I wish the wreck was more intact," she said, thinking about the dive ahead. "Even if he's seen the pictures, I'm sure he'll be disappointed."

"Hurricane Ivan finished her off pretty good," Reg replied. "There was a bit more to it when I first dived her a year or so before that, but she was already mostly broken up."

"Still a great dive with all da critters hiding everywhere," Thomas offered.

"Yeah, yeah," AJ quickly agreed. "I didn't mean disappointed like that. I love diving the OV, but it'd be great if he could see the helm station and picture his grandfather at the wheel."

"You know what's crazy?" Reg asked. "If you search online for the *Oro Verde*, there's not a single picture of her comes up topside. It's like she didn't exist until they sunk her. Now, search for the *USS Palm Beach*, and there's a bunch of old pictures of her in her Navy days."

"I noticed Sally used an old picture of the *Palm Beach* in her article," AJ commented.

"I thought it was bad luck to rename a ship?" Thomas queried.

Reg waved a hand. "Old wives' tale, but yeah, it's said to be bad luck, but they didn't have a choice. Once she was struck from the active list and sold, the private owners weren't allowed to call her the *USS Palm Beach* anymore."

"Had a different name before she was called the *Palm Beach* too," AJ said, looking quizzically at Reg.

"US Army Transportation Corps had her built, I believe," he replied. "Right at the end of the war, right?"

"Yup," AJ said, not giving anything else away. "But what was the name?"

Reg scratched his beard and thought for a moment as Thomas turned around.

"The *Colonel Armond Peterson*," he said, surprising Reg.

Thomas shrugged his shoulders. "I looked it up last night after talkin' wit Andy at da pub," he said with a wide smile. "Army den sold her to da Navy. When da sister ship, *USS Pueblo*, got taken by da North Koreans for spying outside dere waters, dere was quite a mess and da Navy retired da udder ships like her, 'cos dey were all spy ships too."

"Blimey, you did do your homework," Reg chuckled. "There's always been a lot of rumour and wild stories associated with the wreck, but I've no idea how much of that is true."

"I was told the OV was shipping bananas, but she also had a little stash of something else aboard too," AJ grinned. "Officials hauled the weed they found to the east end of the island and set it alight. Wind changed direction on them, and the population of Grand Cayman was stoned for two days straight."

Thomas laughed. "Dat's da story every divemaster on da island bin tellin' forever."

Reg shook his head. "Which way do the winds blow ninety-five percent of the time?"

"I know, I know," AJ agreed. "Out of the east."

"Don't make much sense then, does it?"

"Whatever, killjoy," she teased. "Makes for a better dive briefing than they sank a banana boat as an artificial reef."

Reg chuckled. "Fine. I admit I may have used the same story a few times."

AJ grinned at him. "I know, it was you I first heard it from."

She looked over the back of the fly-bridge to where Andy was still chatting with the other customers. "Must be some of the old timers on the island who remember something about it," she pondered aloud.

"Bob Soto was the one who persuaded the government to let him clean it up and sink it as an artificial reef," Reg said thoughtfully. "His missus, Suzy, might remember something about how it all came about. If not, I bet she'll know who does."

"I wouldn't be surprised if Sally's knocking on her door this very morning," Thomas added. "Dat be da first place I'd start askin'."

Glancing to the shore, half a mile off their port side, Thomas eased back on the throttles as he approached the dive site. The sites were all logged in their GPS, but they rarely needed to check, having been to each one so many times. AJ went to the ladder and turned to shimmy down.

"Don't know what to say in the dive briefing now, seeing as Captain Killjoy has nixed the burning reefer joke," she said, grinning, then scurried down to the deck, quickly moving along the narrow walkway alongside the open-backed cabin to the bow.

"You could tell them if they've had a bicycle nicked lately, they're probably about to find where it went," Reg shouted down over the helm.

AJ used a boathook to grab the rope off the marker buoy and looped the boat's line through the end before securing it to a cleat. She laughed to herself. Someone, long before she'd arrived on the island, had taken a bicycle down and left it by the wreck. Ever since then, the bicycle was mysteriously exchanged for a less-rusty model every few months, much to the chagrin of any cyclist who left their machine untethered. There were many suspects and lots of humorous finger pointing, but the identity of the bicycle thief remained one of the unsolved cases of the Royal Cayman Islands Police Service. As it was usually a fellow divemaster's bike that was nicked, they weren't wasting too many resources on the crimes.

"Okay everyone," AJ announced when she made it to the aft deck. "We're moored to what's left of the bow of the *Oro Verde*."

She glanced at Andy and caught a look of anticipation on his face. AJ was the only child of loving parents and had been close with her grandparents when they'd been alive. She couldn't imagine the void she assumed Andy felt in his life having never known his father or his paternal grandparents. She felt a mixture of delight and pressure for the dive ahead, and hoped he wouldn't be disappointed.

"Most of you have been here before and have heard the colourful story of the ship's demise, so I won't repeat it. Andy, Reg will buddy with you, and I'll stay with the group."

Kristi, Cris's wife, held up a hand while resting her camera on her lap. "Don't feel the need to hang with us, AJ, we've all been to this site a few times. We'll stay in buddy teams and I promise we won't get lost."

"If Andy doesn't mind, I'd like to follow along with them for a bit," Hank, the husband of the second couple suggested. "I'd like to be around for his first visit to his grandfather's ship. I can only imagine what this must mean to him."

The others nodded and Andy appeared to blush.

"I don't mind at all," he said. "But I'm not as experienced a diver as you, so forgive me if I'm not as smooth in the water."

"You'll do great," AJ encouraged. "Okay, gang. Signal me when you lot peel off to do your own thing, please. Back on the boat with no less than 500 psi, don't forget your three-minute safety stops, and we'll max out at an hour if you have the air. Pool's open whenever you're ready." She stepped to Andy's side. "Take your time and we'll jump in after the rest of the group."

Andy managed a nervous smile and nodded. She placed a hand

on his arm. "We'll take you around the wreckage and show you all the identifiable parts. This will be fun."

"I don't know what I'm expecting," he said. "But I know I'm expecting something. Does that make sense? Sounds silly, I know."

"Not at all," AJ assured him, thinking back to the time she had discovered a long-lost U-boat hidden on a deep pinnacle several miles offshore of the island. She'd only had loose ties through her own grandfather to one of the men who'd served on that submarine, but the elation at first laying eyes on the wreck had been unforgettable.

"Relax, and try and enjoy this moment," she told him, squeezing his shoulder.

One by one, the other divers took a giant stride off *Hazel's Odyssey*'s swim step and Thomas handed down their cameras before they slipped below the surface. Reg slapped Andy on the back as he passed by on his way to the stern. "See you down there, mate," he said, then stepped off the boat.

AJ gave Andy's gear a final safety check. She then took a giant stride into the water herself, and after giving an okay sign to Thomas and Andy from the surface, released the air from her BCD and descended ten feet below. Pausing, she took out her GoPro camera, made sure it was turned on and shooting video, then hit the record button. A few moments later, she filmed Butty Butterworth's grandson breaking through the surface, and laying eyes for the first time on the remains of the *Oro Verde*.

15

Gould pulled several bills from his wallet and slipped them into the local man's outstretched hand.

"You know the drill," he said.

The man never looked up, but nodded. "I bin here all day."

Gould gave him a slap on the shoulder as he stepped from the skiff to the dock. Butty wasn't sure whether he should thank the man or not. They'd barely spoken a word and he didn't even know the man's name. He supposed that was deliberate on both their parts, and followed Gould.

"What now?" he asked, catching up to the CIA agent.

"Now, you need to lie low and I need to get to my contact before too many people go crawling all over that ship."

"Your man Rosewater?" Butty asked.

"Him too, but first I need to get to my local official."

Butty thought about his ship sitting abandoned offshore and his pregnant wife back in Miami. Where he should be heading.

"I could sail her to Miami with three crew," he offered. "We could pay double as we won't be paying any of the guys who jumped ship. Maybe we could find some of them?" He added excitedly. "They probably took the tender over to Rum Point. Let's drive out there and ask around. They could be still there."

He kicked himself for not thinking about that earlier. They should have motored over in the skiff on the way back in. Gould paused at the Wagoneer and looked over the roof to Butty.

"Here's a few things you need to understand, my friend," he said, tapping a finger on the hot metal. "That ship isn't important. The guy who owns it ain't important. The people we're concerned about are Herrera, your new pal in Panama, Noriega, and Mister Rosewater. And right now, letting Alfonso Pérez think he's cut off Herrera's supply works in our favour. We don't need an all-out war between drug lords in Miami; it's bad for everyone's business." He slapped the roof and pointed at Butty. "It'll all be fine, Butty Boy, just wait and see. You'll be at the helm of another ship in no time with a hefty pay raise thrown in."

Butty nodded and got into the Jeep, which was sweltering hot inside despite the windows being down. He noted with some disappointment that the mention of more money was the best thing he'd heard in days and the part of Gould's speech which stood out in his mind. He liked money as much as the next guy, and with a growing family, it had been more in his thoughts than usual, but he was jumping into bed with a crazy group of people he barely believed and sure as hell didn't trust. Yet here he was, following Gould and his wild tales of what he claimed was best for the American people. Fighting communism in South America by selling drugs to US citizens seemed like a strange way of going about that. *But what did an English sea captain know?*

Ten minutes later, Gould parked outside an official-looking building. He removed the gun from his holster and reached past Butty to slide it into the glovebox.

"The Caymanians are just like their British uncles," Gould muttered, perhaps forgetting for a moment that Butty was English. "They don't like guns on the island."

"That's crazy," Butty said. "They should let everyone have them and then the island would be safe from violence, just like Miami."

Gould paused as he got out and peered back in the Jeep at Butty. "That was sarcastic British wit, wasn't it?"

"Some might think so," Butty replied. "I assume I stay here and *lay low*?"

"Yeah," Gould said, seemingly thrown by Butty's lack of enthusiasm for his new situation.

The CIA agent forced a smile but closed the door a little harder than necessary. Butty waited until he'd disappeared inside the building before stepping out of the Jeep and leaning against the side, lighting a cigarette.

He pictured Lucia, lying asleep in their bed, just as he'd left her in the middle of the night. Her side of the family worked hard to separate themselves from her uncle's business, and here he was working for the competition. He had a feeling she knew, or at least had an idea he was up to something he shouldn't be, but if he worked directly for Herrera, surely she'd have something to say about it. He let a stream of smoke vacate his lungs in a long sigh. The idea he'd be putting her and their baby in a precarious position made his stomach clench.

After twenty minutes, Gould reappeared and strode down the path to the Jeep.

"Sorted?" Butty asked, getting back in.

Gould grinned as he started the car. "Just like shooting fish in a barrel."

Butty looked at him. "Are you still stuck on the gun thing?"

"What?" the CIA agent answered, pulling away. "No. Means it was easy."

"Oh," Butty muttered. "So what do we need to do now?"

Gould smiled a little wider. "You hungry?"

Butty realised he hadn't eaten all day and hadn't noticed how hungry he was until it was mentioned. Watching his friend die, swimming for his life, and then dumping bodies in the ocean didn't do much for his appetite.

"What time is it?" he asked, after glancing at his own watch, which had stopped after he'd dived into the Caribbean Sea.

"Two o'clock," Gould replied. "I could eat a horse. I know a great place."

Butty hoped he wasn't serious and the restaurant didn't serve up horse, but his stomach was rumbling.

"What's going to happen to the *Oro Verde*?" he persisted, his mind still on what lay ahead after lunch.

Gould shrugged his shoulders. "Don't know, and quite honestly, I don't care, and you need to quit caring too. My contact will let us know when we can relieve the ship of our cargo, and after that, the local government can decide what to do with her. They'll start by contacting the owner and all that jazz. It'll take forever to sort out." Pulling up outside a small shack near the George Town waterfront, Gould parked the Jeep and switched off the engine. "You'll have been to Miami and Panama ten times over before that gets sorted, you wait and see."

"I'm going back to Miami?" Butty asked, getting out and rushing to keep up with Gould as he walked into the little restaurant. "When do I leave? How?"

Gould held up a hand. "Calm down, my man. I told you I'd take care of things and that's what I'm doing. You're on Uncle Sam's payroll now, Butty, so stop worrying about everything. I think Mr Rosewater will be pleased with what we've pulled off this morning. You get on his good side and your ticket is punched, my friend."

Butty had a dozen questions spawned from Gould's statement, but the man was now having a raucous conversation with the chef, who also seemed to be the owner and waiter of the tiny establishment. A cold beer was thrust into Butty's hand as he was herded to a table on a patio overlooking the cerulean blue water.

"Soak it up, Butterworth," Gould said before Butty could formulate his questions. "Doesn't get any better than this."

"My wife would like it, I'm sure," Butty commented, his thoughts still lingering on Lucia and how any of this could play out well for the two of them.

Gould laughed. "See that cruise ship out there?"

Butty nodded. "Sure."

"And you've noticed the airport just outside town?"

"I know it's there," Butty replied, unsure where this conversation was going.

"Between the two, they provide enough beautiful young women to keep us both up to our necks in trouble from now until eternity. And the best part is, they bring 'em in, and they take 'em away again, bringing you a fresh selection every day."

Butty looked over at the man, who gave him a big smile and wink before taking a swig of beer. Not that Butty spent much time evaluating the looks of other men, but he guessed women found Gene Gould to be attractive. He was outgoing, confident, and had a polished, albeit slightly cheesy charm, which seemed to bring the opposite sex flocking. A bit like James Garner selling used Cadillacs, Butty thought to himself.

There was certainly a time, not too long ago, when Butty would have found the man's words wonderfully inviting, but now all he could think about was Lucia and their unborn child. He had obligations to fulfil. Responsibilities. His mind turned circles as the breeze swept off the ocean and a delicious meal of grouper grilled and seasoned with spices was quickly devoured. When they were done, exhaustion caught up with the Englishman, and he was relieved when Gould told him they should head back to the Seaview Hotel. When they arrived, Butty started towards his room, but Gould called after him.

"One more thing before we're done for today."

Butty reluctantly paused and then followed the man to a room just two doors down from his own. Inside, the place looked more like an apartment than a hotel room and it was clear Gould was living here rather than stopping by for a while. Several books were stacked on the dresser and a briefcase sat on a desk off to the side, next to a telephone and a stack of papers.

"Give me a moment to set up," Gould said, and pointed to a wooden patio chair by the window overlooking the ocean. "Beer?"

"I'm good, thanks," Butty said, taking a seat. He was struggling to keep his eyes open already without another drink in the middle of the afternoon.

Gould took a small black case from the closet and set it down on the king-sized bed. Removing the lid revealed a field radio unit of some description. Gould took a lead and plugged it into the electrical outlet, then opened his bedside table and removed a set of headphones and a small microphone.

"Can't use the phone?" Butty asked, pointing to the one on the desk.

"Hell no, we're spooks, my friend. We have to have security wrapped up in security."

To Butty, the day just kept getting stranger and he wasn't completely convinced he wouldn't wake up the next morning and find himself on the *Oro Verde* with a bump on his head and his crew happy he'd come around.

"Neptune, this is Triton. Over," Gould said into the microphone he'd connected to the radio set.

Butty moved to the other side of the bed and sat down.

"Neptune, this is Triton. Over," Gould said again and waited.

"Roger, Neptune. Loud and clear," he finally responded. "I have Proteus for you. Over."

After a brief pause, Gould spoke again. "Roger, Neptune. He'll be standing by. Over."

Gould removed the headset and handed it to Butty who reluctantly took it along with the mic.

"Neptune will be back in a minute or two," Gould said, pointing to a transmit button on the set. "Hit that to talk."

Butty placed the headphones over his ears and waited, unsure who or what to expect. He jumped when the telephone rang on the desk. Gould answered it.

"Yeah?"

He shook his head and looked annoyed. "Okay, okay. I'll be right down."

Gould hung up the phone and Butty slipped the headset aside to hear what was going on now.

"Package I gotta sign for at the front desk. I'll be right back. Listen up for the boss," he finished, indicating Butty should put the headphones back on.

He didn't have long to wait.

"Proteus, this is Neptune. Over." The man's voice was deep, almost booming although he was speaking normally.

"Hello," Butty replied. "This is Proteus, apparently. Over."

"I'm told you're aboard with us. That correct? Over."

"I guess so," Butty replied. "Over."

He heard silence and wondered if the line had gone dead. "We don't guess, Proteus. There's too much at stake. I know you're one of our cousins from across the pond, but I'm hoping as your adopted country, we can count on you. Over."

Butty had no clue what to say. *Count on him for what exactly? Shipping drugs to America?*

"Yes, sir. Over," he said, more because his naval training dictated he agree to a command from a superior officer, although he had no real idea who he was talking to. Mr Rosewater, he presumed.

"We appreciate your service, Proteus. Welcome aboard. Over and out."

The line went dead, and Butty slipped the headphones from his ears, letting them drop to the bed. He sat there with only the cool air from the ducts in the room for company, wondering how everything had become so crazy, so quickly.

It was five minutes before Gould reappeared with a beer in one hand and brown box in the other.

"Did you speak with him?" he asked, sipping the beer and tossing the box on the desk.

"Yeah," Butty replied.

"Go okay?"

Butty shrugged his shoulders. "I've no idea, you'll have to ask him. It was brief."

"That's Rosewater for you," Gould replied with a chuckle. "He doesn't like spending too much time on comms, no matter how secure we tell him they are. He tell you you're in?"

"I think so," Butty muttered.

Gould laughed. "And just like that," he said, "you're now on the CIA payroll under Mr Rosewater's Caribbean and Central American division. Congratulations."

Butty grunted and gave the man a slight nod. Maybe he was supposed to feel grateful, or patriotic, or something meaningful, but all he felt was dog tired.

"I'm going to bed," he said, getting to his feet. "I'll see you tomorrow."

16

AJ watched as Andy slowly descended, staring at the bow of the *Oro Verde*, lying in the sand at an angle. A handful of railing supports remained, covered in coral growth, and gorgonian branchy corals and sea fans reached out from the formerly smooth metal decking. The sides of the hull, once protected by a layer of marine paint, now formed a textured surface where stony coral growth took hold, slowly erasing the seam lines of the steel panels.

Reg began a slow lap around the structure, and Andy fell in line behind him, with AJ bringing up the rear. The others in the group hung patiently away from the wreck, taking pictures of the young man as he surveyed the broken ship. Multiple hurricanes and storms had run the wreck up the sand and into the reef, where she'd been battered apart and redistributed over the sand flats. The bow was the only large segment of identifiable ship left, but all around big pieces of steel plating and parts littered the area.

Arriving at the rear of the bow section, Reg and AJ both took out their dive torches and shone the beams through the opening where the steel had been torn away from the rest of the ship. Sunken into the seabed with sand shoved inside by wave action, the gap was too small to pass through, but their lights showed a mass of silversides - also known as smelt or whitebait - swirling inside the inner space of the bow. Several lobsters shrank back into their daytime hiding holes, and a green moray eel slipped around an inner wall, disappearing into the shadows.

As they backed away, AJ looked at Andy's face and could see the smile behind his regulator, his eyes sparkling inside his mask. She held up an okay sign and he enthusiastically returned the same in answer. Reg continued his lap until they reached the tip of the bow, where AJ slipped over the port side and shone her light through one of the two portholes in the hull. With the frame and glass removed before the ship was ever sunk, the holes were now rimmed with coral growth, but shining her torch inside lit up the school of silversides again. Andy joined her and peered through the hole in the ship, watching the silver flicker of hundreds of small, slender fish passing by.

Moving away from the bow, they passed over the ever-present bicycle, which they all ignored, and moved on to the main debris field. Most pieces were curved and twisted steel plating with supports still welded to the back side, but Reg paused over a larger bulk of machinery which like everything else had a covering of growth masking much of its detail. AJ pumped her fists up and down and Andy's eyes got wider and he nodded keenly, understanding she was signalling pistons going up and down. The diesel engine lay in the sand with the transmission still attached, as though the engine room had been peeled away around it.

The rest of the group scattered amongst the debris, hunting for cool critters to photograph, and Reg led Andy around the remaining wreckage, pointing out the second engine and a few other identifiable parts. AJ looked around and wondered which sections of metal had once formed the pilothouse where Andy's grandfather would have stood at the helm, guiding the *Oro Verde* across the seas. Squirrelfish and snappers looked her way as she rotated upside down to search under the plating, hunting for anything more personal than hunks of broken ship. But anything of use or value had been stripped before she'd been sunk, and the years had not been kind to the freighter.

After forty-five minutes, Andy was down to 700 psi in his tank, so after signalling to the others, Reg and AJ led Andy to the line where they hung at 15 feet on a three-minute safety stop, before ascending to the surface.

Thomas's broad smile greeted them at the stern, and one by one they boarded *Hazel's Odyssey* and shed their gear. Reg and AJ both busied themselves switching their BCDs over to a fresh tank, leaving Andy to gather his thoughts. Finally, AJ couldn't hold back any longer and sat down on the bench next to the young man.

"How was that, Andy?"

He wiped the seawater from his face as it dripped from his hair, and smiled at her. "I'm still not altogether sure what I felt, or even what I'm feeling now, but I was certainly moved."

"Well I think between the lot of us, your first visit was well documented," AJ replied, getting up again to assist the other divers aboard.

Hank and his wife Jackie were first up the ladder, soon followed by Cris and his wife, Kristi. They were all excited to hear how Andy enjoyed the dive, and once the chatter had settled down after a few minutes, AJ announced they'd start getting ready for the second dive in forty-five minutes. Thomas made sure everyone had their water bottles before passing around a Tupperware of fresh fruit slices, and Reg took the opportunity to shepherd Andy up to the fly-bridge where AJ joined them after a few moments.

As she ascended the ladder it struck her that she hadn't thought about Jackson since sometime after leaving the dock. A lump formed in her throat as she realised she'd be returning home to an empty cottage, alone for the first time in years. Single again. AJ bit back the tears which threatened to glisten in her eyes and took a deep breath. It still felt unbelievable to her that two people who fitted so well together and shared a love she'd never doubted from the day he'd moved to the island could be splitting up.

Was she being unreasonable? Anger rose inside as she felt the need to justify and defend her position… *to herself.* The irony was that if she didn't love him so deeply, she'd probably be able to handle the extended time apart, which was the olive branch he'd suggested. *So what did that say about his feelings?* She knew comparing her own emotions to what she perceived another's to be was a fool's errand and pointless at best.

Determined to think about something else, she strode across the fly-bridge to the helm chair while stripping her wetsuit down to her waist. She spun the chair around to face the stern and looked at Reg, who was about to speak.

"The horse may have already bolted on this," he began after he took a seat on the little starboard side bench. "But I wanted to mention something about this whole business with your grandfather."

Andy took the port side bench and eyed Reg with a concerned expression, waiting for him to continue as AJ pulled her long-sleeved shirt on to protect her tattoos from the intense mid-morning sun.

"How much do you actually know about Butty?" Reg asked.

Andy winced. "Very little, I'm afraid, as I've said. There's a copy of a *Miami Herald* article online about the bomb supposedly planted on the side of the OV back in Miami which mentions him; otherwise all I have is what the Navy provided me with, which isn't much."

"That's the Gene Miller article, isn't it?" AJ asked.

Andy nodded. "Who died back in 2005, but I emailed the *Herald* to see if anyone could help me find out more about the story."

"And?" Reg asked.

"I haven't ever heard back," Andy admitted. "And the Navy records are all about his service dates and ranks. That was all before he moved to America anyway."

Reg lifted his ball cap and scratched his unruly hair. "Well, I just wanted to point out that there's a chance what you find out, if you're able to dig up anything at all, might not be all sunshine and roses."

"I read the other stories attached to details about the wreck," Andy said. "They're pretty vague, but I hear what you're saying. There's the chance some of what was rumoured is true, and he was smuggling drugs or who knows what aboard the *Oro Verde*, alongside the bananas of course."

Reg grinned. "Yeah, I think the banana part can be believed."

"What about after the OV was abandoned in 1976?" AJ asked. "Is there any trace of your grandfather after that?"

Andy and Reg both looked at each other. "No," they both replied.

"My mum either doesn't remember or never knew very much about my grandfather," Andy explained, "which isn't surprising as she never spent any extended period of time with Arnie, my father, who in turn never knew his dad anyway. The box of stuff had a few pictures, things from when my dad was a kid, and everything else was bits and pieces which probably meant something to them, but didn't present any clues I could decipher. My mum has always thought my grandfather died around the time my dad was born, but she can't recall how or where."

"I think you'll find this article of Sally's will bring a few old stories out of the woodwork," Reg said. "I wouldn't be too ready to believe all of them, though."

Andy nodded. "You never know, perhaps someone who actually met my grandfather while he was here on the island will come forward."

"Or perhaps they won't," AJ responded and wished she'd kept the thought to herself.

Andy looked at her with a puzzled expression and she knew an explanation was required for a statement like that.

"I'm just wondering about the fact he seemed to vanish after the *Oro Verde* was abandoned back in 1976..." she offered with a smile. "There's one rumour that the disgruntled crew..." AJ stopped and looked at Reg.

"They supposedly did away with the captain," Reg finished for her. "But that's just a story. There's never been any real proof of anything like that, mate."

"Exactly," AJ agreed. "But maybe someone will shed some light on all this for you, and give you a new clue to follow," she said, finishing with an optimistic tone.

But they all knew she'd brought up a valid point. The trail of Butty Butterworth had run dry in Grand Cayman circa 1976.

17

Butty woke, unsure where he was or what was happening. A steady thud echoed around the dark room and he sat up, startled. Someone was knocking on his door. The luminescent hands on the bedside clock told him it was 3:10am. He threw the lightweight cover back and shuffled to the door, looking through the peephole. Gene Gould stood outside, dimly lit by the single hall light left on at night.

"What the bloody hell is going on?" Butty mumbled as he opened the door.

"Get dressed, hotshot. It's time to go to work."

"It's three o'clock in the bloody morning," Butty complained, wandering back into his room. "Thought I was done doing night shifts for a bit."

"Get dressed, my friend. Opportunity knocks," Gould said, turning on the light.

He was far more chipper than Butty had any hope of feeling.

"I don't know about opportunity, but I do know, sure as eggs is eggs, that it's three o'clock in the bloody morning and we're the only two people on the whole island who are awake right now," he said, pulling a shirt over his head.

"Bingo, Butty Boy. That's the point."

The Englishman tugged a pair of shorts on over his underwear. "What are we doing?" he asked, searching for his canvas shoes which had finally dried.

"They already towed the *Oro Verde* into the North Sound," Gould replied. "It's time to retrieve our cargo."

"And this can't wait until the morning when we can see what we're doing?" Butty complained, although he already knew the answer.

"Too many other prying eyes in daylight," Gould said, and Butty followed him from the room.

After a career in the Navy followed by captaining a commercial ship, Butty was used to being roused at all hours of the day or night and sleeping whenever the opportunity arose. But exhaustion had caught up with him and he'd been dead to the world when Gould had come knocking. It took a little longer than usual, but by the time they were driving through the darkened streets of George Town, the cobwebs had cleared, although a strong cup of coffee wouldn't go amiss.

They pulled into the same marina as the day before, and walking carefully under the starlight, they met the same local man in his skiff.

"I'm Butty, by the way," he said, stepping into the boat. "We were never introduced before."

"I know," the man said and pulled the cord on the outboard.

The little motor drowned out any idle chatter, which the man clearly had no interest in anyway, so Butty took his seat on one of the thwarts as they moved away from the dock. How the local man could see where he was going was beyond Butty's imagination. His own eyes adjusted to the darkness but still had a hard time making out anything in the calm body of water ahead. The local had no compass, and half the time his eyes were squeezed closed as he exhaled cigarette smoke which the wind took over his face, vanishing into the air behind them. An orange glow from the cigarette tip was the brightest light as far as Butty could see.

After fifteen minutes, a tall dark shadow began to appear ahead of them. The *Oro Verde*'s profile blocked the stars beyond, which made the still visible pricks of light frame her silhouette. A few minutes later, they pulled alongside, and Gould pointed to the ladder.

"Go first. I'll hand you the tools."

Butty did as he was told, reaching down from the passageway to take a pair of crowbars handed up to him. They were followed by two claw hammers and two lanterns before Gould came aboard.

"We need a crane, mate," Butty pointed out. "There's four big crates."

"Not after we take the crates apart," Gould replied, herding Butty towards the cargo deck.

Butty led the way, finally comfortable moving around in the dark amongst his familiar surroundings. "Your man down there will be making twenty runs back and forth if we're unloading all of it," he pointed out.

"You're gonna have to learn a little faith, Butty Boy," Gould said, sounding unperturbed. "My job in all of this is facilitating and logistics. I'm the *can do* guy. So when I say we're doing something, you'll figure out that it's happening, and it's organised. Our cargo will be tucked away safe and sound by sunrise."

Butty didn't feel convinced, and blindly following orders reminded him too much of his Navy days. He'd grown used to literally being the captain of his own ship for the past few years. He lifted one side of the big cargo doors to reveal the freight below. Gould opened the other door and the hinges creaked loudly in the quiet night. He sat one of the lanterns by the edge of the opening and turned it on.

"Those four, under there," Butty said, pointing to the crates packed with bales of marijuana wrapped in translucent white plastic bags. "But we still need to move at least one of the crates of bananas on top."

"Is the crane electric or diesel?" Gould asked.

"Electric, but it runs off the generator power," Butty replied.

"But it might operate off the battery bank just long enough to hoist one crate up."

Gould nodded. "Let's try it."

Butty moved to the crane hut, taking a lantern with him. He turned on the power and lowered the crane boom over the hold, then went back out to attach chains to the crate. Under the battery power, the crane moved slowly, but as soon as the banana crate had cleared the hold, Butty locked the boom and shut down the power.

"Gravity will lower it," he told Gould once he'd returned to the hold. "But I might not be able to get it quite back in its stowed position."

"Good enough," Gould replied, hopping down onto the top of the first crate, crowbar in hand.

Butty joined him with the second lantern. In the distance he could hear a second outboard engine purring above the sound of the waves gently rolling over the outer reef not too far away.

It took them less time than Butty had thought to break into the crates and lift the heavy bales to the deck. What took longer was busting the rest of the wooden crates apart and handing them down to one of the four skiffs which had shown up. Each crate also had a bale or two which had torn open and strewn some of its contents about the hold, clinging to the rough wood of their crate.

Apart from those small tufts, every trace of the extra cargo was removed, and as the sun cracked the horizon across the East End, Butty lowered the banana crate back into the hold, and raised the arm as high as he could until he ran out of battery power. Gould helped him close the cargo hold doors and they made their way towards the stern, finding the same skiff which had transported them to the OV.

"Hey, I need to run down to my berth and grab my personal belongings," Butty said, realising it might be his last chance.

"I don't know," Gould replied, placing a hand on Butty's arm. "I think it's better they think you just disappeared like the others."

"I at least need my passport, and I have some cash hidden away."

"No, leave your passport behind," Gould said firmly. "And your clothes, wash kit, and a few personal effects, so it looks like you never returned. You can take the cash and anything that won't be noticeable if it's missing."

"But I need my passport to get home," Butty complained.

Gould shook his head. "Don't worry about that, I have you covered. Now hurry up, I wanted to be gone by daylight. We're already late."

As he could bring hardly anything with him, it didn't take Butty long to recover his cash, a picture of Lucia, and another photo of him and his Navy buddies he always kept with him. He'd lost touch with them all over the past few years, but hoped to remedy that one day.

When he joined Gould in the skiff, instead of heading back to the marina the local man steered for Rum Point, where they tied up to the rickety pier a few minutes later. On shore, Butty saw an old flatbed lorry with several men loading the last of the wood from the crates aboard, lashing them down with rope. If the bales had been brought to the same place, they'd already been taken away as Butty saw no sign of them. Except one, which he'd noticed in the skiff he'd been in. Payment, he presumed.

"All these men work for you?" Butty asked Gould, concerned how many eyes had become involved in the proceedings.

"No," Gould replied with a crooked grin. "They work for him," he said, tipping his head towards the local man in the skiff.

They walked towards the lorry. "By the time they smoke and sell their way through that bale, they'll have been stoned for a month and made themselves a pretty penny to boot. You don't have to worry about them."

Gould stepped up and sat on the bed of the lorry behind the remains of the four crates. Butty joined him.

"We're not taking the skiff back?" he asked.

Gould offered him a cigarette, which Butty gladly accepted.

"Need to check on the cargo," he said, clicking his lighter for Butty. "I trust these guys, but it doesn't hurt to be sure."

"What happens to all this wood?"

Gould lit his own cigarette, which wiggled between his lips as he spoke. "That's the other reason we're riding back. They'd love to keep this timber. Although it's cheap wood, it's free, and shipping wood to the island is expensive. But there's a couple of cops who are just nosey enough to keep looking if they suspect something fishy with the *Oro Verde*, so we don't need any loose ends lying around."

"Nosey and not on your payroll," Butty commented.

Gould shrugged his shoulders as the lorry pulled away, billowing diesel smoke from the exhaust as the driver ground the gears in the ancient vehicle.

"Not everyone understands what we do is for the greater good," Gould replied.

The lorry followed the northern coastline until it reached the small town called Old Man Bay which Butty recognised from the first drive he'd taken with Gould the day before. They turned right and bounced along in silence with dust swirling around them and the morning sun inching higher in the sky to their left. After another fifteen minutes, the lorry braked to a stop at a T-junction, then turned right again, following the marl road along the south coast of the island.

It took about the same time again to reach Bodden Town, where the driver turned inland down a small lane and stopped outside a pair of cottages. Sitting on the porch of the first dwelling, an old lady eyed them all suspiciously. She barked something at the men, who climbed from the cab of the lorry. They waved her off and said something back, but Butty couldn't understand their thick local dialect.

Gould and Butty followed the two men into the second cottage, which was surprisingly cool inside. The breeze seemed to efficiently brush through the house, offsetting the balmy tropical heat.

In a back room, the bales of marijuana were neatly stacked, leaving just enough space for the door to swing open and closed. Gould counted the bales as best he could, which meant making an assumption that the stacks were all equal and some at the back hadn't been switched for a box about the same height.

He nodded when he was done but then something caught his eye. Gould pulled a bale from the top of one stack and dropped it to the floor with a squidgy thud.

"What the hell happened to this one?" he asked the closest local man.

"Fell in da water a bit," the man replied nonchalantly.

"A bit?" Gould countered. "It's soaking wet. It's ruined."

"Na, na," the man insisted. "Dry out and it be fine."

"Really?" Gould said. "So you'll switch with the bale I paid you with then?"

The man looked at his friend and they both quickly shook their heads.

"Yeah. I thought not," Gould continued. "Throw it on the truck."

The local reluctantly gathered up the bale, which took them both to carry as it was saturated with seawater, but they did as ordered, sliding it under a few planks of wood on the truck bed.

Gould nodded to the men and slapped the nearest one on the back before hopping up and taking his seat once again. The old lady threw a final barb at the driver as he turned around and trundled the ancient flatbed down the lane.

Turning right, they continued towards George Town, curving slowly around the south-western tip of the island, but when Butty guessed they were still a mile away from the Seaview, the driver stopped once more, this time in a small clearing by the water. Trees shielded the spot from the dusty road and a pile of ashes provided evidence that the location had been used in the past for burning rubbish. A few beer bottles and charred cans lay strewn around the place, the whole scene in stark contrast to the beautiful turquoise water in front of them.

The men began removing the ropes and Gould and Butty helped drag the wood from the lorry, stacking it over the existing pile of ashes and on top of the soggy bale. When they'd finished unloading, one of the local men produced a can of petrol which he sprinkled around the base of the pile before striking a match and setting the wood alight.

They all stood back as the flames quickly took hold of the dry planks, and watched the smoke drift over the water as the north-easterly winds whisked the grey cloud away. Gould handed each man a cigarette, and by the time he'd lit each one in turn, Butty noticed the smoke from the fire was no longer blowing out across the ocean.

"Well I'll be damned," Gould muttered, and looked at the two locals.

They both shrugged their shoulders. "Winds change sometimes," one of them commented.

The second man sniffed the air as the smoke wafted around them. He took a step closer to the blazing fire, and Butty wondered why until the herbal and slightly musky odour reached him. Apparently, the weed was quickly drying out enough to burn and the two locals weren't wasting the available high. The wind slowly shifted until finally settling from the south, blowing the smoke directly north towards George Town.

"You're welcome, everyone," Gould said, looking in the direction of the island's capital with a grin.

18

The second dive was relaxed and while the group wandered around the nearby reef looking for critters to photograph, AJ and Reg once again stayed with Andy at the wreck. AJ sensed he was hoping to find something more than what he'd already discovered on the *Oro Verde*, but there simply wasn't much left intact after years of being beaten by storms.

"I remember one time," Reg began as Thomas piloted *Hazel's Odyssey* north towards the dock, "your grandad and me were charged with getting a newbie a few extra dives in, so Butty tells this kid we'd lost a long weight and he could help us out by finding it. The kid, and I don't remember his name – I don't think he lasted much after this – he asks what a long weight looked like. So Butty rips him up and down about not paying attention in training, telling him he oughta bloody know what a long weight was."

AJ listened from the side, trying to hide her grin, as the customers soaked up to the old sea story. Especially Andy.

"We get the kid ready in standard dive dress, which is drysuit and hard hat gear, and Butty tells him to drop straight down the side of the dock next to the hull of a minesweeper, and he'll find it down there. Now, this was in the Portsmouth Royal Dockyard which was only about 40 feet deep if I recall, but it was nothing but muck down there and you couldn't see your hand in front of your face. 'Don't come back up until you've found it,' Butty tells him, and over the side this kid goes.

"We sat up top, had ourselves a cup of tea, and watched this kid's bubbles as he plodded around down there for nearly half an hour. Finally, he tugs on the line, and we haul him back up. 'I can't find it anywhere,' he says and Butty just shakes his head. 'You're going back down, son, and if you just stand still for long enough, I promise you'll find it.'

"Down he goes again, we get another cuppa, and this time we watch the bubbles and they're coming up from exactly where we dropped the kid in. We leave him down there for half an hour until Butty says, 'That'll do him'.

"We haul him up, pull the kid's helmet off, and he says, 'I sat there just like you said, but I still couldn't find it, sir.'

"'You did just fine, son,' Butty tells him. 'I think that was a perfectly long wait!'"

Cris got the joke right away, and the others soon cottoned on until, pretty soon, Thomas was looking over the back of the fly-bridge to see what all the laughter was about.

"That's the sort of bloke your grandad was, Andy," Reg said. "He never missed the chance for a bit of fun. But he wouldn't go around telling everyone how he'd played a trick on the new kid; he'd had his fun with the lad and after that he'd do anything to help him. It was like a good-hearted initiation, if you know what I mean? Butty didn't have a cruel bone in his body."

AJ looked up and, seeing they were approaching the dock, shuffled along the side of the cabin to the bow, readying the line. She saw Pearl, standing by the little hut, and next to her was Sally Regis, as they'd predicted. Another gentleman stood by them, an older local with a slight frame and stooped posture. His weathered face looked up as the Newton approached.

Thomas deftly brought the boat alongside the dock, where AJ and Reg hopped over and tied her into the cleats.

"You called it," Reg said as they began helping the customers ashore with their gear.

"Dog with a bone, that one," AJ responded.

Once it was only Andy remaining by the boat, Sally walked their way with the gentleman in tow.

"How was the diving?" she asked, looking at Andy.

"Yeah, it was lovely, thanks," Andy replied.

"I assume you made it to the *Oro Verde*?"

Andy nodded. "Both dives."

"I can't wait to hear all about that from you, Andy, but first I have a fellow I think you'd like to meet." Sally urged the old man forward a step. "This is Ormond Willis. Ormond, let me introduce you to Andy Butterworth. He's the grandson of the captain of the *Oro Verde*."

"Pleased to meet you, sir," Andy said, shaking the old man's hand.

"Ormond met your grandfather, Andy, after everyone had abandoned the ship," Sally said, as though she were unveiling the lost city of Atlantis.

"That's wonderful," Andy responded, looking to the old man. "How did your paths cross, sir?"

"It were a long time back," Ormond said with a thick Caymanian accent. "But I recall driving da captain and anudder man from Rum Point into town."

"So this was when he left the ship?" Andy asked keenly, and AJ and Reg listened in.

"Da ship were outside da reef, but den dey tow it inside North Sound, and dat's when I met da man," Ormond replied. "We helped offload some stuff."

"You helped unload all the bananas?" Andy asked, and the old man ran his tongue along his lower lip, looking down at the dock.

"I couldn't say."

Reg grunted a stifled laugh and AJ elbowed him.

"Can you tell me anything about my grandfather, sir? Did you spend much time with him?"

Ormond shook his head. "Tall man, best I remember. I just drove da lorry and somebody tell me he da captain of da ship."

"And where did you take him in town, sir?" Andy continued.

"Seaview Hotel as I recall. Den da udder man I took to da marina on North Sound to pick up a car. Dat was it. Didn't see dem again."

Andy looked from Ormond to Sally, then back again. "Who was this other man?"

Ormond shrugged his shoulders. "I couldn't say."

"Seaview Hotel was south of town on Church Street," Reg said. "They knocked it down mid 2000s if I recall. Built condos there with the same name."

"Dat's da one," Ormond confirmed. "Used to have concerts in da car park, and dat bar was popular back den."

"Is there anything more you can tell us about my grandfather, or the man he was with, sir?" Andy asked. "Was the other man from the ship too?"

Ormond shook his head again. "Da udder man live at Seaview, best I know."

"But you don't remember who he was?" Reg asked.

"I couldn't say. Long time back."

"But somehow you know the other man lived on the island," Reg persisted.

Ormond shuffled uncomfortably. "Guess so. It were all a long time back."

He looked at Sally with a slightly panicked expression.

"Thank you, sir," Andy interjected. "I really appreciate you sharing what you know with us."

"I have a couple more calls I'm following up on this afternoon," Sally said. "I'll touch base with you once I've spoken with them." She put a hand on Ormond's shoulder. "But isn't this wonderful? I told you I'd help get to the bottom of your grandfather's story."

Reg started to say something, but AJ gave him another elbow and he stopped himself. Sally threw him a quick frown as well.

"Andy, would you like to join us for lunch? I'm sure Mr Willis would enjoy talking to you some more."

Reg put a beefy hand on AJ's elbow to save himself from another dig. "We've got plans I'm afraid, Sally," he said, before Andy could respond. "He's tied up most of the afternoon, but how about he gives you a bell later, yeah?"

The journalist glared at Reg then turned to Andy, who was doing his best to remain expressionless.

"That's a shame. But we must speak before the end of the day, Andy, we have much to cover and I'm sure I'll have more contacts for you this afternoon."

"I appreciate your efforts, Miss Regis," Andy replied. "And it was very nice to meet you, Mr Willis."

The old man nodded, then turned to walk up the dock.

"We'll speak later," Sally said, and followed Ormond.

"You're buyin' lunch now," they heard the old man say as the two left.

"Yes, you'll get your lunch," Sally replied impatiently.

Once they were out of earshot, Andy turned to Reg. "I didn't know we had plans, sir. What did you have in mind?"

Reg laughed. "Keeping you out of her clutches was my main objective."

Pearl waved goodbye to Sally, then walked towards them as Thomas stepped over from the boat.

"I'm ready for lunch," he announced. "How about you, Big Boss?"

Reg looked at the young Caymanian. "You're always ready for lunch. But I am a bit peckish, I must say."

"I'm impressed," Pearl said, joining the group. "You got rid of her pretty sharpish. I figured she'd have Andy wrapped up in her web by now."

"She seems very nice," Andy said. "I do appreciate her trying to help."

Reg scoffed. "She's nice enough, all right, but her main objective is getting a story for her paper. Try getting her to answer her bloody phone when she doesn't think you have something useful for her."

Pearl waved a hand at her husband. "Don't mind him, Andy. He can be a cynical old goat sometimes."

"Ain't that the truth," AJ added with a grin.

Reg threw his hands in the air. "Am I wrong about Sally Regis?"

"No," Pearl and AJ said together.

"But you're still an old goat," AJ chuckled.

Pearl stood on her tiptoes and kissed her husband. "But you're a handsome old goat."

Thomas cleared his throat. "Can we get back to da subject of lunch?"

"Come on then," AJ said, patting the side of the boat. "Let's get you fed, and then we'll wash our baby down and put her to bed."

"Where are we going?" Pearl asked.

"Heritage Kitchen," AJ replied as though there were no other options.

"You ought to have shares in that place," Reg responded, walking up the dock. "Do you ever eat anywhere else?"

"Hands up who wants Heritage Kitchen?" AJ said, following along.

They all put their hands in the air, including Reg. AJ looked at Andy, who shot his hand up too although he had no idea where they were going.

"See, even our visitor knows the best food in town," AJ declared.

"I thought you might turn on me if I didn't play along," Andy said, grinning at AJ.

"Wise man," Thomas said, slapping Andy on the shoulder. "Don't get on the wrong side of this lady."

AJ laughed and looked toward the car park where her fifteen-passenger van waited for them to pile in. Why her old van reminded her of Jackson, she had no idea, but it did and a knot twisted in her stomach. He would be boarding the plane soon.

"So seriously, Reg," Pearl asked, opening the van door. "What have you got in mind for Andy this afternoon?"

The question pulled AJ back from the edge of melting down and she brushed a tear from her cheek and climbed into the driver's seat.

"I'm gonna call Suzy Soto at lunch," Reg replied.

"Is that the wife of the man who sunk the *Oro Verde* as an artificial reef?" Andy asked.

"That's the one," Reg confirmed. "And he was also the father of diving here in the Cayman Islands. His fingerprints are on everything to do with the industry around here. His widow, Suzy, is a super lady and still very active in the community, especially with anything she and Bob started when he was still alive."

19

For the second time that day, Butty was awoken by someone else. This time, he was in a lounge chair under the shade of a palm tree, next to the hotel swimming pool, but the person ruining his rest was the same.

"Got you a ship," Gould said, silhouetted by the afternoon sun. "Put a shirt on and let's go."

"Go, as in leaving dock? Or go, as in take a look?" Butty replied, sitting up and yawning.

"Take a look, but leaving tonight so we'll need to provision you for the trip," Gould replied, already walking away.

Butty slipped his canvas shoes on and grabbed his shirt from where it hung over the back of the lounger.

"What about crew?"

Gould waved a hand in the air and didn't turn around. "Logistics is my thing, Butty Boy, remember? It's taken care of."

How the man had dug up a cargo ship and crew in a matter of hours was astonishing to Butty, and he tried to recall even seeing another freighter anywhere around the island, and couldn't. Not even in the little port fronting George Town.

Fifteen minutes later and a short car ride to the same North

Sound marina they'd left from that morning, Butty stood looking at a 42-foot Grand Banks motor yacht.

"That's a boat, not a ship," he said. "It's a lovely vessel for cruising around the island, but I'm not sailing her to Miami."

"Why not?" Gould retorted. "Someone sailed her from Miami to here. Or somewhere else to here."

"I bet they didn't do it at the beginning of winter."

Gould looked out across the North Sound which with the reef protection would sometimes whip up little one-foot waves on a very windy day.

"We have a great weather window."

Butty scoffed. "What's the cruising speed of this thing?"

Gould shrugged his shoulders. "You're worrying about the wrong stuff here, Captain. This ship…"

"Boat," Butty corrected.

"This boat made it to the island, so it'll have no problem making it back," Gould continued unperturbed. "The part we need to discuss is how the missing captain of the *Oro Verde* can remain hidden and avoid any further scrutiny by authorities."

Butty put his hands on his hips and stared over his sunglasses at Gould. "You are the bloody authorities! What do you mean *further scrutiny?*"

Gould waved his hands as though it were all simple details. "We're one branch of a complex grouping of law enforcement and government agencies who don't all play nicely sometimes, that's all I'm saying. I have a solution, Butty, but it means an adjustment for you."

"An *adjustment?*"

"Look, all we have to do is get this boat to Miami with our goods and then you'll pick up a proper cargo ship, some new paperwork, and be back in business. In a few weeks from now we'll be drinking mai tais by the pool and laughing about all this."

"You mean I'll be at sea while you'll be sitting by the pool sipping bloody mai tais," Butty replied. "Who's going with me? You said you had crew."

"Yeah, yeah. I'll introduce you to him back at the hotel. He's one of our agents. Great guy."

"He know how to crew a boat on the open ocean?" Butty asked.

"He grew up in San Diego," Gould replied. "Everyone in San Diego can sail."

Butty was about to step aboard the boat, but paused. "Are you sure we can't figure out a way to get the *Oro Verde* back? She has everything we need."

"Except a crew," Gould pointed out. "Besides, she's wrapped up in island red tape now and your owner friend hasn't been answering his phone. If he's in the wind, it'll take months, maybe even years to settle all the paperwork. We're lining up another ship in Miami for you. We'll control it this time, and we'll round up a crew you can trust."

Butty looked at Gould suspiciously, then stepped over the gunwale onto the wooden motor yacht. It was a nice vessel, the kind a family could spend long weekends cruising the coastline in comfort, enjoying cool drinks and basking in the sun. The Grand Banks was capable of making an open ocean crossing, in perfect conditions, but that certainly wasn't what she was designed for. He poked around, checking the galley was adequate and then lifting the doors to the engine bay. It had twin diesels which didn't look particularly speedy, but likely reliable.

"When do we leave?" Butty asked, returning to the cockpit and peering over the transom. He noted the boat's name was *Straight Shooter*.

"Tonight," Gould replied, glancing at his watch. "I'll have her loaded around midnight, and then you can leave."

"Seriously?" Butty exclaimed. "Your plan is for me to find my way out through the reef at night in a boat I don't know? You're bloody bonkers."

"I'll have a local lead you out of the North Sound and then you'll be all set," Gould replied. "Logistics, Butty Boy. It's my thing."

Butty shook his head and sighed. "Fine. Whose boat is this anyway?"

Gould lifted his straw trilby and scratched his head. "A guy who worked for us. But he's retired now."

Butty stepped over to the dock. "If he's retired I'm guessing he'll be looking to spend more time on his boat."

Gould walked towards the Jeep in the car park. "Not that kind of retired."

Butty spent the rest of the afternoon attempting to gather provisions. It was Sunday and every shop on the island was closed. Gould led him to the restaurant at the Seaview Hotel, where with the manager's permission, he raided their stores. As the Grand Banks didn't have a refrigerator, he was limited to canned goods and fresh produce. He estimated the journey would take a little over three days, running at the nine knots cruising speed quoted on the paperwork he'd found in a drawer near the helm. He was provisioning for a week, to cover them for unforeseen delays.

Gould promised he'd supply plenty of extra diesel in cans as well as filling the tank before they left. Butty reminded the CIA agent that the closest land option they'd have for ninety percent of the journey would be Cuba, and urged him not to skimp on the fuel as he doubted he'd be allowed to leave if he was forced to set foot on Cuban soil in an American-owned vessel. Butty asked repeatedly to meet the man who was supposed to accompany him, but Gould had yet to introduce him. The trip would be far more comfortable with three to rotate watches, but Butty was praying the one he was getting was at least a seaman of some description, so he didn't push for a third. The longer Gould delayed in producing the man, the less confident the captain was in his help being of much help.

After a filling meal in the Seaview restaurant on Gould's tab, Butty retired to his room to catch a few hours' sleep before leaving.

He knew it might be his last chance for restful shuteye in the next few days. For the third time within twenty hours, he was startled awake by Agent Gould. Rising from his bed, Butty gathered his belongings, which were limited to his two photographs, the clothes he'd been bought from the hotel shop, and his wallet which still hadn't dried out yet. Once again, he followed Gould to the Wagoneer, and they drove the dark streets of George Town to the marina.

A man wearing a sport coat and neatly pressed trousers met them at the Grand Banks and Butty tried not to laugh. All the guy needed were the dark shades and he'd be the stereotypical spook.

"You're kidding me?" Butty muttered, turning to Gould.

"He's not officially here on the island; we need him stateside, and you need crew, so this works out perfectly."

"You're kidding me?" Butty repeated.

"Fieldman, this is Raymond Butty Butterworth," Gould said, ignoring the Englishman's complaints. "Butty, meet Agent Fieldman."

The man extended a hand, which Butty reluctantly shook.

"Check the port side bilge is pumping for me, would you Mr Fieldman?" Butty said, and in the dim light he could see the man was completely baffled. He turned to Gould again. "Everyone from San Diego knows boats, huh?"

"I'm actually from El Cajon, sir," Fieldman volunteered. "It's in the hills inland of San Diego."

"Not much boating in those hills, I'm guessing," Butty responded.

"You'll train him up in no time, Butty Boy," Gould said. "Now, time's wasting, so let's get under way. Just head into the sound and follow the light."

"What light?" Butty asked, looking around without seeing another boat ready to leave.

"You'll see, don't worry," Gould assured him.

They spent the next ten minutes loading the provisions and Butty started the engines, letting them warm up. He tried going below deck to the berths but discovered the cargo took up the entire area below the main deck, leaving the pilothouse as the only habitable space. With no access to the head. Butty was about to complain, and then stopped himself. *What was the point?* He could pee over the transom and aim the other over the side or go in a bucket and dump it over. He'd dealt with worse before.

He reminded himself that in three days' time he'd be home with his pregnant wife, and he'd decide how to proceed from there. Regardless of what he'd told Gould and the mysterious Mr Rosewater, maybe he'd talk Lucia into going to the UK for a year or two, until all this mess calmed down. No way she'd want to leave her family, but if it meant their child would be safe, he figured she might agree if the move wasn't permanent.

After explaining the bow from the stern and the port side from starboard to Fieldman, Butty had him and Gould cast the lines, and he idled away from dock without a look back to the CIA agent. If he never saw Gene Gould again, he'd be okay with it, no matter how much they were promising to pay him.

Once *Straight Shooter* was in the middle of the canal leading to the sound, Butty heard the purr of an outboard over the dull drone of the diesels, then saw the orange glow of the local man-with-no-name's cigarette. A white light from a small torch appeared at his stern and Butty aimed the Grand Banks in pursuit, edging the motors up a few hundred rpms to keep the distance equal.

Fieldman stood alongside Butty and remained silent for most of the smooth trip across the sound, accepting the cigarette Butty offered him.

"Just explain what you need me to do, and I'll do it, sir," the young man finally said.

Butty sighed. He seemed like a decent kid and if nothing else, he might be good company as they trudged across the Caribbean Sea.

"Know how to read a compass?" Butty asked.

"Of course," Fieldman replied.

"That's a start, then," Butty said, his tone softening. "Know what these gauges are for?" he added, nodding to the engine gauges inset into the wooden dashboard.

Fieldman leaned over. "Temperatures on each engine. Rpm gauges. Fuel level. And looks like oil pressure," he said, pointing to each round gauge in turn.

Things were looking up, Butty thought. His attention returned to the white light ahead as it began to rock side to side and then rise and fall over the waves. He eased into the two throttles a little more to keep the Grand Banks on course through the cut in the reef which he couldn't see. After another minute of building seas, the torch ahead flashed twice, then went out, leaving them alone in the open ocean off the north side of the island. Butty pushed the throttles forward a little further, watching the rpms slowly climb until the speed read nine knots.

Steering to port, he moved onto the compass heading he'd plotted earlier from the chart, and settled in for the rest of the night. The seas were rolling in from the north-east as the *Straight Shooter* took a north-westerly track, so pretty soon the boat was gliding into the troughs and yawing and rolling over the crests sweeping underneath them. Butty noticed Fieldman becoming slightly agitated, but before he could ask if he was okay, the young man bolted for the transom and released his dinner into the dark water.

"Great," Butty mumbled to himself. "So much for things looking up."

20

Reg finished his phone call and walked back to the group, who were sitting at a long wooden table in the shade next to the brightly coloured shack signed Heritage Kitchen. Overlooking the water from the inland side of the narrow Boggy Sand Road, AJ passed by the little restaurant every time she came to and from her cottage at the south end of the street.

"Suzy's meeting us at the dock in fifteen minutes," Reg announced. "She happened to be in West Bay already, doing research for a history book about schooners she's working on."

"And she met my grandfather?" Andy asked, wiping his lips with a napkin and placing it on his empty plate.

"I don't think Suzy ever met him, but she's pretty sure her husband, Bob, did," Reg replied. "Either way, I guarantee she'll know someone who can help us."

"How was everything?" Ronaldo, the restaurant owner asked, scooping up empty plates from the table.

"Bloody terrible, as you can tell by all the leftovers," AJ joked, picking up a few plates herself and following his laughter into the kitchen.

"When you gonna bring me some lionfish?" he asked AJ, taking the plates from her and placing them in a large stainless-steel sink.

"I might be able to hunt a bit tomorrow morning, depending where my customers want to go," AJ replied. "I'll text you if we catch any."

"Make sure it's enough for a lunch special," Ronaldo called after her as she re-joined the group heading to the van. "Not just your lunch!"

She turned and laughed. "Priorities, mate. My lunch always comes second."

"Dat's right," Thomas added. "Mine comes first!"

AJ nodded her agreement.

Ronaldo wiped his hands on his apron, shaking his head. He gave them a wave and went back to work as more customers arrived at the serving window in the front of the shack.

Three minutes later, AJ parked the van and they clambered out, stretching and complaining how full they were.

"Feels like nap time," Thomas said as AJ steered him down the dock towards *Hazel's Odyssey*.

"As soon as we give her a good wash, you can sleep all afternoon," she assured him.

Reg's boats were back at the dock, refilling tanks for the afternoon trips or readying for the next day, and AJ and Thomas said hi to the crews before stepping aboard her Newton. She peeled off her sun-shirt so she didn't get it wet and tossed it onto the shelf at the front of the open cabin. They began their daily routine of spraying down the decks with fresh water and cleaning their own gear as well as the rental BCD Andy had used.

AJ looked at her watch. A Rolex Submariner her friends and family had clubbed together to buy her on her thirtieth birthday. Jackson had been there for the party, which felt like forever ago. It was 1:30. Jackson would be boarding the plane. Probably in his seat by now. She wondered what he was thinking. Excited about everything that lay ahead, or sad about leaving? The whole situation still felt surreal, as though she was watching an episode of a show and the writers had made a big mistake, separating the two main characters that were clearly meant for each other.

"AJ, you remember Suzy Soto, yeah?" Reg's booming voice echoed around the boat.

She turned and saw an elegant blonde-haired lady on the dock wearing a flowing summer dress.

"Of course," AJ said, quickly recovering from her melancholy thoughts. "Nice to see you again."

Reg offered a hand and Suzy stepped aboard, followed by Andy.

"Thought we could chat in the shade," Reg said, indicating the fibreglass bench seats beneath the open cabin.

"Not much of a conference room, I'm afraid," AJ apologised, and beckoned Thomas to join them.

"I've been on a boat or two in my time," Suzy said with a broad smile. "I'm as happy on water as I am on land."

They all sat and Thomas handed out water for everyone, before the group looked towards Suzy expectantly.

"Has anyone else called you about the *Oro Verde* lately?" Reg asked.

Suzy laughed. "I'm guessing so," she replied. "I missed a call from Sally Regis of the *Daily News* this morning, and seeing her article in the paper today, I'm guessing that's why she was after me."

Reg nodded and AJ knew he was hiding a smirk behind his bushy beard. "I dare say you're right. Sally's been hounding poor Andy here."

"Well, I've been thinking," Suzy began. "I don't recall ever meeting the captain, but I was married to Bob by the time he began serious plans to sink the abandoned *Oro Verde* as an artificial reef. It took him years to convince the government to let him do it."

"Did your husband ever talk about meeting the captain, Mrs Soto?" Andy asked.

"Please, it's Suzy," she insisted with a genuine smile that made her eyes sparkle. "I recall he did meet the man, but I honestly can't remember when or why he did. I am sorry, but we're talking about a few years back."

"That's completely understandable," Andy replied.

"There are a few fellows we can ask, though," Suzy offered. "One of Bob's friends who's still around today, for starters. He's a businessman who owns a dive resort and marina and a few other things. Oh, and we might start with Curly. He's an Australian who worked for Bob in his dive shop. He still lives on the island."

"Curly Roper?" Reg asked.

"That's him," Suzy confirmed. "Do you know him?"

"I've bumped into him once or twice over the years," Reg said guardedly. "Usually in a bar."

Suzy grinned. "He's a bit of a character, but he might well remember something from back then. Although we should probably catch him before happy hour. To be honest, I think the sinking in 1981 got more attention than the ship first being abandoned here, but it doesn't hurt to ask."

"That seems to be mostly what pops up when you search the internet for details," AJ agreed. "It's all rumour and tall tales from 1976, which is when we believe Andy's grandfather was here."

"I don't think many people did know much about the ship or why it came to be left afloat," Suzy continued. "It was on the north side, if I'm remembering correctly. I was busy running a hotel and the Caribbean Hotel Association at the time, but I recall a lot of chatter about this cargo ship that showed up one day. It was news for a week or two and then it sat inside the North Sound for years."

Suzy took out a mobile from the pocket of her brightly coloured dress and found the contact she was looking for. After a few moments, AJ listened to her side of the conversation.

"Hello Curly, it's Suzy."

She gently shook her head as she listened.

"Don't worry about that, I took care of it."

She closed her eyes as though she were urging herself to be patient.

"Like I said, not to worry, Curly. I was calling you about something else, not your bar bill…"

Apparently he didn't let her finish and she waited for another opportunity to speak.

"No, nothing like that, don't worry. I have a couple of friends who'd like to talk to you about the *Oro Verde*. I don't remember much about it until the sinking, and they're after information about when it first arrived here."

Suzy once more waited to get another word in.

"You don't need to tell me, Curly, tell them. I'm sending them over to your place now, so listen for a knock at the door."

She held a hand in the air.

"Okay, My Bar it is then."

It took another minute for Suzy to wrap up the conversation and be able to politely end the call, after which she sighed and slipped her mobile back into her pocket.

"He lives in a cottage across the road from Sunset House," Suzy explained. "Not Maureen and Maxine Bodden's home where they do their amazing Christmas lights, but the little run-down place next door. It used to be a darling little traditional island cottage but he hasn't been able to keep it up over the years. Anyway, he said to meet him in My Bar, but if he's not there, go knock on the door at the cottage."

"Can you come with us?" Andy asked.

Suzy stood and straightened her dress. "I have another appointment, I'm afraid, and you'll get more out of Curly if I'm not there." She smiled and blushed a little. "I think he always had a bit of thing for the boss's wife, so he tends to be distracted when I'm around."

"I can't blame a bloke for admiring beauty," Reg said, standing himself.

"Oh stop it," Suzy replied, blushing more and swatting him on the arm. "Anyway, I must be off for now." She extended a hand to Andy. "Good luck young man and please let me know what you find out. I'm very curious now, and you never know, maybe it'll be the subject of my next book."

"Thank you," Andy replied, then Reg offered Suzy a supporting hand as she stepped over to the dock.

"Lovely to meet you again," AJ said, hopping to the dock herself to retrieve the hose.

Suzy paused and pointed to AJ's bare arms. "I like your tattoos," she said with a smile. "I'm a painter myself, so I admire beautiful art in all its forms."

Now AJ blushed, looking down for a moment. "Thank you." And then she picked her head up. "I hope we can meet again. I'd love to hear more about your husband."

"Have you read my book about him?" Suzy asked and AJ's cheeks turned a brighter red.

"I'm embarrassed to say I haven't, but I promise I will," she responded, thinking she was about to have a lot more free time in the evenings now she'd be living alone again.

"Reg has my number," Suzy said. "We'll have a chinwag over a glass of wine some evening, as you Brits say."

AJ watched the woman walk away and thought about the magnificent life the woman had lived, and all she was still doing to impact the islands in a positive way. She hoped to have that much energy and cheer when she reached Suzy Soto's age.

"You gotta take Andy," Reg said, and AJ looked his way.

"I need to finish washing the boat first, and then I can."

Reg waved her off. "Pearl says I have a bloke coming to talk about a charter, so I have to stay here. I'll help Thomas finish up until he shows up. You can toddle off."

AJ looked at Thomas, who waved her towards the car park.

"Alright then, if you two are sure?"

Reg and Thomas both nodded and pointed at her van.

"Fine, I'm going," she said, quickly hopping back aboard and grabbing her shirt. "But don't let that old goat slack off and leave you doing everything," she said to Thomas.

Reg picked up the hose to spray her, but she'd sprinted halfway up the dock before he could. She'd learned that lesson a long time ago.

21

Butty had been concerned about leaving Grand Cayman's North Sound at night, but he was even more worried about sneaking into Tavernier Creek Marina in the upper Florida Keys under cover of darkness. It was 5:00am and a few fishermen were preparing to make an early start; otherwise the place appeared deserted. Exhausted, unshaven, and badly in need of a shower, he carefully piloted the *Straight Shooter* across the shallow coastal waters and into the channel leading to the marina.

Fieldman had dry retched for the first four hours of the journey after depositing every ounce of his stomach's contents into the sea within five minutes of leaving the North Sound. Following that, he'd slept, groaned, and sipped water all day. Sometime into the first full night at sea, he'd managed to relieve Butty at the wheel for a few hours, and from then on he'd taken a turn for an hour or two out of every six. He'd finally found his sea legs in time for them to reach Tavernier.

With their cargo in mind, Gould had instructed Butty to avoid Miami and instead find the little marina where someone would meet them. As Butty idled into the dock under the dim light of one yellow bulb on a tall pole, he couldn't see a single soul around, and wondered whether he'd come to the right place. A sign confirmed he was, so Fieldman jumped to the dock and tied the bow line in. Butty drew the stern against the dock until the fenders squeaked in protest, then Fieldman tied the stern line in and Butty shut the engines down for the first time in over three days.

"Who are you?" a man's voice asked in Spanish.

Butty couldn't see anyone and Fieldman spun around trying to locate the source of the question.

"Proteus," Butty replied, assuming he should stick with his codename.

There was silence for a few moments.

"Who?"

"Proteus," Butty repeated.

"What the hell kind of name is that?" the voice asked.

Butty was too tired to play these games. "Look, are you Herrera's man or what?"

A figure stepped forward from the shadows beside a building. He was a heavy-set man with swarthy skin, dark hair and a moustache. Butty didn't recognise him from the few men of Sal Herrera's he'd met before.

"Butterworth?" he asked, in what Butty knew was a Cuban accent.

"Yeah," he replied. "Where do we unload?"

The man pointed across the marina to a rickety wooden pier on the far side, away from the boat ramp and newer dock.

"Over there. I'll bring the van around."

Butty and Fieldman moved the *Straight Shooter*, and a large box van manoeuvred into position at the foot of the wooden pier. A second man opened the back doors and the two Cubans wheeled a pair of hand trucks over. The four men worked silently, removing the bales from the boat and loading them in the van. When they were done, the hand trucks wouldn't fit, so they put them on the boat.

"What now?" Butty asked in Spanish.

"He takes the boat, you two come with me," the moustached man replied, and hopped into the driving seat.

Butty had hoped he'd seen the last of the drugs, so riding to Miami in a vehicle crammed full of weed wasn't what he'd planned on, but it was that or be left in Tavernier without transportation. Fieldman got in the van without hesitation, so Butty reluctantly followed. Foremost on his mind was getting home to Lucia. Quite what he'd tell her about everything that had taken place he wasn't sure, but simply hugging her and touching her swollen belly containing their unborn child would be a great start.

Falling asleep against the passenger door, Butty woke when the van pulled into a warehouse, lit by the sunlight pouring in through the roll-up door. He guessed they were in Miami, but it could have been any of the outlying towns or suburbs. Butty opened the door and picked up the familiar scent of diesel and seawater which suggested they were near one of the docks.

The warehouse had industrial steel shelving down both sides with a variety of crates and pallets stacked on most of them. From an office in the far corner, Sal Herrera walked towards him and held his hand out. Butty shook.

"I have a new ship for you," Herrera said without any verbal salutation or preamble.

"And I have a shower and a bed waiting for me," Butty replied, too tired to give the Cuban the deference he undoubtedly expected.

Herrera waved a hand in the air. "Of course, take some time. I understand that bastard Pérez has made things difficult for us, but that will change very soon."

Butty certainly wasn't in the mood to discuss the politics of Miami drug lords, so he simply nodded.

"Can I get a ride home?" he asked.

"Of course," Herrera replied and snapped his fingers towards the office. Another man instantly appeared. "Take them where they need to go," he ordered then turned back to Butty, holding out a piece of paper. "Here's the dock and the name of the ship. Be there tomorrow at noon. We'll sort out the paperwork."

Butty took the paper and without looking at it, stuffed it in his pocket. Everyone seemed to be making a lot of career decisions for him, and assuming he'd play along, but he was far from sure. Walking away from all this chaos felt like a much better option, especially in his exhausted state. He nodded one more time to Herrera, then followed his man towards a Buick parked outside the warehouse.

Fieldman had stayed quiet and Herrera had completely ignored his presence. As they walked to the car, Fieldman whispered to Butty.

"Who's that guy?"

"Sal Herrera," Butty replied, not offering anything further. "Where do you need to get to?"

"The CIA field office in town, I guess," the young agent replied.

Butty laughed as he opened the front passenger side door. "I wouldn't ask this chap to take you there."

Fieldman looked bemused for a second and then nodded. "Right. Probably not. Perhaps a bus station or somewhere I can take a taxi from would be best."

Switching to Spanish, Butty gave the driver his address, then asked him to drop Fieldman by a decent hotel along the way. The Cuban glanced disdainfully at the man in the back seat, then nodded and started the car.

Twenty minutes later, the young CIA agent had been dropped off, and the Cuban driver turned onto the street where Butty rented a small cottage for him and Lucia.

"Hold up," Butty said in Spanish, looking down the road. "Pull to the side."

The driver did so and they both stared at the row of bungalows along the tree-lined suburban street. Outside a home about six buildings away from where they watched, was a Miami-Dade Police Department car.

"That your place?" the driver asked, finally speaking.

"Yeah," Butty replied, without taking his eyes off his home.

"Looks like you're screwed, man," the man said without an ounce of sympathy in his voice. "How about you get out here so I can leave?"

Butty nodded. "Fine," he replied, and exited the Buick, closing the door quietly despite his temptation to leave it open so the Cuban had to get out to close it himself.

With his head down, Butty moved down the pavement until he was two houses away and screened by a Volkswagen bus, parked by the kerb. A pair of officers stood at the step into the bungalow, where Lucia held the door open but remained inside. She was shaking her head a lot, and one of the officers occasionally made a note on a small pad of paper. After a few more minutes, the two policemen turned and walked to their car, pausing to have a conversation across the roof before getting in. Butty was too far away to hear what they said and he leaned against a tree behind the VW bus until they'd driven down the road and turned out of sight.

His mind whirred and wondered what they'd been calling about. It could have been a follow-up about the homemade bomb on the *Oro Verde* which felt like it had been a lifetime ago, but was actually less than a month. Or more likely, it had something to do with the ship being abandoned in Grand Cayman. He was the captain according to the paper trail leading from Miami to Ecuador and back, so it wasn't surprising that the authorities would come knocking. The Caymanians would have found the ship's paperwork in the wheelhouse and started calling. It wouldn't have taken long to track him down. Or at least his house.

Butty jogged across the road and scanned the street before walking up the footpath to his house. He dug around in his pocket for his front door key he'd remembered to grab from the *Oro Verde* and turned it in the lock.

"It's me," he said, opening the door and stepping inside. "Lucia?"

His wife appeared from the kitchen, looking at him across the living room. He quickly closed the door behind him and smiled. To him, she looked radiant, and a sight for sore eyes. The change in close to a month away was remarkable. Her slender frame looked like she'd traded a football for a basketball under her blouse, where both her hands rested on her tummy. He wished he had a camera to capture that very moment. If he could bottle the feelings running through him in that instant, he'd savour them every day and never go to sea again.

"It's so good to see you, love," he said, his voice slightly hoarse.

Her dark eyes glared at him, her brow creasing into a frown. "What the hell have you done?" she greeted him in return.

22

A large thatched-roofed, open-air bar overlooked the ocean from a raised terrace in the Sunset House Dive Resort on the south side of George Town. The resort had been around for decades, and the bar was popular with locals as well as guests and other visitors. A patio extended to a low wall above the ironshore-lined ocean front, and as AJ led Andy to the bar, she noticed the place was mostly deserted. The lunch crowd had moved on, and now a dive instructor sat at a table to one side going over classwork with two students, three men sat on stools at the bar, and one older man occupied a table under an umbrella near the edge. The old man was tall, skinny, with a completely bald head.

"Are you Curly by any chance?" AJ asked the man, despite the lack of any visible curls.

The man turned, looked AJ over, and smiled. "I am, love. And I'm very pleased to meet you," he said with an Australian accent.

"I'm AJ Bailey, and this is Andy Butterworth," AJ replied, moving to the opposite side of the table. "Suzy Soto sent us your way."

Curly looked past Andy, searching for anyone else with them. "Where's Suzy at then?"

AJ and Andy sat down. "She had another appointment. It's just the two of us."

Curly's face looked disappointed for a moment, but then he took a sip of his cocktail and eyed AJ once more. His face softened and his stare lingered in the general vicinity of her chest.

"Suzy mentioned you were around when the *Oro Verde* arrived here back in 1976," AJ quickly said, drawing his gaze up a little higher. "Andy is the captain's grandson and we're trying to find out anything we can about what happened."

Curly sat back in his chair, cocktail in hand. "That's a while back, mate," he said, finally looking Andy's way. "Bob was the one who talked the government into letting him sink the bugger."

"Yes," Andy replied patiently. "Miss Soto was able to tell us a little about that."

"What do you recall from 1976 when the *Oro Verde* first arrived?" AJ pressed, wondering if the man could keep two thoughts straight in his mind.

His eyes flicked back to her. They had a playful sparkle and AJ decided he might be a little lecherous, but seemed harmless, and was probably a good bloke or Bob Soto wouldn't have kept him around.

"It was strange," he began. "The ship just turned up one day, and by the time anyone got around to investigating it, the whole crew were gone." He gesticulated in the air like he was releasing a puff of smoke. "Vanished."

"What did the authorities do with the ship?" AJ asked.

"Towed her into the North Sound and left her there at anchor," Curly replied. "But she drifted a bit and sat on a sand bank. That's where she stayed until Bob organised to sink her."

"And no one ever saw or heard from any of the crew?" Andy asked.

The old man shook his head. "Vanished."

"But Suzy indicated you may know something about the captain?" Andy continued.

Curly grinned. "I met him."

AJ and Andy both leaned forward a little in their seats and Curly took a long sip, finishing his cocktail and clearly relishing the attention his comment received.

"Can I get you two anything?" a waitress asked, appearing by their table.

Curly rattled the ice cubes in his empty glass.

"I'll have a Strongbow, please," AJ replied, wishing the waitress's timing had been better. "No glass."

"I'll have the same," Andy said.

"Start a tab for us," AJ said before the waitress walked away. "His can go on ours," she added, nodding towards Curly.

"That's the spirit, love," Curly said with a broad smile.

"The captain," AJ continued, trying to get the old man back on track. "Where and when did you meet him?"

"You know about the rumours, right?" he said in way of reply. "About that ship?"

"Sure," AJ said. "They were smuggling weed and the crew got pissed off at the captain. There's the whole government burned the dope and got the island high story too."

Curly chuckled. "Yeah, that was a good day."

"It's true?" Andy reacted in surprise.

Curly shrugged his shoulders. "Sort of."

The waitress returned with their drinks and they all sat back while she set them on the table.

"Anything else for now?"

"We're good, thank you," AJ was quick to reply before Curly ordered a prime rib on her bill.

Once she'd left, AJ and Andy leaned forward again and Curly took a long drink from his fresh glass. AJ wasn't sure what he was drinking, but by the dark golden colour, she guessed it was rum and Coke, with the emphasis on the rum.

"You were saying…" AJ encouraged the old man, who put his half-empty glass down and smacked his lips.

"I don't know what happened to the crew of the ship, but I can tell you the captain..." Curly paused and looked at Andy. "Your grandfather, mate?"

Andy nodded.

"Yeah, well he was alive and kicking when I met him, and that was a week or so after the ship showed up."

"Do you recall where this was?" AJ asked.

"At the Seaview bar. That's where he was staying."

"Isn't that where the other fellow said he dropped him?" Andy remarked, turning to AJ.

"Yup," she acknowledged. "Was he with anyone else?"

Curly's expression changed and he picked his glass back up, tipping it to his lips.

AJ and Andy waited. The old man finally put the glass down having almost drained it of its contents. AJ realised she was yet to touch her own drink, but she didn't care. She could sense they were close to actually learning something about Butty Butterworth.

"I don't know about anyone else," Curly mumbled and stared out across the blue water.

AJ glanced over at Andy, who shared her puzzled expression.

"Okay. So you met the captain in the bar, just the two of you?" AJ asked, trying not to sound like she was grilling him.

"No, no. There were other people there," Curly said. "I just remember Bob telling me that a guy at the bar was the captain of the *Oro Verde*."

"Did you speak with him?" Andy asked.

Curly looked thoughtful and AJ guessed he was beginning to be careful with what he revealed. Why he should be doing so puzzled her, and she wanted to wave the waitress over to liquor him up a little more, but then felt guilty.

"Maybe a casual hello in passing, I reckon," Curly finally replied and then swallowed the remaining rum in his glass.

"You said this was a week or so after the *Oro Verde* arrived," AJ said. "Had the authorities been questioning the captain or detained him at all? As best we know, there's no record of that," she added, making a mental note to ask her friend Nora to search the police records.

"It was too long ago," Curly said. "I don't remember."

Sod it, AJ thought to herself, and gave the waitress a subtle wave behind Andy's seat. The woman appeared to get the hint and went behind the bar to fix another cocktail.

"What were you doing for Bob at the time?" AJ asked and sensed Andy's confused look, no doubt wondering why she was drifting off topic.

"I helped him run the dive shop," Curly replied, his voice brightening with the change in subject. "Best op in town, we were. Ran dive trips, sold gear, taught lessons, the lot."

The waitress slid a fresh cocktail in front of Curly and he quickly snatched it up.

"I might be in love with you," he told her, lifting the glass straight to his lips.

The waitress winked at AJ as she walked away. AJ and Andy both took a swig of their cider while Curly polished off half his glass again.

"Was the Seaview a popular hangout for the diving crowd back in the day, Curly?" AJ asked, carefully bringing the questions back to the subject they'd driven across town for.

"Oh yeah," he replied. "Holiday Inn on Seven Mile Beach wasn't bad either. But Seaview had live music sometimes, and these costume parties. They were a bloody riot." He shook his head. "Like everything else though, it changed over the years, then they tore it down and built more condos there. Just what the bloody island needs is more of them rabbit hutches."

He scoffed and tipped the glass back. AJ felt a pang of guilt once more. She was enabling a man who she guessed was probably an alcoholic, and for what? A bit of info about Andy's grandfather. She was certain Curly was holding back something he knew, but she couldn't tell what. He'd pretty much confirmed that drugs had been involved in some shape or form, so perhaps he'd had a hand in moving or selling them? Surely, after all these years he wouldn't be worried about any legal ramifications? In her mind, the police certainly wouldn't care.

"We know Raymond Butterfield, the captain who went by the nickname Butty, was with another man after leaving the ship, Curly," AJ pressed, hoping the liquor had done its job. "It would be a great help to us to know who that might have been."

Curly scoffed, his head bobbling as though his neck muscles had turned to jelly. "You just think that'd be a help, love. You don't know what you're sticking your nose into."

"What on earth do you mean by that, sir?" Andy said, pouncing more urgently than AJ wished he had.

Curly held up both hands, his rum and Coke swirling in the glass as the ice cubes clinked against each other.

"Nothing, nothing, mate," he slurred. "I just saw your father the one time. I can't tell you anything else, mate."

"Grand..." Andy began correcting, but AJ rested her hand on his arm and he stopped.

"We appreciate what you've given us, Curly," AJ said instead. "We'll see what we can dig up from the Seaview records. Someone will likely have them stored away."

The old man pushed his chair back. "I wouldn't if I were you," he mumbled, getting to his wobbly feet. "I need to go home."

AJ and Andy both rushed around the table to help Curly, who felt like a spindly creature in AJ's grasp, making her feel even more guilty about aiding his condition.

"Help him towards the road while I settle up," AJ said to Andy and let go of his arm once she was sure Andy had the old man steady.

She moved to the bar where the waitress printed out their bill.

"He come here much?" AJ asked, handing her a credit card.

The waitress nodded. "For years, the owner used to let him run up a tab, but he'd never pay it off, so now he doesn't come by so much as he has to bring cash."

AJ knew the owner was a Caymanian who'd been close friends with Bob Soto, so she wasn't surprised he'd been lenient on Curly.

She signed the bill, leaving a healthy tip, then jogged after the other two. They hadn't made it far. Curly was plodding slowly along, leaning heavily on Andy. Taking his other arm, they steered him up the gentle slope towards South Church Street, turning left through the car park so they didn't have to walk on the road itself.

When they reached the north end, AJ could see the cottage Suzy had told them about, directly across on the other side of the two-lane road. South Church Street was wide enough for cars to pass by each other comfortably, but a pair of vans or anything larger would need to slow to avoid wiping off a wing mirror or bumping the low wall edging the car park. AJ looked left and waited for two cars coming that way, while a glance to her right showed nothing coming.

The two cars passed by and they all took a step forward before hearing an engine note roaring from the right. Where the battered old car had come from, AJ had no idea, but her feet slipped on the loose gravel at the side of the road as she tried her best to back up, pulling Curly with her. Falling backwards, all three of them sprawled to the ground as a spray of loose pebbles and dust consumed them. As she dropped, AJ heard a dull thud over the whoosh of the car hurtling by.

23

For an hour, Butty tried his best to explain what had transpired in the past few weeks. Lucia slowly calmed but remained in the chair opposite the sofa where he sat. Her tone was accusatory at first, mellowing to inquiring by the end, yet her expression never yielded to a point that indicated she was remotely pleased to see him. The police had indeed been asking after the captain of the *Oro Verde*. She'd told them that as far as she knew he was still at sea on that very ship, which until he'd walked through the door after they'd left was the truth.

Leaving her to think over all she'd just learned, he excused himself and took a shower. As the water cascaded over his body in murky rivers swirling down the drain, Butty felt a temporary reprieve from his exhaustion, and his head began to clear. He needed a plan, and there wasn't much time. His primary task was one he dreaded, but it had to be done, and once he'd completed that he could focus on what lay ahead for him and Lucia. He had no intention of captaining the new ship Herrera had lined up. Between the drug lord, Mr Rosewater, and Agent Gould, he'd had enough of the clandestine madness and wanted out. Which meant persuading Lucia to leave Miami. Leave America.

Putting on clean clothes, Butty trotted downstairs and found his wife sitting in the same chair where he'd left her.

"I won't be long," he said, and kissed her forehead.

She didn't turn away, which felt like progress, and he left the house with the hope she'd continued accepting all that had transpired. Their pale blue 1964 Ford Falcon was parked farther down the street and he wound down all the windows while the engine warmed up, letting the breeze flush the stagnant, stuffy air from the interior. He caught a brief scent of Lucia's perfume and a tingle of nervous anticipation flooded through him. It was hard to push aside her hardened and irritated stare, as he hadn't seen her beautiful smile since his return, but he was determined to change that.

The drive wasn't far, and if time had been on his side Butty would have walked the six blocks, giving himself a little longer to prepare. But instead, he arrived before he was ready and knocked on the front door of a single-storey home. After a few moments, a short Hispanic woman in a brightly coloured blouse opened the door and beamed a smile.

"Captain," she said in Spanish. "How lovely to see you."

Her eyes flicked beyond Butty as though she expected someone else to be with him. Butty managed a weak smile in return.

"Mrs Sanchez, is your husband home?"

The women sensed her visitor's sullen demeanour, and her face took on a concerned expression.

"No, he's at work, Captain. Please, come inside," she said, ushering him towards the living room. "Something to drink?"

"No, no, thank you," Butty said, pointing to the dining table. "Take a seat."

She did as instructed and he sat on the opposite side of the table, noting the six chairs. One for each family member.

"Mrs Sanchez, I'm sorry Mr Sanchez isn't here so I can tell you both together, but I'm afraid I don't have much time."

She rested one hand on the polished wooden tabletop and the other fell to her chest, covering her heart. Butty swallowed the lump in his throat.

"I'm so sorry to tell you, Mrs Sanchez, but Pepe is gone."

———

An hour later, Butty got in the Falcon to drive home. As much as he'd wished for the time to walk to the Sanchez's house, he wished a hundred times more to be able to walk back. Consoling a mother over the loss of a child was the worst thing he'd ever faced in his life. On the heels of Vietnam, it had been an all too familiar sight in homes across America during the past decade. Parents dreaded that knock on the door to tell them their sons, or in some cases their daughters, weren't coming home.

Butty turned onto his street, trying his best to push aside the vision of Rosa Sanchez sobbing in his arms, and for the second time that day saw a strange vehicle outside his house. He pulled over and parked. The car was a gold-coloured Cadillac Sedan DeVille which took up a space and a half along the kerb. An Hispanic man leaned against the side of the long hood, smoking a cigarette. Butty didn't recognise the car but he knew the look of the man. No one wore a sport coat outside in this heat unless they were selling door to door or concealing something. This guy was the latter, and probably the driver for someone else.

Stepping out of the Falcon, Butty moved down the pavement on the opposite side until he could see his own front door. It was closed, but a second 'heavy' stood guard. If it was Sal Herrera paying a visit, he was treading on dangerous ground, visiting a relative of Alfonso Pérez in broad daylight for all to see. Butty had no doubt Pérez had nosey neighbours on every street in the neighbourhood, reporting anything suspicious going on. This was far more likely to be a visit from Alfonso Pérez himself. The drug lord had probably expected to see the *Oro Verde* by now, or at least hear from his man, Jorge.

Butty weighed his options. He could stay out of the way and wait for the man and his hoods to leave, or he could walk into his own home and face whatever Pérez had in mind. As he settled on the latter, it became a moot point. The bodyguard leaning on the Cadillac saw him and shouted to the other man at the door. Before they could start running around, causing a scene on the quiet street, Butty waved and walked across the road towards them. Both men had a hand under their jackets, ready to draw their weapons at any moment. Approaching the first guy, Butty raised his arms and let the driver pat him down.

"Who's the visitor?" Butty asked in Spanish.

The man ignored him, nodding to the door guard once he was done checking for weapons. The second man pushed the door open and spoke to someone inside, then waved Butty over, signalling for him to enter his own home.

Inside, Butty's eyes adjusted to the dimmer light and saw Lucia was now on the sofa, and a stoutly built bearded man wearing sunglasses sat in the armchair. She didn't look any happier than when he'd left, and the man stared at him with disdain.

"You know who I am?" the man asked in heavily accented English.

"Alfonso Pérez would be my guess," Butty replied, moving to the sofa and sitting next to his wife. "Are you okay?" he asked her.

Lucia nodded, but her expression suggested otherwise.

"How can I help you, sir?" Butty asked.

"Where's the *Oro Verde*?" Pérez asked.

"Grand Cayman."

The man's eyes narrowed. "Why?"

"I had crew trouble," Butty said, using the truth to begin. "Ended up having to leave the ship there."

"What kind of trouble?"

Butty wanted to say 'The kind you caused', but he held himself back. Anger percolated, having just come from telling Pepe's mother that her son was dead, and it was unlikely she'd have a body to bury. He'd lied and told her he'd gone overboard, instead of the truth that the man sitting before him now had planted a killer aboard the *Oro Verde*.

"They were unhappy about pay and left the ship. Without a crew, I couldn't sail her to Miami."

"How did you get here?" he asked.

"I hitched a ride on a pleasure craft heading to Florida," Butty replied, loosely hanging on to a portion of truth.

"When are you going back to get it?" Pérez asked.

Butty shrugged his shoulders. "I don't know if I will. I haven't heard from the owner and I'd like to be home for the birth," he said, glancing at Lucia.

Pérez's eyes moved to her. "Leave us alone," he barked in Spanish. "I have business to discuss with your husband."

Lucia didn't move. "I wanna hear whatever it is you have to say."

Her uncle sat forward in the chair. "Go for a walk, Lucia, or I'll have my men take you for a walk," he growled.

She started to protest, but Butty put a hand on her arm. He gave her a smile and a wink, which he hoped conveyed his intention of filling her in once Pérez had left. Whether she'd got that message or not, she got up, stomped around collecting sunglasses and her purse, before slamming the front door behind her.

Pérez settled back into the armchair. "She gets that fire from her mother, my brother's wife," he said, although his eyes remained cold despite the pleasant family reference. "You're working for Sal Herrera."

His words were phrased as a statement instead of a question, as though he were challenging the Englishman to contradict him.

"I'm not working for anyone at the moment," Butty replied, trying to find a way of denying the claim without telling the drug lord he was wrong.

"That's about to change," Pérez responded. "As of today, you work for me."

For a moment, Butty couldn't believe his ears, and then he slowly shook his head. "I mean no disrespect, mate, but I'm done with all of this mess. I want nothing to do with any of it."

Pérez tilted his head to one side. "You say that like you have a choice."

Butty groaned. "Come on, just let me and Lucia be. Please. We don't want any part of this."

"You should have thought of that before you ran product for Herrera," Pérez snapped back, spittle flying across the coffee table between them. "You speak of respect; well, let me tell you, gringo, you already disrespected me, and the only reason you're not dead right now is because of Lucia. If you weren't married to the family, I'd use your severed balls to chum for sharks then throw you to them." He lurched forward in the chair and pointed at Butty. "Now, you're going to do exactly what I tell you, or you'll never see that kid of yours."

"Keep them out of this," Butty responded, struggling to keep his anger in check. "Your problem's with me, not with them. Like you said, she's your family, and her child will be your family too."

"Family only goes so far," Pérez replied. "They'll be fine as long as you do what I tell you."

Butty sighed. "And what's that?"

"What does that bastard Herrera have you doing now your ship is stuck in Grand Cayman?"

"It wasn't his ship; it belonged to someone else," Butty replied. "He told me he has another ship he wants me to captain."

Pérez smirked. "Then that's what you'll do. Then you'll tell me everything about your trip. Who, where, when, everything. Understand?"

The phrase "between a rock and a hard place" sprang to Butty's mind, and he couldn't think of a way out. If he crossed Herrera, he'd not only piss off the other drug lord, he'd be turning on a CIA operation.

"There's more to Herrera's deal than you know," Butty said, wondering whether he was digging himself a deeper hole or finding a way out. "He's involved with people you don't want to mess with."

Pérez rose to his feet and for a second, Butty thought he'd

crossed a line he didn't know existed with the man. He expected him to pull out a gun or call for one of his goons. Instead, he sneered.

"Let me worry about Herrera's imaginary friends," Pérez growled. "Just make sure you bring me every name and detail from wherever he sends you. Are we clear?"

Butty nodded. He certainly understood what was now expected of him, and knew the other side would do worse to him and his family if they found out. Which inevitably they would.

He was screwed, no matter what.

24

AJ rolled to her side and bumped into another body she assumed was Curly.

"Are you okay?" she spluttered, with dust in her eyes and throat.

The old man grunted something in return, so she rolled the other way and scrambled to her feet, leaning over him.

"Curly, are you okay?" she repeated.

He looked up at her, blinking. "I think so," he said hoarsely, coughing a few times and pushing himself upright.

AJ looked beyond Curly and saw Andy several yards away, clutching his left arm.

"Stay there a minute," she instructed Curly. "We'll help you up when you've caught your breath."

She stepped around him and crouched down by Andy. "Are you okay?"

He turned her way, looking dishevelled and stunned. "What the hell was that?" he asked.

"Someone not paying attention, I guess," AJ replied, as he carefully tried extending his elbow.

Curly scoffed, but her attention stayed on Andy.

"Was the thud I heard your arm?"

Andy nodded. "I unintentionally showed his wing mirror who's boss."

AJ gently took his arm in her hand and felt from his wrist to his elbow. "I don't think it's broken," she assured him. "Probably turn some impressive shades of blue and purple though."

Taking his uninjured arm, she helped him to his feet and then between them they hauled Curly up.

"Let's get inside before they come back," Curly muttered, sounding a lot more sober than he had a few minutes before.

"Come back?" AJ questioned, steering across the street after carefully checking both ways. "You think that was deliberate?"

Curly scoffed again. "What do you think, love?"

"I think it was probably someone looking at their mobile instead of paying attention to where they were going. I wish I'd got their bloody registration plate."

"Bit strange how it came out of nowhere," Andy said as they walked up to Curly's front door. "There was nothing on the road to our right, and by the time the cars from the left went by, that guy appeared."

"That's 'cos he was waiting for us," Curly said, opening the door.

"Why on earth would someone want to run us over?" AJ asked, about to follow Curly inside until he started closing the door behind him. "Oh," she said, stopping abruptly. "Will you be okay, sir?"

"Safer I reckon," he said and shut the door.

"Blimey," AJ muttered. "Not even a thanks for the drinks, let alone pulling him out of the road."

"Something's got him really rattled," Andy added. "I know he almost got run over, so anyone would be upset, but he was already acting strange before we left the bar."

"He wasn't telling us everything, that's for sure," AJ agreed, jogging back across the road, looking for speeding motorists as she went. "But I can't imagine why anyone would try to run us over. I'm sure that was just someone not paying attention."

"Didn't even stop to check on us," Andy said.

"If they weren't paying attention, they may never have seen us," AJ replied, unlocking the van.

"Pretty sure they heard their wing mirror being smacked," Andy pointed out.

AJ started the engine and put the windows down. "That's true. And I think you'd automatically check the rear view if you'd just swerved off the road, right?"

Andy nodded, rubbing his arm. "I would."

"We'd better get you an X-ray," AJ suggested, watching the young man wince.

"Suppose so," he agreed.

Sitting around at George Town Hospital for a few hours was exactly what AJ didn't need. After an hour, she realised a better plan would have been to leave and find something to keep her busy before coming back, but by then it seemed too late. So she sat in the waiting room, answered emails on her mobile, and stewed in her own juices about how her personal life had fallen apart.

When Andy reappeared, he reported that nothing was broken, and he'd been advised to ice his arm for a few days to help with the swelling. AJ glanced at her watch. It was almost five.

"Fancy a drink?" she asked, and immediately wished she'd phrased it differently.

"That sounds good," Andy replied, not showing any indication that he'd taken her question as a romantic invitation.

On the way to the car, AJ texted her friend Nora and invited her to join them, figuring a third wheel ought to dispel any wayward ideas.

Just north of the downtown waterfront, Rackam's catered to

tourists from the cruise ships during the day and locals in the evening. A long deck stretched over the ocean and water lapped at the ironshore below, a constant audible backdrop accompanying the music playing from the bar. By the time they found a place to park in a car park down the road, the patron switch was complete and happy hour had begun.

AJ ordered a Seven Fathoms rum over ice and Andy said he'd try the same. They found an open spot in one of the outdoor lounge areas and settled into the comfortable chairs. Andy began talking about the day, and AJ was glad of something to pull her mind from her own woes.

"You're probably right," he said. "It was someone not watching where they were going. I mean, what reason would anyone have for running us over?"

"None that spring to mind," AJ agreed. "Especially poor old Curly."

"He seemed to think there was more to it," Andy added, swilling the ice around his tumbler before taking another sip.

"Yeah, but he'd also knocked back a few and I'm not sure he's overly compos mentis at the best of times," AJ replied. "He was paranoid about the car, but he might be one of them conspiracy nuts."

"I'm sure you're right," Andy said. "So what's on for tomorrow?"

"You think your arm will be okay for diving?" she asked.

Andy rubbed his forearm and elbow which was turning dark shades of purple and even green. "I reckon so."

"Hey," came Nora's voice and they both stood.

AJ gave her a quick hug and Andy seemed unsure whether he should hug her or shake her hand. He stepped forward and she placed a hand on his chest.

"Hello," she said. "But I'm not a hugger."

Andy looked mortified and stepped briskly back. "I'm sorry," he mumbled, "but you two hugged, so I thought…"

"She's different," Nora said, taking a seat.

"Oh," Andy blurted. "I didn't realise you two were…"

"Were what?" Nora asked, her blue eyes piercing his skull.

AJ leaned over and gave Nora a playful slap on the arm. "Leave the poor bugger alone, he's had a traumatic day." She turned to Andy. "No, we're not a couple. Nora's not a hugger, but she tolerates me doing it because she gave up trying to stop me."

Nora sat back in her chair and winked at Andy, who added blushing red cheeks to his various skin tones.

"You stumble over the *Oro Verde*?" Nora asked, pointing to his colourful arm.

"Some wanker tried to run us over," AJ blurted. "Just down the road near Sunset House."

"Get a plate?" Nora asked. "Or a description?"

She'd changed out of her uniform into leggings and a T-shirt, but she was quick to switch back into her police mindset.

Andy shook his head. "Happened too fast. Some sort of older car. Maybe brown, but I couldn't be sure."

AJ shrugged her shoulders. "I thought it was yellow, but could have been brown. There was dust thrown up everywhere."

Nora asked a series more questions but neither Andy nor AJ could tell her anything more meaningful about the car, so the conversation shifted to the dive that morning. Before long, the sun was setting and they'd ordered food, picking at their meals as they watched the sky turn glorious tones of orange and red.

For AJ, it was another reminder of why she'd chosen to make the island her home and couldn't imagine living anywhere else. Which of course led her thoughts back to Jackson. Unless she joined Sea Sentry and they allowed her to crew the same boat as him, it didn't matter where in the world she lived; they'd only see each other three or four times a year at best. Just like before, when they were dating. Would that feel like enough compared to never seeing him again?

"I have to go," Nora announced, and AJ realised it was dark and she was the only one with food still on her plate.

"We probably should too," she said, although the idea of going home to the empty house made her shudder.

Andy tried to pay for everyone, but the women insisted on splitting it three ways, so once the bill was settled, they walked to North Church Street and Nora stopped as AJ and Andy turned left.

"I'm parked over here," she said, pointing south.

AJ walked back to her and gave her another hug.

"You okay?" Nora whispered in her ear.

"Not really," AJ admitted.

"Come by if you'd like," Nora offered.

"I might," AJ replied, a sense of relief flooding through her.

Nora nodded, then left the embrace, heading for her Jeep parked down the street.

AJ re-joined Andy and they walked north.

"She's a unique woman," Andy commented humorously.

AJ laughed. "That she is. Pretty fit though, yeah?"

Andy was quiet for a moment and AJ was sure he was blushing again. "She's stunning, and she's not even trying to be," he said.

AJ scoffed. "Tell me about it."

"But you're gorgeous too, AJ," Andy stammered, and she laughed.

"Well she's single and probably closer to your age." She left out the part that she was also apparently single as of that morning. "But the reason she had to leave was to get home to her teenage kid."

Andy stopped walking. "What?"

AJ took his arm and they crossed the street, carefully watching for traffic both ways. "It's not how it sounds," she chuckled. "She fostered a young local girl. The kid was living on the streets and Nora kinda saved her, so now Jazzy won't agree to live with anyone else. It's a temporary foster home situation as Nora's too young to officially adopt a teenager, but it's become pretty permanent."

"Wow. That's brave," Andy responded as they reached the van.

"I know, eh? Beautiful, and superhuman," AJ joked.

The next thing AJ knew was a painful thud as she hit the gravel car park. With the wind knocked out of her, she gasped and felt the sharp sting of grazes on her hands and knees.

"Stay down," came a heavily accented voice, and a foot pushed against her back.

She wheezed and coughed, acting a little more incapacitated than she was, before rolling over and swinging her leg in the direction she hoped the man was standing. She hit something, but it was firm, like a thigh, so she thrashed both feet, hoping for more contact. All she hit was air.

Struggling to her feet, she heard the man curse then grab her by the shoulders from behind, shoving her face first against the side of the van. She flailed both elbows, catching him in the ribs a couple of times, which loosened his hold on her. AJ whipped around, swinging her clenched fist in an arc that landed on the side of his face. Around his neck, a gold chain glinted in the meagre light as it flailed from the weight of a medallion attached to the end. The man staggered back before regaining his footing, but she followed up with a kick, aiming for his groin. His arm deflected the attack, knocking her off balance, and she dipped her head and braced for the punch which she saw was coming. Connecting with the top of her head, he grunted loudly as she continued to the ground, landing hard on her left side.

Certain she was in for a good kicking now he'd put her down again, AJ curled up and tried to protect herself as best she could. But instead of a boot in her side, she was surprised to hear feet pounding on gravel as the man ran away. She unwrapped herself and took a few deep breaths.

"Andy?" she called out, easing herself up.

"Yeah," he moaned from the other side of the van. "I might need another X-ray."

AJ made her way around the van in the dimly lit car park and found Andy curled up on the ground, blood seeping from a wound on his forehead. Crunching sounded from behind them and AJ swung around ready to start throwing more punches.

"You okay?" Nora asked, breathing heavily with her police Taser in her hand.

AJ nodded. "I'll be fine but they gave Andy a good going over."

The two women helped him to his feet and inspected him for other damage. He touched a finger to his forehead, staring at the blood on his fingers.

"What did they take?" Nora asked.

Andy shrugged his shoulders and AJ shook her head.

"Nothing from me," she added, feeling her mobile still in her pocket.

"Was it you that scared them off?" Andy asked, looking at Nora.

"Yeah, but they heard the Jeep stop and ran before I could zap one of them," she replied holding up her Taser.

"Well, thanks," Andy told her.

"Maybe they planned to steal the van," AJ suggested. "But it's crazy; stuff like this doesn't happen here."

"They weren't after the van," Andy said.

"Why do you say that?" Nora asked.

Andy let out a long breath. "Because they told me I wasn't welcome here. They said I should leave the island."

25

Butty spent the night on the sofa. Lucia couldn't see beyond the fact that the problem started with her husband agreeing to transport extra cargo on his ship. If he'd said no at the beginning, they wouldn't be in the situation they were in now. He had little defence. She had a point.

The fact that his motivations were based around her and their unborn child didn't make the poor decision more forgivable, and the consequences had he said no were unknown, and therefore unarguable. According to Lucia, at least. She also wouldn't hear of leaving Miami. He pleaded with her to leave that morning to spend a year or two in England with him until things settled down, but she flatly refused.

In the morning, Butty packed, wishing he'd been able to take more of his things off the *Oro Verde*. Important gear, like his foul weather clothes, which were expensive to replace. There was also the question of his passport, which Gould had assured him wasn't a problem.

When he hugged Lucia goodbye, she showed her first signs of softening, embracing him in return.

"Be careful," she whispered, and kissed his cheek.

He touched her stomach. "I'll be thinking about you both," he told her. "No matter what happens, I'll be thinking about you both."

With that, he walked outside to the waiting taxi, resisting the urge to run back inside the house and wrap her in his arms, never to let go.

The new ship was called the *Silvia Azul*, a 94-foot single engine cargo vessel with less length, capacity, and crew required than the *Oro Verde*. Built in the mid 1950s, she appeared to be in good shape, albeit better suited for lake, inter-island, or coastal passage than long runs across the Caribbean Sea.

"Proteus?" a man asked quietly, appearing behind Butty as he stood on the dock.

"We're back on that rubbish again, are we?" he asked in response.

"Excuse me?" the American responded with a frown.

He was the only person anywhere near the docks wearing a suit, so Butty assumed he was with the CIA.

"Yeah, I'm Proteus. You Gould's man?"

"No names," the agent hissed back. "Here," he said, and handed Butty an envelope.

"What's this?" Butty asked, opening the clasp before the man could answer.

Inside, he saw a passport, driver's licence, and what appeared to be a sizeable wad of cash. Butty pulled the passport out and the first thing he noticed was that it wasn't British. Opening it, he stared at a photograph of himself, but the name read James Lofton.

"I guess my citizenship came through early," he joked, but the agent didn't smile.

"I also have a package for Triton, to be delivered immediately," the man said sternly. "You'll take it to Grand Cayman on the way to Panama, where you'll drop the cargo."

"It's not on the way," Butty said, examining the Florida driver's licence with the same fake name.

"Excuse me?" the agent questioned.

"Grand Cayman," Butty said, looking up. "It's not on the way to Panama. It's about 150 miles off our course."

The agent stared at him blankly. "You'll go by Grand Cayman on the way to drop your cargo in Panama. You'll collect more cargo in Panama, stop by Grand Cayman on the return, then deliver the goods here in Miami. Is that clear?"

"Fine," Butty replied, wondering if he was being watched by Pérez's people.

"We'll return later today with the other package," the agent said, and he walked away, leaving Butty alone feeling twice as paranoid.

The guy had said 'we', but Butty couldn't spot another suit anywhere nearby. Who he did see was Herrera's man who'd driven him home the day before. He approached down the dock with three other Hispanic men in tow. Butty quickly stuffed the envelope he'd been given into his duffel bag before the group reached him.

"This is your crew," Herrera's man said in Spanish, nodding to the men behind him without introducing them individually. "Get the ship ready. We'll start loading shortly."

Butty sighed and looked at the crew he'd been given. "Let's see what we've got here then," he said in English, and watched all three frown and look at each other. He repeated his words in Spanish and they all smiled, nodded, and shook his hand.

As they boarded the ship and looked around, he learned Jesus was the most experienced sailor, Felipe was a dock worker and diesel mechanic, and Basilio was his teenage cousin who was a keen fisherman but had never been beyond local waters. He introduced himself as Butty rather than using his new moniker. Quite how he'd split watches up amongst the group was beyond Butty, as only Jesus had any experience at the helm of a ship this size, but after what he'd been through recently, it seemed the least of his problems.

The captain's quarters were tight but comfortable, and Butty stowed the few things he'd brought aboard. Finding Felipe, he took him below and they inspected the engine. Butty would have much preferred to see two engines for the amount of time they'd spend in open water, but the diesel appeared well maintained and they couldn't find any obvious issues. It fired up on the first crank, which was also promising, and Butty left Felipe to familiarise himself with the engine room while he returned topside.

The *Silvia Azul* had her own crane, but a larger unit on the dock was already swinging crates of cargo into the hold. Trotting down the steps, Butty found Jesus and Basilio manhandling the crates to the sides of the hold after they'd been lowered through the narrower opening above.

"What are we carrying?" he asked, lending a hand.

"Looks like starter motors for tractors," Jesus replied, tapping on a cardboard box that was visible between the slats of the wooden crate.

It made sense they were carrying heavier items as the hold wasn't as spacious as most international cargo ships. Butty looked to the front of the hold, where a dozen crates of a different shape were already stacked.

"Those are not starter motors," Jesus said, wiping the sweat from his brow.

Butty walked over and tried to see what was in the long narrow crates but their boxes were made of higher quality wood without gaps. He had a bad feeling about what they contained.

"I assume we need to hide those under and behind everything else we're loading," he commented, and Jesus nodded.

"That was my plan, captain."

Butty nodded, and they went back to arranging the freight as it was lowered their way, Butty wondering how on earth he could extricate himself from this mess which was getting worse with every step. Or more importantly, how to remove himself without harming Lucia and their child.

By late afternoon, the cargo was loaded and after cleaning up, Jesus and Butty gave the ship a more thorough inspection, including the lifeboats, which sat under davits behind the wheelhouse. They appeared functional, but only as a means of staying afloat. Neither had outboards, or any supplies. Butty made a note to add water jugs and some form of sunshade to complement the oars which wouldn't be much help in the open ocean.

Basilio had been designated cook and sent out with a list to provision for the trip. When he returned, Butty had just stepped to the dock to help carry the goods aboard when the CIA agent appeared out of nowhere. This time, the man carried a black holdall with a chain extending from inside the bag to a handcuff on his wrist.

"Take me to your room," he instructed.

Butty laughed. "I don't play for that team, mate," he replied. "But I'm flattered you asked."

The agent glared at him. "We need to do this out of sight. Let's go, damn it."

Butty shrugged his shoulders and led the man aboard. "Berth," he said. "If you'd like to avoid any confusion in the future, not to mention sounding like a plonker, I suggest you rephrase your statement. The word for a room on a ship is a berth."

They stood shoulder to shoulder in the tiny space and the agent flung the bag on the small desk and unlocked the handcuff. From inside the holdall he pulled a large Halliburton briefcase.

"This is for Triton," he said. "Keep it safe, and hand it only to him."

"I'm confused," Butty pretended. "I'm taking guns and money with me?"

The agent twitched as though he'd been shocked by an errant electrical current.

"Your job is to drive this ship…"

"Pilot," Butty interrupted. "Or skipper is also acceptable."

The man's brow creased and a nerve in his cheek spasmed. Butty was sure the agent was contemplating all the ways he could shoot, slice, bludgeon, and dispose of him at that very moment, but his hands were as tied as Butty's were.

"Do your job. Stop asking questions and indulging in frivolous conversation. Your life and the lives of others may depend upon it."

"You're exchanging guns for the drugs you're selling to the American people," Butty replied through gritted teeth. "Don't lecture me on being reckless with lives. I'll skipper your ship, because I have no choice, and I won't tell anyone about it, because I have no choice. But I'm not listening to your sanctimonious bullshit, because I sure as hell don't have to do that. Now, if there's nothing else, get off my ship."

Every muscle in the agent's body tensed, but he quickly gathered his wits and let out a long breath.

"Cayman. Panama. Cayman. Miami," he said, then turned and left.

Butty watched him climb the steps to the main deck, then once he was certain the agent had gone, tried the locks on the case. As expected, it was secured, and he noticed the barrel locks were all set to zeroes. Shoving the case in the back of his locker where it barely fitted, he walked up the steps and found Jesus helping Basilio stow their provisions.

"How long before we can leave?" he asked.

Jesus thought for a moment. "Are you planning on travelling tonight, Captain?"

"I'm planning on moving us into Biscayne Bay and anchoring near Dodge Island overnight. We'll leave at first light. It'll give us a full day to get used to the girl before our first night at sea."

By Jesus's nod and brief smile, Butty gathered his plan had been met with approval.

"Give me one hour, Captain, and we'll be ready."

"Thanks," Butty replied. "I assume you all understand that we are under-crewed for what we're doing, right?"

Jesus nodded, so Basilio nodded too, although Butty doubted the kid had any idea whether they were appropriately staffed or not. At least he shouldn't face any mutinous issues from this group as they were all selected and employed by Herrera, but he wanted to be sure they knew what they were in for.

"Join me at the helm tonight, Jesus. We'll figure out how she steers together. In the morning, Felipe can join me and I'll train him at the helm. You and I will take four-hour watches, and if he can take two hours, that'll give us six hours of rest between shifts. Sound good?"

"Yes, Captain," Jesus agreed. "Felipe is a good man, he'll learn fast."

"Okay. One hour then. I'll see if I can clear our paperwork by then," Butty said, turning to leave.

"I don't think that will be a problem, Captain," Jesus said, making Butty pause at the door. "The customs agent will come to us. His name is Herrera. He is the uncle of El Jefe."

"Figures," Butty muttered as he stepped outside for a smoke.

26

Nora steered Andy and AJ through the process of filing a police report about the assault, which they all knew would net nothing. Neither of them could provide much of a description of their assailants, and although AJ was certain from the one man's voice that he was Jamaican rather than a local Caymanian, the police had almost nothing to go on. But at least filing the report registered the incident in case it came up later.

Andy was staying at the Hampton along Seven Mile Beach and between the three of them, they decided he was probably safe at the hotel. The thugs had delivered their message, and the earliest he could leave would be the following day, so there seemed little chance they'd approach him again. Especially in his room at a nice hotel with a security man on duty all night.

Nora followed in her Jeep, and AJ stopped at the Hampton to let Andy out, promising to pick him up first thing in the morning. His hire car could stay in the car park at her dock where they'd left it until then. She watched him walk inside before pulling out to West Bay Road and waiting for a clearing in traffic. Pulling out, she glanced in the mirror and watched the distinctive headlights of Nora's CJ-7 fall in line behind her.

The question AJ and Andy had tossed back and forth without a logical answer was why anyone would want him to leave the island. Of course, some locals didn't care for the number of foreigners visiting and living on their once quiet little island, but she'd never heard of anyone being intimidated like that before. Besides, unless she was mistaken, the man who'd pushed her down wasn't even a local. The thoughts swirled around her mind as she drove north, and it wasn't until she entered West Bay that she was reminded of what she faced. Her cottage would be empty.

Jackson would have landed in Miami hours ago, yet she'd received nothing from him. No call, text, or email. *But why should he?* It was over, which had been of his doing, yet she'd been forced to make the final decision. A now familiar anger and frustration rose inside her and AJ thumped the steering wheel. She drove over the crossroads instead of turning left onto Boggy Sand Road towards her home. She'd take Nora up on her offer, and stay with her and Jazzy for tonight. It would mean getting up even earlier in the morning, but the thought of pushing the challenge of stepping through her own door further away was desperately appealing.

Up ahead was the left turn onto North West Point Road and the dock, but it was quicker to go through the middle of West Bay to reach Nora's shack on the north side. AJ glanced in the mirror when the Jeep's headlights flashed once behind her, and noticed Nora's left indicator was on. She quickly turned left and slowed, checking her mirror again. Nora turned her indicator off for a moment, flashed her headlights again, and put her left indicator on once more. AJ braked and turned into the sloped car park for the dock she shared with Reg. Andy's hire car was the lone vehicle there, and she parked next to it.

"What's up?" she asked, climbing from the van as Nora pulled alongside.

"Pretend we're picking something up from the hut," Nora said, getting out, but leaving the Jeep running.

AJ began walking across the tarmac to the little hut. "What's going on?"

"I think we were followed from the hotel," Nora replied.

AJ unlocked the door and they both stepped inside. Nora stopped AJ from turning on the light and watched the road from the crack in the door.

"What are we looking for?" AJ asked, trying to peer around her friend.

"That car," Nora replied as a golden-brown Mazda Protege rolled slowly along North West Point Road and sat at the T-junction.

"It's going the opposite way," AJ pointed out.

"Because he went past then turned around," Nora replied.

Under the streetlights, the paintwork looked sun faded and the right front hub cap was missing. The profile of one figure could be seen inside the vehicle. The Mazda pulled away, turning right in the direction they'd just come.

"Is that the car that tried to run you over?" Nora asked.

"Maybe," AJ replied, closing her eyes and trying to visualise the scene from that afternoon. "It's honestly hard to say. I didn't get a good look."

Nora stepped outside. "Okay. Leave your van here, we'll take the Jeep."

"I have to be up pretty early tomorrow," AJ said, locking the hut. "I hate for you to have to get up with me."

"We might not be going home yet," Nora replied. "Get in the Jeep."

AJ quickly locked the van then hopped in the passenger side of the left-hand-drive CJ-7. Nora backed out, then pulled up the slope, stopping at the road. From the right, the Mazda reappeared, moving slowly towards the left turn.

"Bloody hell," AJ muttered. "Look at the mirror."

The Mazda's left side mirror hung like a wounded bird from its mount on the door, swinging loosely. Nora let out the clutch and the Jeep lurched from the car park. The gold car instantly acceler-ated, staying on the main road which became Town Hall Road.

"Clear!" AJ yelled, checking traffic from the right as Nora barely paused at the intersection.

The 4.2 litre inline six-cylinder engine was a workhorse, but certainly not a racing machine, propelling drive through hefty 33-inch tyres on the lifted Jeep, but fortunately the old Mazda wasn't either. Greyish-brown smoke billowed from the car's exhaust as the driver floored it in his attempt to get away. Nora rowed through the gears and pretty soon they were doing 75 mph along the narrow, house-lined street, and slowly gaining on the car ahead.

They were on what was considered a *main* road by the island's standards, but AJ reckoned if the driver knew his way around West Bay, he'd take to some of the even smaller lanes as soon as he could. Twisting and turning would suit the car far better than the Jeep with its high centre of gravity. They soon reached the first intersection where the street teed into another. The road to Hell was to the left, the ancient dark-coloured ironshore tourist attraction, and Reverend Blackman Road ran right, heading deeper into town and towards the dual carriageway out of West Bay.

The Mazda chose right, screeching its tyres through the intersection and causing another car to swerve in avoidance. Nora braked and slowed, then barrelled through the T-junction once she saw it was clear. Hanging on to the rollover bar with one hand, AJ wrestled her mobile into camera mode and began shooting video of the car they were chasing.

"If my sergeant or Detective Whittaker ever sees that, I'll be helping school kids across the road for the next five years," Nora complained, accelerating back up to speed.

The Mazda suddenly braked, slowed, and turned hard left down a small road.

"Ha!" Nora grunted, a slight grin appearing on her face as she hit the brakes to follow.

"What's down here?" AJ asked, shouting over the wind and engine noise.

"Not much," Nora replied, swinging the Jeep down Dill Lane

according to the street sign they flew by. "I've arrested someone here before."

AJ wasn't sure whether that was comforting or not as up ahead the tarmac became dirt and disappeared into the darkness beyond street and house lights. The two red rear lights of the Mazda bounced and jolted as the car hit the rough gravel single track lane, then disappeared to the left. Nora never lifted off the throttle.

"I hope you know where you're going!" AJ yelled as the CJ-7's tyres crunched on the loose terrain and the Jeep slid as Nora veered left, the headlights picking out a building amongst the trees.

They came into a clearing which appeared to be a car park and the Mazda had stopped up ahead. As the Jeep's lights flooded the area, the car took off again, curving right.

"This won't be good," Nora muttered, and before AJ could ask why, she saw for herself.

They brushed past the branches of a few trees and burst into a wide-open grassy area, which AJ recognised as the locals' beloved cricket field. The pale brown Mazda was sliding across the grass, kicking up dirt and fresh grass clippings, hunting for a way out. Figuring his best bet was the way he'd come in, the driver continued in a wide arc which was easy for Nora to predict. The two vehicles ended up facing each other in the middle of the field, both slipping and sliding on the neatly trimmed grass, with a game of chicken afoot.

"Oh, bugger," AJ moaned as Nora aimed straight for the oncoming car without backing off at all.

The Mazda tried dodging to his right at the last moment, but it just meant the CJ-7's beefy bumper bar hit his passenger door instead of head on. The car spun like a top and AJ was jarred into her seatbelt by the impact, but the Jeep was completely unharmed. Nora swung around and pinned her bumper against the driver's side door as the man inside sat stunned with a deflated airbag in his lap. Nora grabbed her Taser and jumped out, leaving the Jeep in neutral with the emergency brake on.

"Back the Jeep up when I tell you," she shouted to AJ, who shuffled over to the driver's seat.

"Okay, now," Nora ordered, and waved her hand.

AJ reversed the Jeep away from the Mazda and hoped the man wouldn't try to drive away, although the engine wasn't running and the car looked too smashed up to get far. It took a few hard tugs for Nora to swing the driver's door open, then she reached in and pulled the man out, letting him tumble to the grass.

"This one of them?" she asked, looking at AJ, who hopped out and joined her in the area illuminated by the Jeep's headlights.

"Yup. That's the wanker who pushed me down," AJ replied. "I remember that gold chain thingy around his neck. Check the knuckles on his right hand."

The man tried to push himself up.

"Police. Stay down," Nora ordered.

He ignored her, muttering obscenities and continuing on to his knees, looking up at her. His right eye was bruised and starting to swell shut.

"I'm a police constable. Stay down," she repeated.

"You're no..." he began, about to step up, but Nora jabbed the Taser against his shoulder.

The man's body shook and quivered while groaning sounds vibrated from his lips as he slumped to the turf.

"Blimey," AJ said. "Those things really do work."

"I'd prefer a gun, but this is pretty cool," Nora said nonchalantly.

"I don't think they'll let you loose with a bloody gun any time soon."

Nora shrugged. "Probably not. But a girl can dream."

AJ picked up the man's arm and examined his battered knuckles. "I have a hard head, don't I?" she declared.

Nora jabbed a foot at the man on the ground. "Why did you attack her, and why were you following us?"

The man struggled for breath, panting hard. "Dis illegal, man. You can't just attack me."

"Why? You attacked her," Nora rebutted. "And I'll zap you again unless you tell me why."

His eyes danced between the two women then ended up staring at the Taser in Nora's hand.

"It has enough juice for at least two more good hits if you're thinking of testing me."

The man shook his head and hauled himself to a seated position against the front tyre of the Mazda. "I don't know his name. I swear. Da udder guy I wit say we bin hired to put da scare on dat English guy. Dat's all I know, man."

"Where's your friend?" Nora asked.

"I drop him to watch da hotel."

"Watch or do something else?" AJ quickly asked.

The man shook his head. "Just watch. He told me to see where you go," he replied, flicking a hand towards AJ. "Den go back and pick him up."

"Get up," Nora demanded. "You're gonna take us to him."

He shook his head again. "I called him when you saw me and told him we'd bin made. He gone now."

Nora took out her mobile with her free hand, found a number, and hit *call*, handing the device to AJ. "Tell them where we are, and to send a unit."

AJ waited for someone to answer.

"What did your friend say about this guy who hired you?" Nora quizzed. "Black? White? Local?"

The man shrugged. "He white I tink. He didn't say much 'bout him, and I didn't ask," he said, then looked up. "He did say he was an old man."

Someone was talking over the phone in AJ's ear, but she was too busy looking at the Jamaican on the ground, her mouth agape. "An old white guy?" AJ mumbled. "Bloody hell. This keeps getting stranger."

27

The passage to Grand Cayman passed without incident, albeit far from restful. It took two of the four days before Butty became comfortable with leaving Felipe at the helm, but the man proved a quick study and knew his way around a ship, so most of the instruction revolved around navigation. Once they had three of them taking watches, things settled down, and with the early winter seas being kind, they made slow but steady progress. Seven knots was the cruising speed on the single screw, so the *Silvia Azul* was in no hurry to go anywhere.

It was Wednesday morning when Butty dropped anchor outside Hog Sty Bay in Grand Cayman and a tender picked them up, ferrying the four men to shore. Butty held his breath as he handed over his shiny US passport, and kept reminding himself of his new name. He needn't have worried. It took five minutes to stamp them all in and send them on their way to a waiting Gene Gould.

"How's your new ship, Butty Boy?" the agent greeted him.

"Slow," he replied. "But it got us here."

Gould slapped him on the back. "Good to hear, good to hear. Let's get you to the Seaview. You boys can clean up and spend the day by the pool."

"Okay," Butty replied, as they all crammed into Gould's Wagoneer. "How long are we here for? And more to the point, why are we here?" he added.

"Got a case for me?" Gould replied, looking over at his passenger as he left the paved road and bumped down the gravel lane towards the hotel.

Butty nodded. "On the ship. Didn't think it'd be a great idea to walk through customs with it."

"See," Gould grinned. "That's why you're the perfect man for this job, Mr Lofton."

Butty frowned and shook his head. He couldn't imagine ever getting used to being called a stranger's name, and he certainly didn't feel perfect for what the CIA had going on.

"They should have told you to leave it on the ship," Gould continued. "But they didn't, right?"

"They missed that part out," Butty replied.

"Exactly. But you figured it out. Same as you knew how we needed to handle business last time you were here."

The idea that Gould thought he'd been willing, complicit, or agreeable to anything that happened with the *Oro Verde*, or Pepe, gnawed at Butty's gut, but he kept quiet. He'd spent many of the hours in his berth when he was supposed to be catching much-needed sleep staring at the dark ceiling of his tiny cabin, searching for a way to detach himself from his predicament. Without hurting Lucia or their baby.

That was the hard part. There were lots of ways he could slip away and disappear, but family or not, Pérez had made it clear Lucia and their child were pawns in this ruthless game. They would suffer if Butty simply abandoned the task he'd been given. On the other side of the fence, Herrera had no family obligation to cause him even the slightest hesitation in taking out his displeasure on Butty's wife.

After all his deliberation, he'd realised he only had two options, and neither were in the least bit appealing. He could toe the line and play along, which had a short future as both drug lords expected him to do their bidding. It was a house of cards, waiting for the softest of breezes to bring it crashing down. And that was if he didn't get caught by the authorities — the ones outside the CIA's control — and Butty had no doubt the agency would vehemently deny any knowledge of him. Butterworth or Lofton.

The other option was his own demise. His death left all parties with no reason to take anything out on Lucia and their shortly to be born child. He considered the odds of him meeting his end at the hands of Noriega or his enemies in Central and South America were quite high, or the ship being taken by anyone learning of their cargo. They were defenceless against pirates, and powerless against Panamanian authorities who could turn deadly at any time.

Taking his own life was incredibly unappetising, but he'd trade his own skin for that of his wife and baby's every day of the week, and twice on Sundays. Maybe the whole situation would take care of itself in short order, bearing in mind the nature of what he was doing, but that was no guarantee. He'd need to conceive his own demise. The idea felt ludicrous and more than a little tragic, but it was the only avenue Butty could see where Lucia and the baby would be free.

"Are you coming?" Gould was saying, and Butty realised they were parked at the Seaview.

He grabbed his overnight bag and followed Gould to the front desk, where keys were handed to each of them. His crew couldn't believe they were getting their own rooms at an oceanside resort and eyed the swimming pool with anticipation as they rushed to clean up and change.

"Tonight," Gould said. "We'll retrieve the case and I'll take care of my end of things. Enjoy your day, my friend. Sign your food and drink to the room, and I'll meet you at the bar around six."

Butty nodded. "We leave tomorrow?"

"I have to check with Mr Rosewater," Gould said quietly, "but that was the plan."

Butty glanced at the pool, where island music wafted from speakers and suntanned bodies lazed on loungers or in the water.

Quite the life, for some. He was being tortured with a brief dip of a toe into the pool of sun-filled leisure in a carefree world. He pictured himself in one of the chairs, with Lucia in one of those skimpy French bikinis and their young son gleefully playing with a toy between them.

"Better keep a leash on the crew, Butty Boy," Gould joked. "Don't let them have too much fun."

Butty grunted and left the agent waving to a young woman by the pool. Torture indeed. Along with the crew, Butty knew Gould's reminder was also aimed at him. Tonight they'd sneak out to the *Silvia Azul* and in the morning they'd weigh anchor and be back on the high seas. For some, the brief glimpse into life at the Seaview Hotel would be an incentive, but for Butty it was a reminder of everything he wouldn't get to enjoy with his family. He was beginning to really dislike Gene Gould.

The day passed quickly. Butty chose sleep over the poolside festivities, wandering downstairs in the early afternoon and enjoying a late lunch of seafood. He caught up with his crew, who were spending the afternoon in the shade, sleeping off their overindulged morning of sun and beer. Jesus was in better shape than the other two, and Butty took the opportunity to let him know they'd be pulling out at dawn. Jesus promised to have everyone sober and functioning by then.

Rather than lounge at the hotel, Butty walked into George Town in search of anything to take his mind off the hornet's nest he'd found himself in. Without a cruise ship docked, the town was quiet with locals and long-stay visitors ambling around the waterfront stores and buying fish from a little market set up on a patch of sandy beach. A sign caught his eye, and Butty wandered into a shop advertising scuba diving trips.

"Can I help you?" came a soft voice with a hint of a local accent.

Butty looked over, spotting a broad-shouldered man with thinning hair swept back, holding a dive regulator in one hand and a screwdriver in the other.

"Just browsing," Butty replied with a smile. "I've done a bit of diving in my time, but our gear didn't look like this stuff."

He looked at the simple harness to hold the scuba tank in place and the regulators and gauges in the display cabinet by the counter.

"It's come a long way," the man said. "Navy?"

Butty nodded. "Just short of ten years. Hard hat stuff."

"That's how I got my start," the man replied, placing the screwdriver down and extending his hand. "Bob Soto. Pleased to meet you."

"Ray…" Butty began, then recalled he was supposed to be using his new identity. "Friends call me Butty," he said, unable to bring himself to say James.

"Royal Navy?" Bob asked.

"Yup. Mainly ship repair, mine removal, that sort of thing. I was lucky not to see any real conflict during my time. Mostly splashed into cold, mucky water and blindly fumbled around until someone tugged on the line."

Bob nodded out the window. "You should come out with us here. You can see for hundreds of feet, and you won't believe the reefs."

"Proper Jacques Cousteau stuff, eh?" Butty joked, picturing the amazing footage from the few episodes of *The Undersea World* he'd caught on television.

Bob looked up and grinned. "He was here earlier this year, but I didn't tell you that," he said and winked. "Stayed down the East End of the island with some friends of mine. All hush-hush as otherwise he gets hounded by the press. He said he liked the diving here."

Butty laughed. "That's a pretty good recommendation I'd say."

"Want to give it a try?" Bob asked.

"I wish I could," Butty replied. "Leaving in the morning."

"Shame you didn't come by earlier in your stay."

Butty laughed again. "Well, that was this morning. Maybe I'll have more time on my next visit."

Bob looked out of the window. "That cargo ship yours?"

"Not mine, but I'm her captain."

The shop owner put the regulator he'd been working on down. "Know anything about that other cargo ship that showed up the other week?" he asked.

Butty flinched.

"The *Oro Verde* it's called," Bob continued. "Crew left her off the north side. She's anchored in the sound now."

"I heard about that," Butty replied, feeling like his lie was written all over his face.

Soto seemed to be a good sort, so he hated not being truthful with the man, but he had too much at stake.

"I'd better be off," he said, wishing he could stay longer.

"Raymond Butterworth," Bob said quietly, and Butty turned back to face the man. "I was told that was the captain's name."

Their eyes met, and a slight grin formed on Bob's face.

"Cousteau tried to keep his trip under wraps, eh?" Butty responded. "I can relate to that."

Bob nodded. "I have this crazy idea to sink the *Oro Verde* as an artificial reef. You know, attract coral growth and create an environment for the fish. Make a fantastic dive site."

Butty raised his eyebrows. "As a captain, it makes me shiver to think about a ship going under, I have to admit, Bob. But that might be a nice way to retire the old girl."

With that, Butty left the shop and made his way back to the Seaview Hotel. If he made it to Grand Cayman again, a dive with Bob Soto sounded mighty appealing. But he wasn't sure what he'd make of meeting the *Oro Verde* on the sea floor.

28

AJ stirred and instantly knew her surroundings were foreign, propelling her fully awake with a start. The glow from a light on the coffee maker was enough for her to recognise she was in Nora's shack. It was more like a cottage, really, but the old fellow who'd given it to Nora called it his shack, so she did too.

AJ fumbled on the floor by the sofa and found her mobile, tilting it so the screen lit up and showed her the time. 6:24am. She'd set her alarm for 6:30am, so she cancelled it, threw the sheet back, and swung her legs to the floor, yawning. The other thing which resonated from her mobile was the lack of text messages. She hadn't heard from Jackson since he'd left. Of course, she hadn't sent him anything either, but that was different. He was the instigator. He was the one leaving.

AJ heard a button click from the kitchen, which was only a few yards away as the shack was basically one big room plus a bathroom. She made out the silhouette of Nora and wondered how the young woman could move so quietly that the sound of the button click was the only indication another human was present. AJ plodded to the bathroom, far less stealthily, although she closed the door quietly, hoping not to wake Jazzy.

Ten minutes later, the two women sat on the deck, listening to the tide tickling against the ironshore coastline and sipping coffee.

"I don't get it," AJ said. "Why would anyone want to scare Andy off?"

"Pretty amateur attempts, too," Nora commented.

"Didn't feel very amateur when I was being run over or shoved around," AJ complained. "But I suppose you're right. Not exactly professional hitman stuff. The first one with the car could have been an accident, I suppose."

"You said it was the same car that followed us," Nora pointed out.

"Oh, that's right. I can't be a hundred percent sure, but I think it was," AJ replied. "Bit coincidental if it wasn't."

"Maybe Andy's grandfather is still alive and been in hiding all this time. Wants to stay that way," Nora suggested.

AJ let out a sigh. "I could tell last night that the thought crossed Andy's mind. Could you imagine? You go in search of learning something about your grandad who you've never known, and he tries to bump you off for your troubles."

"People suck," Nora said flatly, and sipped her coffee.

AJ naturally retained a slightly rosier outlook on the world and its inhabitants than Nora, but some people certainly did suck. Still, it was hard for her to imagine a grandfather actively and violently scaring off his grandson, especially as all he had to do was stay quiet and Andy would be back home in the UK within the week. After all, it was unlikely a few old timers on the island were about to suddenly reveal anything new after all these years.

"Wait," she blurted. "What if the car was after Curly, not Andy?"

"Why?" Nora rebutted.

"Curly had something he wasn't telling us. What if Raymond Butterworth *is* still around, and he's worried Curly might reveal something?"

"Then why did the guy follow us?"

AJ frowned. "I don't bloody know. Maybe to see what we did. Figure out if we learned anything we weren't supposed to know."

Nora didn't look convinced. "We'll take another run at the driver from last night, but he was quick to lawyer up. Doubt he's changed his mind this morning and he swears he wasn't driving the car earlier in the afternoon."

"We need his accomplice," AJ muttered, lost in thought.

"The car registration was years out of date, but we'll follow up this morning with the last owner."

"Probably nicked though, right?" AJ asked.

"Most likely. Wasn't reported, but we'll see when we go by the registered owner's address," Nora replied, then got to her feet. "We need to go."

AJ frowned at her. She needed more coffee to function after the little sleep she'd had. "What's the big rush all of a sudden?"

Nora moved to the door and paused. "If the accomplice was the one dealing with the old man. And the accomplice was the one driving the car in the afternoon. Then the accomplice is still out there, and Curly might not be safe."

"Oh, bugger," AJ swore, jumping to her feet.

Dawn was breaking over the island by the time they'd picked Andy up from his hotel and driven to Curly's house on the south side of George Town. AJ's conviction about the urgency of their visit had ebbed away with the air rushing over the topless Jeep, and by the time Nora parked in Sunset House's car park, she was riddled with doubt.

"What if we're about to scare the crap out of the poor old bloke?" she said, reluctantly hopping from the CJ-7 to keep up with Nora. "Maybe it's better to come back at a decent hour to check on him."

"There's a light on," Andy said, pointing to the little home.

Nora jogged across the road and AJ followed, after carefully checking both directions. The young constable banged loudly on the front door and the three waited. Silence.

"He must leave a light on when he goes to bed," AJ said. "He's still asleep."

Nora banged on the door one more time, then moved to her right across the porch and cupped her hands to the window, peering inside. She moved to the next window and did the same.

"*Dritt!*" she groaned and ran back to the front door.

"What?" AJ asked. "What did you see?"

"He's on the kitchen floor," Nora breathed, trying the door handle, which was locked. "Go that way," she ordered, pointing to their left. "Find a way in."

AJ and Andy ran along the wraparound porch, checking the windows as they went. Along the rear wall of the house they spotted a back door and arrived a step after Nora, who'd run around the opposite side. The door was unlocked, and Nora held up one hand before taking a step inside.

"Police!" she shouted. "I'm coming in the house. Make your presence known."

She was met with silence beyond the creak of the old floorboards under her feet. The three hurried across the living room to the kitchen where Curly was face down on the floor, blood pooled by the side of his head from a cut on his scalp. AJ knelt down and placed two fingers on his neck.

"Bugger. I can't feel a pulse."

She moved her fingers around, searching for a sign of life.

"Maybe... I think I feel something."

Nora called 911 on her mobile, giving them the location and asking for an ambulance. Andy knelt next to AJ and held a dishcloth he'd run under the tap against Curly's wound.

"He's still warm," AJ said, "and I think I feel a weak pulse."

Nora hung up the call and helped the other two roll Curly over onto his back. Andy ran to the living room and grabbed a cushion from the sofa, placing it under the old man's head. His tanned and wrinkled face looked pale and his lips were barely parted.

"I should have thought of this last night," AJ groaned. "We could have been here sooner. I think he's been on the floor all night. These are the clothes he had on yesterday when we left him."

Nora leaned down and listened near Curly's mouth. "He's still breathing."

Andy dabbed at the head wound and winced as he dared a look. "He took a right good bash on the head. You think he fell over somewhere?" he said, looking around the kitchen.

Nora stood and checked the edges and corners of the counter tops, as well as a table with two chairs off to the side. Finding no trace of blood, she walked through the opening into the living room.

"Here," she said, examining the rear wall between the back door and the opening to the kitchen. Speckles of blood spatter peppered the light teal paint. "Someone hit him. Maybe came through the back door as he was walking past here and whacked him over the head. Right handed," she added, positioning herself where she figured the assailant had stood and swinging her arm.

"All because he spoke with us?" Andy wondered aloud. "He didn't tell us anything new, really."

"Except he confirmed the captain was on the island after the *Oro Verde* was abandoned," AJ pointed out. "Puts to bed those rumours about the crew killing the captain and tossing him over the side."

Andy's eyes widened. "I thought you didn't believe that story?"

AJ looked at him apologetically. "Yeah. We may have played that one down a bit. It's always been believed that's what happened."

Sirens wailed in the distance, quickly growing louder as the ambulance neared from the hospital, only a short distance away. Nora moved to the front door and pulled her shirt sleeve over her hand to open it. Two constables were getting out of a patrol car they'd parked just beyond the house.

"It's going to be a crime scene," she told them, without wasting time on pleasantries. "The victim is still alive, but barely."

"Hey Nora," One of the constables said with a local accent, stepping inside. "Where's the vic?"

She pointed towards the kitchen. "Two others with me. Non-law enforcement."

The man moved carefully across the living room while his partner stayed outside and called in on his radio. Sirens screamed, destroying the still of the early morning as the ambulance pulled up out front. The EMTs killed the wailing before jumping out and opening the back doors to retrieve the gurney.

AJ stayed with Curly as the EMTs, one male, one female, eased him onto the gurney and set an oxygen mask over his face, the bottle laid by his frail body. Once they'd wheeled him to their vehicle, the gurney was slid inside and an IV started.

"You riding with him?" the female EMT asked.

AJ nodded, although she wasn't sure why. Guilt, she decided as she took a seat in the back.

"We'll meet you there," Nora said, looking in from the street. "Once I finish here."

"Keep Andy close," AJ replied, as the driver shut the back doors.

She felt like everything had changed now. Escalated. She'd been worried last night, but they'd only been shaken up. Threatened. Now, an old man lay before her, desperately hanging on for his life. The attacker likely thought he'd killed him and simply left. She'd seen no signs of a robbery. No emptied drawers or scattered possessions from a frantic search for valuables. The ambulance pulled away and the siren wailed once more, but it was actually quieter inside the vehicle than it had been from the outside. The EMT kept checking Curly's wrist for a pulse. She was about to say something when they both heard a groan.

"Curly? Can you hear me?" AJ said, leaning over the old man.

His eyes flickered open, and he grunted again.

"You're okay," she told him. "You're in good hands."

Curly's lips moved under the oxygen mask but whatever he

was trying to say came out as more muffled grunts and groans. His hand fumbled with the mask and pulled it aside.

"You need to keep dat on, sir," the EMT instructed, but he frowned and left his feeble hand over the mask, holding it askew.

AJ leaned closer, putting her ear near his face while trying not to bump him as the ambulance jolted and leaned side to side.

"Heaven?" Curly wheezed, his voice barely audible.

AJ couldn't help but chuckle. "Not yet, mate. You're in an ambulance. We'll get you patched up at the hospital. You're going to be right as rain in no time."

His brow creased into a frown as though he was confused. Or disappointed. His other hand weakly pulled on AJ's shirt, tugging her ear closer to him. A word came from his lips like the whisper of the wind through the trees, then his hands fell away and the EMT guided the mask back over his nose and mouth. For a second, AJ thought he was gone, but his chest softly and slowly moved up and down, and she sat up, relieved.

The EMT tapped on the monitor. "His heart rate is slow, but stabilising," she said. "Hard to know what damage is done wit a blow to da head, but I tink we got dere in time."

AJ let out a long sigh. She hoped the lady was right.

"What he say to you?" the EMT asked.

AJ thought for a moment, replaying the sound she heard in her head. "I can't be certain, but it sounded like he said, rose water."

"Dat mean someting to you?" the woman asked.

AJ shook her head. "No. Not a thing."

29

A few minutes before six, Butty walked downstairs from his room and found a seat at the Seaview bar. A band were setting up and he spotted his three crew members at a nearby table eating dinner. He ordered a Carib beer and after a few minutes Gene Gould took the seat next to him. The agent ordered himself a rum and Coke, then leaned in close.

"Mr Rosewater is very pleased everything is back on track."

He sat up straight as the bartender slid the drink his way, then leaned in again once the man had retreated.

"That's a win for you, Butty Boy," he whispered, holding up his glass.

Butty clinked his beer bottle and managed a nod, but struggled to fake much enthusiasm.

"Any sign of the *Oro Verde* crew?" Butty asked. "They can't have just vanished."

"The lifeboat was ditched at Barker's on the opposite tip of the North Sound from Rum Point, but no one's seen the men," Gould replied. "I had the boat taken care of."

Butty sipped his beer and thought things over. *Maybe the crew had found a boat heading off island, or were still here*? He told himself it was no longer his problem, which brought him back to the things that were.

"Where is Rosewater, anyway?" he asked. "He's here, right? Where does he stay?"

Gould sat his glass down. "Keep it down, man. There's too many eyes and ears around this place."

Butty glanced around them and scoffed. "Seriously? We're surrounded by holidaymakers and locals I've seen here every time I come by."

"You never know," Gould insisted. "There's a lot of people who'd love to see this operation fail. In this game, lives depend on discretion."

Butty took another look around, pivoting on his bar stool. No one was paying them any mind, until his eyes fell upon a recently familiar face. Bob Soto sat at a table by the pool. The man looked towards the bar and raised a finger in subtle acknowledgement. Butty nodded in return.

"How do you know him?" Gould asked, his voice still a whisper.

"He runs the local dive shop," Butty replied, noting another, younger man with curly hair sitting with Bob.

"I know who he is," Gould hissed. "Everyone around here knows Bob. But how and why do *you* know him?"

"I stopped in his dive shop earlier today," Butty replied, refusing to reduce himself to whispering about something that seemed so ridiculously unimportant. "You think he's working for the commies?" he mocked.

Gould shook his head. "Damn it, *Lofton*," he replied, emphasising Butty's new name. "Of course Bob's not working for the commies or anyone else we're worried about, but you don't know that. What we can't afford is anyone piecing you together with the *Oro Verde*. You'll be coming by here to and from every trip to Panama, so we need James Lofton to keep his head down and not start any rumours or fuss."

"Bloody hell, Gould. I dropped by his dive shop and looked at the gear. That's all," Butty said, hoping Bob would be discreet. "Seemed like a good bloke."

"Bob Soto is salt of the earth, don't get me wrong," Gould responded. "But his business is on and under the waters around this island so there's not too much he misses when it comes to ships. Especially abandoned ships."

Butty was about to mention Bob's comment about sinking the *Oro Verde*, but he decided better of it. In Butty's view, the sooner they moved on from Gould's paranoia-driven cloak and dagger rubbish the better. Laughter echoed around the pool area and he noted the curly headed man with Bob was cracking up over something.

"Sink the bloody thing?" he cackled, and Butty detected a distinct Australian accent.

Great, he thought, they are talking about the *Oro Verde*.

"When are we heading out to the *Silvia Azul* then?" he said, spinning around and lowering his voice.

How or when he'd brought his skiff around from the North Sound, Butty had no idea, but it was the same nameless local who had motored them out to the OV under the cover of darkness. Butty knew better this time to attempt anything more than a greeting nod before taking his seat. The man picked them up right out front of Seaview, and within fifteen minutes they'd made a wide arc away from shore and tied up alongside the *Silvia Azul*.

"That's the best hiding place you could come up with?" Gould asked as Butty dragged the Halliburton from his locker.

"Who am I hiding it from?" Butty retorted, handing the case to the agent. "There's only four of us aboard, and the other three work for Herrera."

Gould moved into the mess where a handful of tables with bench seats provided space for the crew to eat alongside the galley. He looked at Butty, who'd followed him in.

"Give me a minute here," he said, and Butty looked at the empty black duffel bag the man had brought with him.

"Okay," he said, and stepped outside, staying on the opposite side from shore and lighting a cigarette.

"Butty!" he heard from inside after a few minutes, and returned to the mess. "Here," Gould told him, handing him the case back. "That's for Panama. I'll tell you the code but you can't write it down; you have to remember it, okay?"

Butty took the case. It felt lighter than when he'd pulled it from the locker, and Gould's duffel was no longer empty. He nodded his assent and the agent read off four digits for him to commit to memory. Butty returned the case to his locker and promised to find a better spot for it on the way to Panama.

"I'll have time on my hands. This tub's as slow as molasses," he explained as they made their way to the stern.

Butty looked at the black duffel again. "So, where's that going?"

Gould shook his head. "You haven't quite grasped the *need-to-know* side of this operation, have you?"

"I spent nearly ten years in the Navy being told where to go, what to do, and how to do it, with no explanation why," Butty said. "Nowadays, I've found I prefer to know what's going on. Especially when my bloody neck's on the line."

"I'm a middleman, just like you," Gould said. "I'm given orders and that's what I follow. Mr Rosewater tells me to jump and the only thing I ask is how high."

"So that bag goes to him?"

"This bag goes to him," Gould replied. "What happens after that is above my pay grade and well outside the scope of what you're privy to."

The agent dropped the bag into the skiff, then climbed in. Butty followed, glad to take one more night in an air-conditioned room before setting off once more. They rode back to shore without a word or any lights beyond the orange glow from three cigarette tips, accompanied by the whine of the little outboard motor. The Seaview bar was still in full swing, but Butty was glad to see no sign of his crew. Maybe they'd be ready for work in the morning after all.

"When do I get to meet Rosewater?" Butty asked, before the two men parted ways outside their rooms.

"Why would you wanna do that?" Gould said in way of reply.

Butty shrugged his shoulders. "That's what I'm used to, I suppose. We always got to see the officers on the ship. The captain would be there for inspections and all the other pomp and ceremony the Royal Navy saw fit to put us through. His voice would address us over the ship's comms. Even us lowly divers got to have some idea about the man at the helm, you know? Made a difference, knowing who had your life in their hands."

Gould nodded slowly, pausing with his key in the door to the hotel room he called home. "This ain't the Royal Navy, Butty Boy. This is a world of secrets and lies and espionage, played behind the scenes. Undercover. In the dark. Anonymity is everything. The whole idea is for no one to know you exist. Same as Raymond Butterworth needs to disappear into the shadows and, for now, James Lofton can move around the Caribbean without raising suspicion."

"You're not hiding from anyone," Butty pointed out.

The agent grinned. "Gene Gould isn't."

It had crossed Butty's mind that Gould might not be his real name, but he guessed he had an answer now.

"So that's a no on meeting Mr Rosewater?"

Gould opened his room door. "Trust me, Butty Boy," he said, glancing down the hallway at the Englishman. "If you ever meet Mr Rosewater, there's a good chance you won't know it's him you're meeting, and it'll probably be the last thing you ever do."

With that, Gould entered his room and closed the door, leaving Butty standing in the hallway wondering about the mysterious voice he'd spoken to over the radio. Gould's words should have left him wanting to avoid Mr Rosewater at all costs, but Butty's curiosity was piqued even more. After all, he'd already decided he needed to take himself out of the picture, so what did he have to lose?

The early dawn light cast a long shadow off the port bow of the *Silvia Azul* as she headed south-west, away from Grand Cayman. Butty sipped his coffee and scanned the waters for fishermen, their small skiffs often easy to miss although the morning swells were small. It became even harder when the winds picked up and created chop, and it always amazed Butty how far from land the island fishermen would sometimes go in their tiny boats.

"What should we expect in Panama?" Jesus asked, standing by the door to the wheelhouse drinking his coffee.

"I'm not sure," Butty admitted. "I presume it'll be like what I did before on the *Oro Verde*, except we don't have to continue on to Ecuador. Although why we're travelling all the way through the canal to the Port of Balboa, I have no idea. It would be much easier to deliver our cargo in Colón."

Jesus held up his hand and rubbed his thumb and index finger together. *Money.*

Butty shrugged his shoulders. "It costs more money to go through the canal twice."

"Not the money for the tariffs," Jesus clarified. "Money for the officials."

"You think they've paid off the officials in Panama City? At the Port of Balboa? So why don't they do the same in Colón?"

"They've paid off officials everywhere, but they must be more reliable in Balboa. Might be something to do with our return cargo too."

Butty nodded. "It's all above my pay grade, as someone recently reminded me."

"Mine too, that's for sure," Jesus replied with a grin.

Butty looked the man over. He liked Jesus. He reminded him of Pepe a little bit. The Cuban seemed like a hard-working bloke who could be relied on, and Butty had to remind himself that Herrera had placed him on the ship.

"How long have you worked for Herrera?" he asked.

A slight frown creased Jesus's brow. "A few years, I guess. Before, I would just have a package or two on the fishing boat I worked. This is the first time I'm... more involved."

For a reason he didn't know, Butty had assumed Jesus to be a long-time employee and trusted soldier of Herrera's. But that didn't appear to be the case.

"Need the money?" Butty asked, trying to sound casual.

Jesus scoffed. "Everybody needs the money, Captain. I live with my own family, my brother's, and a cousin's, in a house built for one small family. They pick oranges in the fields, which barely earns enough to keep the lights on, and two of our wives clean houses. One takes care of all the kids. So yes, I need the money."

"And that's better than living in Cuba?" Butty asked, astonished at how they were barely keeping their heads above water.

Jesus nodded softly. "No one will come drag us from our home in the middle of the night because of something we said, or they think we said. We only have the INS to worry about, and the worst thing they do is lock us up, feed us three meals a day, then send us back to Cuba. So yes, living in destitution in Florida is better than living in destitution and fear in Cuba."

The INS wasn't the worst thing Jesus had to worry about now, Butty thought to himself, and wondered how much the man knew about exactly who they were dealing with. Not only in Miami, but the Cayman Islands and Panama. *Maybe he'll change his mind once he meets Manuel Noriega.*

30

AJ called Reg, who gave her a hard time but agreed to skipper her boat for the morning with Thomas as she was stuck in town. Detective Whittaker, the lead investigator for the Royal Cayman Islands Police Service and a friend of theirs, came to the hospital to listen to what they knew so far. Which was very little. He had one suspect in a cell at the station not saying a word, a victim in the hospital under sedation, and a visiting Englishman with a link to the story of the *Oro Verde*.

"You sure he said rose water?" Whittaker asked AJ again.

"I'm not very sure at all, to be honest," she replied. "But that's what it sounded like."

Nora took out her mobile and searched online for rose water.

"Bunch of *dritt* on here about making flavoured water from rose petals. Says it's good for your skin. Popular in Iran."

"I didn't notice any rose bushes in his garden," AJ commented. "You know, maybe he was giving us some kind of clue."

"His garden was overgrown weeds," Nora responded, putting her mobile in her pocket. "But we should search his house for anything related."

"Why don't you do that," Whittaker said, looking at Nora. "I'll let West Bay station know you're working on something for me today." He turned to Andy. "My apologies that your experience on our island so far has not been ideal. I promise you, it's not usually like this here."

Andy managed a smile. "Seems like I've stirred up a bit of a commotion, Detective. I'm perplexed as to why, but it appears we need to get to the bottom of it now."

Whittaker nodded. "We'll certainly try, Mr Butterworth. I suggest you let AJ take you diving and try to enjoy yourself, I'll pursue the angles we have. Perhaps we can persuade this fellow in custody that he's better served helping us with our inquiry."

"He's Jamaican, isn't he, sir?" Nora asked.

"He is."

She shrugged her shoulders. "He's going to be deported anyway, right? So not much incentive to help us."

"That's true," Whittaker agreed. "But the charges coming his way and the manner in which he's sent home can vary based on his cooperation, so we have something to bargain with."

"Andy didn't get a good look at the bloke who threatened him as it was darker on his side of the van," AJ said. "But I bet he's the one who clobbered Curly on the noggin."

"We'll certainly try to persuade our Jamaican to give up his friend, and his hiding behind a lawyer might be a good thing in this case," Whittaker explained. "He'll be advised to cooperate as that will be in his best interests."

"*His* lawyer, or court appointed?" Nora asked.

"Court appointed," Whittaker confirmed. "I verified that earlier in case someone we might be interested in was providing defence for him."

The detective said his goodbyes, and the three walked out of the hospital into the bright mid-morning sun.

"I guess we need a ride?" AJ realised as they approached Nora's Jeep.

"I'll take you after I search the house," Nora said, climbing in and starting the CJ-7. "I should probably change into my uniform at some point."

"I suppose I should grab some clothes from the cottage," AJ said, sniffing her shirt she'd been wearing since yesterday. "Andy will go home telling everyone we're nice in the Cayman Islands, but you might get mugged and the women pong a bit."

Nora let out a sound which may have been a rare snicker or laugh, and AJ turned to Andy who'd climbed into the back seat, expecting him to at least politely chuckle at her humour.

"I may have found something," he said instead, staring at the screen of his mobile. "Rosewater. That name came up in the Iran-Contra Affair investigation, back in the 80s."

"I don't know what that is," Nora said, letting the engine warm up at idle and turning in her seat.

Andy leaned forward. "It was a big deal in America, back when Reagan was president. The CIA were involved, and it was a huge scandal."

"I remember Reg telling me about it one time," AJ said. "But I can't say I remember anything he actually said. It was before I was born, and as I'm the oldest one in the car, it means it was before any of us were born."

"So what does Iran have to do with rose water and Grand Cayman?" Nora asked.

"Good question," Andy replied. "I'd say it's a tentative connection at best, but it's something."

Nora reversed out of her parking spot, then drove through the car park to Maple Road and turned left. She drove slowly so they could hear each other over the loud tyres and wind.

"From what I recall in a class I took at uni," Andy began, "it all started because Reagan was passionate about stamping out communism…"

"Why?" AJ interrupted. "What's it gotta do with him? Or was he worried about a communist party in America?"

"No, I think he just didn't like the idea of it," Andy replied.

"I think it's one of those great theories that doesn't really work in practice, yeah?" AJ said, shrugging her shoulders. "But I still don't see why it was any of his business."

"Well, apparently he made it his business," Andy replied.

"Let him tell the story," Nora said impatiently.

"Yup. Sorry."

"No problem," Andy said politely, and continued. "So, the whole trial thing afterwards was very much about what Reagan actually knew, versus what was done behind his back and he didn't know. A guy called Oliver North ended up taking the fall for the mess, but it's generally believed he fell on the sword for the sake of the president.

It started in the early eighties with a secret arms deal with Iran who were under an international arms embargo. The excuse was a trade for hostages who were being held in Lebanon by an Islamist paramilitary group called Hezbollah."

"Wait, Lebanon," AJ interrupted again. "Not Iran?"

"Hezbollah was being controlled at least in part by Iranians," Andy responded, and Nora flashed AJ another scowl.

"Alright, alright. Keep your hair on," AJ said, then waved a hand at Andy. "Carry on, you're doing splendidly."

"Okay. This part was brokered by an expat Iranian arms dealer — a dodgy bloke whose name I don't remember — and succeeded in freeing a few hostages, but then Hezbollah turned around and kidnapped a few more, so the Americans never got ahead."

"Weren't the Contras South American?" Nora asked, and AJ playfully punched her arm.

"Who's interrupting Andy, now then?"

"He said Iran-Contra and I haven't heard any Contras mentioned yet," Nora said defensively.

"That's next," Andy responded.

"See. That's next if you'll just wait, Miss Ants in Her Pants."

Nora looked down at her seat. "I have ants in the Jeep again? *Dritt.* I don't see any ants."

AJ shook her head. "Continue, Andy. If you please."

"Sure," Andy said, trying to hide a grin while keeping the story straight in his head. "So the second part is the Contras, who were fighting the communist Sandinistas for power in Nicaragua from, I think, 1979 until about 1990. The man who helped the US funnel money to the Contras was a Panamanian called Manuel Noriega."

"I've heard of him," AJ said.

"Me too," Nora agreed.

"He had a long history with the US authorities and especially the CIA, who for years had Noriega on their payroll as an informant and agent in Central and South America."

"Didn't the US end up arresting and putting Noriega on trial?" AJ asked.

"They did," Andy confirmed. "US forces invaded Panama after tensions peaked with a marine being killed there, and Noriega was eventually caught and arrested. But that's a whole different story. Related, but different."

Nora pulled into the Sunset House car park. Across the road, in front of Curly's little house was a police car and a van. Nora parked, turned off the engine, and waited for Andy to continue. Before he could, AJ's mobile rang and she checked the caller ID.

"It's Sally Regis," AJ announced, wrinkling her nose. "She can go to voicemail. Carry on Andy."

"The thing about the Contra part was that US Congress had prohibited the funding of the Nicaraguan Contras through the Boland Amendment, which was a couple of legislative amendments made in the early eighties. So not only were the Iranian arms deals under the table and against an embargo, but the funding of the Contras was against America's own policies. It was a huge scandal with a lot of complicated moving parts, which is partly why the investigation took so long, and in the end, a handful of people were given probation and Reagan was off the hook. Soon after, Bush, who'd been Reagan's vice-president throughout all this, became president himself, and pardoned everyone."

"That's all very interesting," Nora said flatly. "If you happen to be interested in this sort of thing. But what does it have to do with your *farfar*? Everything you explained happened several years after the *Oro Verde* was abandoned here."

Andy shrugged his shoulders. "I've got no idea. But AJ thinks Curly said 'rose water' and the only reference I can find online for anything even remotely connected to the island involving the name Rosewater is PDFs of court transcripts and documents related to the affair which I found in a Brown University study. Twice, Mr Rosewater is mentioned in regard to the money transfers from Iran to Noriega. It says he was a CIA agent based in the Cayman Islands."

"So we're looking for a CIA agent who was in the Cayman Islands in the seventies and eighties?" AJ posed as a rhetorical question. "Blimey. That would make him an old guy, wouldn't it?"

"Did this Rosewater guy testify in the trials?" Nora asked.

Andy shook his head. "There's so much to read through here, but from what I can find so far, the CIA denied any existence of a Rosewater on their payroll. They claimed the person may have been posing as an agent, but they had no one based in the Cayman Islands during that period of time."

Nora got out of the Jeep. "Be helpful if Curly could tell us something more."

AJ and Andy followed.

"I reckon he told me that 'cos he thought he was about to peg it. I bet he clams up again once he's sitting up in a comfy bed at the hospital. He was dead panicked after that car ran our toes over."

They crossed the street and walked up the path to the front porch of the cottage.

"I read all the rumours about the *Oro Verde* having drugs aboard," Andy said, and the two women stopped by the front door to hear what he had to say. "And you said there are stories floating around about that, right?"

"Yeah," AJ replied. "And Curly alluded to it being at least partly true. But you know how that stuff goes. A comment back in 1976 becomes a joke, which turns into a story at the pub, and next minute it's punted around as fact."

"And that could be the case," Andy agreed. "But one thing Manuel Noriega was known for in the seventies was running drugs from Central America."

"That could be the connection to our timeline, then," AJ suggested.

"And he was on the CIA's payroll when he was doing that?" Nora asked.

"Yup," Andy confirmed.

31

At the port of Balboa outside Panama City, the *Silvia Azul* was met by Díaz, the tall man Butty had always dealt with. The two greeted each other warmly, and Díaz looked over the ship from the dock.

"I think you downgraded," he said with his boyish grin, hand-rolling a fresh cigarette as he spoke.

Butty laughed. "I agree, but the *Oro Verde* is currently indisposed in the Cayman Islands. This is what they gave me."

Díaz lit his cigarette and slapped Butty on the arm. "Let's get you unloaded, then we'll see about the refit."

"Refit?" Butty asked. "I didn't know anything about a refit?"

Díaz had begun walking towards the crane but stopped. "I have orders to create some new cargo spaces," he said, and winked at Butty. "The main hold is too small for everything you need to carry."

It was true, the hold wasn't big, and Butty had been wondering how they'd be hiding their extra goods amongst the legit freight, but no one had mentioned a refit.

"What about the engine? This thing runs at seven knots on a flat sea and doesn't have much interest in trying harder."

Díaz shook his head. "Nothing about the engine, my friend.

Let's get you unloaded, then moved to another dock where we'll do the work."

"Okay," Butty agreed. As usual he didn't have much choice.

It didn't take long to unload the cargo, including the long crates which were stacked separately, then Díaz gave him directions where to move to. The new dock was in the low rent district of the port, with ships and boats in various states of disrepair scattered about the water and land. The smell of diesel, oil, and metal being welding filled the hot, humid air. Once the *Silvia Azul* was tied alongside, Díaz arrived with several other men in tow. One of them wore a uniform, and Butty thought he recognised him from his prior trip. He'd been with Noriega's men. The third man, he soon learned, ran the marine repair shop and would be doing the work.

Butty sent the crew away to find food while the visitors came aboard. Díaz introduced the officer as Lieutenant Flores. The man had a permanent look of anger on his face and said very little until they were on deck and ready to inspect the boat for modifications.

"You have something for me," the lieutenant said, sternly phrased as a statement.

"I have something for Noriega," Butty responded, not wanting to aggravate an already aggravated man, but he also had no desire to hand a lot of money over to the wrong guy.

"Lieutenant Colonel Noriega!" Flores barked. "And I'm his representative. You'll give it to me."

Butty looked at Díaz, who gave him a subtle nod. It was all out of Butty's league, but he'd go with the okay of the one man in Panama he thought he might be able to trust.

"Come with me, then," Butty replied, and the officer followed him down to the captain's meagre berth, where Butty pulled the case from his locker.

After half-heartedly looking around for a better hiding spot, and not finding one, he'd left it in the locker. Setting the case on his little desk, Butty rolled the numbers of the combination and opened the lid. He'd resisted the urge to peek inside on the trip down, and was now stunned by the sight of so much cash. Hundred-dollar bills were bound in stacks, which filled three-quarters of the Halliburton briefcase.

Flores elbowed Butty aside and began counting the stacks, then paused. "Go sort the modifications out; I'll take care of this."

The man waited and when Butty didn't move, he turned and repeated the order. "Leave. Now!"

Butty knew he should be counting the money with Flores, or should have looked inside and counted it on the way down. He sensed with every tingling nerve ending that something wasn't right. But once more, he was a passenger on the journey with no control over anything which really mattered. He slipped from his own cabin, and went to find the other two men.

The forward bunk room was designated as the easiest and largest area to convert into cargo space. Butty couldn't argue; it was both of those things. It was also where the three crew slept as it was in the bow as far away from the rumbling engine as they could get. The three men would now have to share two berths in rotation in the main cabin structure towards the stern. Next to the galley. Above the engine and generator. It was where the captain's berth was already, but Butty was used to being close by the helm in case of emergencies and had learned to sleep through the noise.

Work began that day, so when Jesus, Felipe, and Basilio returned having eaten lunch and bought food for their unexpected stay in the shipyard, they found all their possessions in the galley instead of their berths. Butty then explained the situation and each man stoically gathered his clothes and they divided up the locker space available in their new digs.

The Panamanian shipyard workers were neither subtle nor quiet. With gas axes, grinders, and hammers, they tore the forward berths apart, including the head and adjoining space, all the way to the ship's hull. They worked long into the evening, and just as Butty wondered if a night shift would take over, the noise ceased, and their voices faded with their footsteps across the gangway.

Next morning, the same faces returned before sun-up, and woken by the renewed racket, Butty took a look at their progress with coffee in hand. The men had opened up a space adding a significant amount more capacity, and were in the throes of concealing the access hatches. One from the crane hut above, and the other from the cargo hold behind. One of the men predicted they'd be finished by the end of the next day. Butty had never seen so much work done to a ship in such a short amount of time. It wasn't the fine craftsmanship of the QE2, but certainly functional for the purpose at hand.

Butty returned to the galley, where his crew were eating breakfast. He topped off his coffee, scooped a plate of eggs and bacon together, and joined them. They were all eager to get underway once more, although Butty's future weighed heavily on his mind. He still had to invent a way to get out of his situation and keep Lucia and the baby safe. Nothing new had sprung to mind, so he dreaded returning to Miami to face the expectations of two rival drug lords. *Maybe, for a trip or two, he could satisfy them both before his duplicity became obvious?* It felt like a tenuous thread but short of throwing himself overboard on the trip, he was out of ideas. *Or, was too cowardly to do what had to be done.* That thought didn't sit well at all.

Raised voices came from the dock and he spun around to see what the commotion was about. Dawn had broken and a soft, low light threw long shadows across the shipyard, where a dozen or so men in uniform lined up, guns in hand.

"What's going on down there?" Jesus asked nervously.

"No idea," Butty replied, rising from his seat and wiping his lips with a napkin. "I'll go down and find out. Stay here for now."

"No problem," Jesus replied, clearly happy to remain as far away from the soldiers as possible.

Butty ran down the steps and when he reached the deck, was met by Flores and two of his men.

"Come with me," the officer ordered.

"Do you mind telling me what's going on?" Butty asked without moving.

Flores glared at him and with the subtlest of nods, one of the soldiers drove the butt of his rifle into Butty's midriff. The Englishman crumpled to the deck, gasping, but the two soldiers hauled him back to his feet.

"When I tell you to do something, you do it," Flores growled in English. "No questions. No delay. Understand?"

Butty nodded his assent as he didn't have enough breath to utter a word. Flores turned and strode across the gangway, then the guards shoved Butty along behind him. On the dock, they paused, and the two soldiers tightly gripped an arm each as the rest of the soldiers stood to attention. From the building emerged Manuel Noriega with the same two personal bodyguards Butty recalled from their first encounter. The chief of military intelligence marched up, returned a salute to Flores and his men, then stared at Butty.

The Englishman again noted the man's textured complexion, and wondered if Noriega had been teased at school. He was also much shorter than Butty, especially when Butty straightened up, recovering from the blow to his stomach. Perhaps the combination had paved the path to his acidic demeanour.

"Where's the rest?" Noriega asked flatly.

"I'm sorry, sir, the rest of what?" Butty replied, although he guessed what the man had in mind.

Flores stepped forward with a clenched fist, but Noriega held up a hand, stopping him.

"My money."

"Sir, I gave the case I brought with me to Lieutenant Flores yesterday. That's what I was given and it hadn't been opened until I gave it to him."

Noriega looked at Flores, who smirked.

"I didn't open it. He did," the Lieutenant said smugly. "He knew the combination code. I counted it and brought it to you, sir."

Noriega turned back to Butty. "Where's the rest of my money?"

"I have no idea," Butty pleaded. "I was given that case in Miami. The agent in Grand Cayman took it, then gave it back to me before we left port. I gave the case to him," he said, nodding to Flores. "I have nothing to do with that side of things, sir. I'm just the ship's captain. I deliver whatever you chaps give me to deliver."

Noriega nodded. Butty knew he was on thin ice. The easiest thing for the two Panamanian officers to believe was that Butty had taken the missing money for himself. Which of course he hadn't. Either Gould had creamed too much, or Flores was on the take.

"Search the ship," Noriega ordered, and Flores began organising his men and sending them aboard. "And bring me the rest of the crew," Noriega added.

For forty minutes, Butty, Jesus, Felipe, and Basilio stood in the growing heat while the soldiers tore the *Silvia Azul* apart, looking for hidden cash. Noriega leaned against a shipping container, remaining in the shade, drinking orange juice and chatting casually with Flores. When the soldiers finally disembarked, they had one envelope they handed to Flores, who showed Noriega. It was the cash Butty had been given in Miami. The man shrugged his shoulders and walked over to the captives.

"Either you stole the missing money, or they sent you with less than was arranged. Regardless, this is unacceptable. So I must let them know." Noriega turned and looked at Flores. "Take them to Cárcel Modelo and shoot one of them. The other three can be returned to the ship when it's ready to leave."

Noriega spun around and began walking away.

"Wait! Why are we being punished?!" Butty blurted. "We're not responsible for the financial side of all this."

The man paused and looked back.

"Perhaps, perhaps not. But they must know this deceit is unacceptable. Personally, I don't think any one of your lives is worth one hundred thousand dollars, so I'd shoot all of you, but that leaves no one to take the ship and my product back to Miami. It's a lucky day for three of you."

"Then it should be me!" Butty shouted.

"You're the captain, no?" Noriega questioned.

"I am, but Jesus is more than capable."

Butty glanced over and saw Jesus looked mortified. Felipe gritted his teeth in silent defiance, and Basilio had tears running down his cheeks. This was Butty's chance, and he knew it. With one bullet, he could set Lucia and his unborn child free.

Noriega shrugged his shoulders. "Fine," he said, and walked away.

32

The Royal Cayman Islands Police Service scene of crime officer, Rasha, met Nora in the living room of Curly's cottage. AJ and Andy lingered in the doorway, waiting to see if they would be granted permission to enter.

"I'm almost done here," Rasha told Nora. "You're welcome to search the rest of the house; just stay clear of the back entrance and kitchen for now."

"Mind if they help me look around," Nora asked, thumbing towards the two at the door.

"Hi, AJ," Rasha greeted her. "No, that's fine. Everyone needs shoe covers and gloves though, and please photograph and catalogue anything you think might be relevant."

The SOCO trudged back to the kitchen in her pale blue Tyvek suit while the three donned shoe covers which they actually put over their bare feet after kicking off their flip-flops.

"What are we looking for, exactly?" AJ asked, staring at the sparse old and musty furniture. The LED television appeared to be the only item from the current century.

"The box labelled 'Rosewater and important clues'," Nora

replied as she began opening drawers of the sideboard underneath the TV.

"Ha, bloody, ha," AJ groaned, and walked into the first of two bedrooms. Andy took the other one.

AJ was surprised to find the bed neatly made, and while the carpet was old and the paint on the walls faded, the room was clean and tidy. Above the bed was a framed movie poster from *The Deep*, with Jacqueline Bisset, and AJ wondered if it was original from 1977. Searching for anything which seemed relevant to the 1970s was going to be laborious, as she was sure most of the possessions and furniture matched that criterion.

Starting with the bedside table, she began the hunt, finding several old, cheap watches, reading glasses, and a copy of Bob Soto's biography by his wife, Suzy. It was another reminder for AJ to buy a copy herself. In the cupboard below, she found more old paperback books. Mainly Clive Cussler, and a few by John D. MacDonald. There was also a half-empty bottle of cheap rum.

After carefully looking through the wardrobe, using a ballpoint pen to nudge Curly's clothes aside in the dresser, then checking for anything on top — where she found nothing but thick dust and dead bugs — AJ was about to leave the room. She paused at the doorway and realised she hadn't checked in everybody's favourite catch-all for stuff they didn't know where else to put. Kneeling on the beige carpet, she peered underneath the bed. An ancient looking canvas kit bag partially blocked her view of a pair of boxes. She pulled the bag out, which was falling apart from age, and completely empty.

Moving to the other side of the bed, she reached under for what she could now see were two shoe boxes. Flipping the lids off revealed both were stuffed full of photographs. Old photographs, if the top ones were the last added to the collection.

"I've got a boatload of old photos in here," AJ called out, and heard the other two's footfalls as they joined her in the bedroom. "You have any luck?" she asked them.

Andy shook his head. "Spare room is full of old dive gear, a bunch of books, and dive magazines."

AJ immediately sat up. "Old dive gear? I wanna see!"

Nora pointed at the photo boxes. "I bet you do, but it won't help us solve anything, so what's in these?"

AJ frowned at her friend. "Killjoy. Photos. Hence me yelling to you that I had a load of photos in here. Tons of them. How we'll know who's in any of them, I have no idea."

"Are they marked on the back?" Nora asked.

"Oh," AJ responded, picking up a picture. "I haven't looked."

She flipped the first ten over, but none of them were marked. They also weren't in any form of chronological order as one showed Curly as a young man, standing outside a dive shop with Bob Soto. AJ recognised Soto from the many pictures she'd seen of him around the island over the years. There was a whole section dedicated to him in the Cayman Islands Museum in George Town. Another picture showed Curly at a similar age, sitting in a small fishing skiff with a dark-skinned man. Curly was beaming, but the other man appeared to be less amused.

"These people could be anyone," AJ complained. "We have no idea."

"I'm sure some are long gone, too," Andy pointed out.

AJ took a photo with her mobile of the picture of Curly and the local man, then texted it to Suzy Soto. Nora reached down and picked up one of the boxes, dumping it out on the bed.

"Here," she said. "Now look for anything related to the *Oro Verde*, marked with a name, or anything else which catches your eye."

She turned to leave.

"Where are you going?" AJ asked. "This is needle in a haystack stuff. You not helping?"

"When I'm finished in the living room," she answered and waved her hand at the scattered pictures. "Better get started."

AJ stuck her tongue out at Nora, who cracked a slight grin and left the room answering her mobile, which rang as she left.

"Probably be a lot easier if Curly was here to help," Andy said, sitting on the far side of the bed and picking up a handful of photographs.

"Except he'd probably sit and reminisce about each one, so it would take even longer," AJ replied, sitting on her side of the bed and gathering a few pictures in her hand.

Andy held one up to show her. "I think you're right."

AJ looked at the photograph. A younger, shirtless Curly with his arm around a pretty woman wearing a bikini. The George Town harbour was in the background. Andy held up two more photos. Similar shots with different backgrounds, and different women.

"Bit of a playboy, our Curly," AJ laughed.

Using a system of piles, they began sorting through the pictures, using their best guess to divide them into 1970s and 80s, earlier, and after that time periods. Many of the photos in the second box were of Curly as a child. Or at least they presumed it was Curly, as they were mostly black and white pictures of the same kid. After twenty minutes, AJ and Andy had made a dent in the pile when Nora re-joined them.

"That was Whittaker who called," she said, sitting on the end of the bed. "The Jamaican guy gave up his friend in return for a deal. A Haitian national. They have an address."

"Should we go there?" AJ quickly asked. "I mean, this is super exciting, but shouldn't we be there when they nab the bloke? Andy can ID him."

"I'm not sure I can," Andy admitted. "It was dark and I barely saw him."

"Later," Nora said, firmly. "Whittaker will keep us informed. We should finish here."

"This is odd," Andy said, holding up a faded polaroid photograph of trees lining a gravel road. He flipped it over. "Here's an address written on the back."

"Is it this address?" AJ asked. "Might be the land here before the cottage was built."

Nora leaned over. "No it says it's on Rum Point Drive."

AJ took out her mobile. "Read me the address, Andy."

"2112 Rum Point Drive."

AJ's map app took her to the road running from the village of North Side to Rum Point itself, but couldn't find the house number. She clicked on few rental condos and guest houses along the route until she narrowed it down to a house on the water a few hundred yards before the road turned left and split into Water Cay Road and Sand Point Road. AJ zoomed in and showed the other two.

"Got a street view?" Nora asked.

AJ clicked on the feature then touched her finger to the screen in front of the home she guessed it to be. A long driveway from the road led to a large, older home facing the ocean on the north side of the island.

"I'd say that's out of Curly's league," AJ remarked, holding out her mobile for the others to see again.

"Maybe it wasn't in the 70s," Nora pointed out. "That was long before the big development started on the island."

AJ gave her a look. "He'd hardly be living in this place, which, by the way, is worth a pretty penny for the land alone these days, if he owned that palace overlooking the water."

"Hey, we don't even know why this is in here," Andy said. "Could be he fancied buying the land forever ago and kept the picture."

AJ looked around. "You're probably right. He kept everything else from back then."

Rasha poked her head in the door. She'd changed out of her Tyvek suit and now looked more comfortable in cotton shorts and a T-shirt. "Five minutes and we'll be out of here. Do you need more time?"

Nora looked at AJ and shrugged her shoulders. AJ shook her head. They were clutching at straws with the photos.

"We'll finish up and leave with you," Nora said.

"Five-minute warning," Rasha reiterated, and left the room.

They began gathering the pictures back up and shovelling them into the boxes by hand.

"Think it's worth running up to Rum Point and seeing this place?" AJ asked, keeping the picture to one side.

"We have a better chance of learning something from the Haitian man if they pick him up," Nora said, putting a lid on one of the boxes and handing it to AJ.

"What are we doing next, then?" she asked in return, sliding the box under the bed, then placing the second one next to it.

Andy shoved the old canvas bag under the other side, and the three walked out of the bedroom into the living room.

Nora was about to answer when her mobile dinged with a text. "It's Whittaker. They have the guy in custody," she said, looking up from the screen. "I should take Andy to the station."

"Bloody hell," Andy mumbled. "I hope I recognise the guy when I see him. I suppose it's all on me now, eh?"

"Pretty much," Nora said.

AJ shoved her. "Hey, what about fingerprints from the car that tried to run us over?"

"My team is pulling prints this morning, and whatever else we can find from that car you bashed into," Rasha said, hauling a big forensics bag out the front door.

"See," AJ said, frowning at Nora.

"A positive ID will help a lot," Nora rebutted.

"I'll do my best," Andy added. "Let's go see this bloke and maybe he'll seem familiar. I got a good whiff of his breath if that helps."

"Not really," Nora replied.

AJ was about to tell her friend to stop being so literal and try encouraging her witness when her own mobile buzzed in her pocket. It was Suzy Soto.

'That looks like Cuda Crestwell. He was always up to no good back in the day. Nothing serious, but ran with a bad crowd. Still alive, last I heard. Lives in North Side.'

"Are you coming?" Nora called out from across the road, standing by her Jeep.

AJ was still out front of Curly's place rereading the text. She jogged across the road.

"Drop me at the bus station on the way. I should go and get my van."

Nora looked unsure, but climbed in the Jeep and started the engine. "Okay."

33

Handcuffed and shoved into the back of a canvas-covered military troop lorry, the four men rattled and shook their way across Panama City. The soldiers with them smoked, chatted amongst themselves, and laughed as though it was just another day. Which for them, it probably was. Through the open flaps at the back of the lorry, Butty watched the city pass by, crowded, noisy, and hot. He could tell when they'd reached their destination as the soldiers began stamping out their smokes and lowering their voices. After waiting for a few moments, the lorry pulled through an entrance and entered into a compound surrounded by a tall mesh fence topped with spiral razor wire.

Ordered out of the transport, the four men were pushed by rifle stocks and rough hands through a doorway into a stark, bare room with steel bars protecting prison clerks. The paperwork process was brief and superficial by what Butty could tell, and he felt like a man being removed from the functioning planet. Life continued outside the wire, but inside Cárcel Modelo, people ceased to exist, whether they continued to breathe or not.

Moved to a holding area, they were all thoroughly searched,

although it had already been done before they'd been placed in the lorry; then they were left alone to wait.

"I've never been in charge of a ship this size, Captain," Jesus whispered. "How will we run it with just the three of us?"

Butty thought about asking if he'd rather trade seats, but he didn't. Jesus was a good man and had a right to be concerned about what lay ahead.

"Get out of the docks and through the canal. You just came through with me and saw what to do at the locks. Just have your paperwork ready. You could ask around at each stop, see if you can pick up a seaman who'll join you. One additional man will make it work if he can take the helm for a few hours in rotation. Lean on Felipe; he's a good bloke. I planned to give him full shifts at the wheel on the return home."

Felipe nodded his appreciation, but didn't look up.

Jesus had listened intently, then they all fell silent for several minutes. Eventually, Jesus spoke again.

"You shouldn't have volunteered, Captain. You had one in four odds. It would have been fair to take the same chance as us."

Butty leaned a little closer. "It's better this way, believe me. I needed a way out, and this is a shitty way out, but it'll work."

"I don't understand," Jesus responded.

"That's okay, mate, it's not important, but I will ask a favour of you."

"Anything, Captain. You're laying down your life to save one of us. I'll do anything you ask."

"If I give you my address, will you drop by and tell my wife I couldn't make it home? Don't upset her by saying how, but tell her I love her and I hope our baby is strong, healthy, and as beautiful as she is."

"Maybe you should write her a letter, man."

Butty shook his head and smiled. "They won't give us a pen and paper. Can you tell her that for me?"

"Of course," Jesus replied, and crossed himself. "I swear on my mother's life I will deliver this message for you, Captain."

Butty squeezed the man's arm. "Be safe, Jesus. And if there's any way to get yourself out of this mess, take it. Picking fruit will be better than ending up in this place," he said, looking around the filthy holding room.

"What about the Cayman Islands?" Jesus asked. "Do I have to stop there on the way back?"

Butty shrugged his shoulders. "I wouldn't. Unless Noriega or Flores tells you to, I'd go straight to Miami. That guy in Grand Cayman is probably the one who skimmed the money. Or Flores," he added, then thought it over. "Or both of them."

"What happens if they do that again?" Jesus asked. "If Herrera makes me come again."

"Get out," Butty repeated. "I'm telling you, Jesus. Get as far away from all this as you can."

Jesus nodded, and fell silent once more. A few minutes later, the lock on the door clunked open and two guards came in, truncheons in hand. Following them was Flores.

"Get up," he ordered, and the four nervously stood.

Butty leaned over and gave Jesus his street address in Miami. Jesus repeated it back to him and the two men nodded to each other.

"Out," Flores ordered, and the prisoners filed through the door of the holding room into a series of hallways which smelled like disinfectant, sewage, and sweat.

After descending a flight of steps, the guard leading them stopped and pointed into a small, dingy room. A single light fixture was affixed within a protective cage to the ceiling with a metal conduit running to the wall where it disappeared through a hole. A rusty brown stain streaked down the wall below the hole.

"You," he told Butty, and shoved him inside.

"Captain!" Jesus called out, but another guard hit him in the kidneys with his truncheon before pushing the group past the room.

Flores entered and pulled the door closed, leaving one guard outside. The lieutenant lit a cigarette, while walking back and forth.

He indicated for Butty to sit in the lone chair which Butty noted was fixed to the chipped and stained concrete floor. The room was cooler than the last place they'd been held and he guessed it was below ground.

"Did you take the money?" Flores asked in English.

"You know I didn't," Butty replied.

The man smirked. "I don't know that. But I suspect your friend in Grand Cayman was a little greedy." Flores continued pacing. "Why did you volunteer to die?"

Butty sighed. This all felt like a waste of time and he wished they'd just shoot him and get it over with. He really hoped Flores didn't think torture would gain him any valuable insights. Butty had nothing to hide at this point.

"Sal Herrera, the drug dealer in Miami who your shipments go to, wants me to be the captain of his supply ship. His rival is Alfonso Pérez, and he says he'll hurt my family if I don't feed him information on Herrera and the supply chain. I can't serve both, so the best thing to do is remove myself from the picture altogether. Your boss offered a way for that to happen."

Flores stopped pacing. "You would rather be shot by a firing squad than figure out a way to choose a side in Miami?"

He made it sound simple. It didn't feel simple to Butty.

"I'm out of my depth, man," Butty replied. "I'm no match for these maniacs. One or the other is going to get cheesed off with me and then they'll hurt my wife, and she's pregnant with our kid. How can I avoid it?"

"Leave. Go somewhere else. America is a big place. You're not even from there. Go back to England and drink your tea and live."

Butty almost detected humour from the officer, but then again, it was at his prisoner's expense, so sadistic humour seemed right for Flores.

"She won't leave," Butty explained. "She's Cuban, and all her family are there in Miami. She'd never leave."

"Don't ask. Take her and leave," Flores said, waving a hand, sending cigarette ash sailing through the air. "My wife does what I tell her to do."

"I bet your wife isn't Cuban," Butty responded, and Flores surprised him and broke into a grin.

"That's true."

"I didn't take your money," Butty said, ready to get his fate over with.

"I know," Flores replied.

Butty looked up and Flores shrugged his shoulders.

"It doesn't matter," the officer added.

"Sort of matters in Noriega's eyes," Butty pointed out.

"That bastard in Grand Cayman needs to be taught a lesson," Flores said, his eyes losing any hint of amusement. "He is not in control of this game."

"Just so you know," Butty replied, "killing me won't teach Gene Gould anything. Might inconvenience him for a minute, but he won't care if I live or die."

Flores shook his head. "Gould is nothing. Rosewater is the son-of-a-bitch I'd like to get my hands on."

"He'll care even less about me," Butty scoffed.

"No matter," Flores said with another wave of his hand. "If I keep shooting his boat captains, he'll get the message. Besides, you want to die anyway, so I'll oblige you."

"I don't *want* to die," Butty rebutted. "I just don't see another way around it."

Flores looked at Butty and frowned. "I've met men who have taken the worst torture you can imagine, because they felt so strongly about their principles. Men die often in this part of the world defending their beliefs and their leaders. But I've never come across a man willing to be shot because he doesn't have a better idea."

"Doesn't sound too smart when you say it like that," Butty admitted.

"Get up. Let's go," the officer ordered, and opened the door.

Butty stood and walked to the door.

"This is a shame," Flores added, guiding Butty into the hallway. "You seem like a useful man."

"I used to be a Royal Navy diver," Butty said, not knowing why he'd brought it up. Perhaps because he'd once felt somewhat useful back in those days.

"That looks like difficult work," Flores said, leading the way with the guard falling in step behind them.

"Fumbling around in the muck and darkness most of the time," Butty replied. "But I learned to weld underwater, plant explosives, and remove them. That's useful, I'd say."

Flores went up a flight of old concrete steps and outside into what was little more than a broad alleyway. At one end, a set of five posts stood before a wall which was peppered with bullet holes and stained with blood splatter. Butty's knees felt weak and he took a half stumble before regaining his footing. The time had come. He was about to die.

"So this is it?" he said, his voice wavering.

"This is it," Flores said. "Your part is easy. You just stand there and die."

"I expect I'll manage that," Butty breathed.

"Captain?!" came Jesus's voice from a building nearby.

Butty saw the knuckles of several hands clutching window bars but the angle was too acute for the men to see each other.

"It's important our message is delivered," Flores said dispassionately. "I won't force them to watch, but they must witness your punishment."

Five soldiers arrived in the alleyway, rifles in hand, and Flores pointed to the centre post.

"Should I bind you?" he asked. "Blindfold?"

Butty walked to the post and turned around. He wasn't completely convinced his legs would hold him up, but tying him and covering his eyes would just delay the proceedings and he wanted it to be over with. The more time he had, the more he'd think, and the time for thinking had passed. A brilliant scheme to dodge the drug dealers and runaway with Lucia was useless to him now.

"Be safe, lads," he called out.

"May God have mercy on your soul," Jesus called back.

Flores quickly gave the five soldiers his instructions, before they raised their weapons, and Butty closed his eyes and pictured Lucia.

Flores yelled, "fire", and gunshots echoed around the alleyway.

Jesus heard his captain's body slump to the ground with a thud.

34

AJ rode one of the little buses from George Town to West Bay. By the time she stepped to the kerb opposite Foster's market near her cottage, she'd made three new friends, one of whom was a Cayman brown hound a little smaller than Coop. She treated herself to a coffee-flavoured energy drink and a sticky bun for lunch, stopping in the grocery shop instead of Heritage Kitchen as she was in a hurry. Collecting her van from the dock was the smarter move, but she felt like taking a ride, so she made the five-minute walk down Boggy Sand Road to her cottage, where she put her protective motorcycle gear on.

Letting the Ducati Multistrada warm up for a few minutes, AJ went back in the house and found a window cleaner spray bottle to clean the bugs from her visor. Apparently she'd been remiss in her post-ride duties recently. She paused in the kitchen and looked around. Her home appeared the same, but different. Every personal item belonging to Jackson was gone. Just like that, it felt like random words were missing from the pages of her life. Holes in the fabric of her existence.

Her breath caught and AJ hurried to the wardrobe and found her drinks bladder backpack. Opening the fridge, she poured ice water from a jug into the bladder, trying her best not to spill it, despite her shaking hands. She closed the fridge door and faced the array of photos held in place by colourful magnets. Two pictures were missing. *What did that mean?* A surge of anger surpassed her gut-wrenching sadness. It meant he had taken a few photos with him when he'd walked out of her life, that was all. Gone was gone, and trying to find the man's motivation and reasons were completely pointless.

AJ slung the drinks bag over her back, fastening the chest strap and tucking the drinks tube into its clip on the harness. Returning to the Ducati, she affixed her mobile to the holder on the handle-bars and opened the map app where she'd plugged in the location Suzy had texted her for Cuda Crestwell's home. She didn't have an address, but "teal green house next door to the grocer's" was enough to get her close.

Leaning the motorcycle against her hip, AJ steered it through the gate and on to Boggy Sand Road. She put the side stand down then hopped on, only able to touch the ground on one side at a time. With practised skill, she tilted the bike, taking the weight on her right foot, kicked the stand with her left heel to swing it out of the way, then dropped it in gear and pulled away, heading for the north side of the island.

Midday on Sunday meant the traffic wasn't too heavy through George Town, and by the time she left the dual carriageway and neared Bodden Town, AJ began to enjoy being out on the bike. For years there'd been talk of building a road on the east coast of the North Sound, linking the capital with Rum Point, but it had never happened. The wetlands between the two created a construction nightmare, as well as a serious environmental problem, disturbing or removing acres of precious mangroves. So the trip remained a ride along three-quarters of the southern shore of the island to Frank Sound Road, which took her straight north into Old Man Bay on the north coast. The little village of North Side was only a few miles west from there.

Arriving, AJ pulled into the gravel car park of the grocery store, which was closed on Sunday. The teal-painted house to the left was impossible to miss. It wasn't large, just a block-built single-storey, typical of local Caymanians' homes, but the teal was eye catching. She put the stand down on the Ducati, sat her helmet over one of the mirrors, and slipped her gloves and jacket off. The vented, protective gear was cool enough with the wind rushing over her, but she was soon sweating once she'd come to a stop.

The teal house appeared quiet, but the front door was open and net curtains fluttered behind the open windows. AJ walked up the front yard and knocked on the door.

"Hello? Anyone home?"

"Doubt it," came a gruff voice from the shadows inside. "What you want?"

AJ could smell cigarette smoke from inside, despite the wind coming from behind her off the water. It wasn't simply the odour of a currently lit cigarette, but the musky aroma embedded in the house from decades of constant participation in the habit. She turned her head to capture more of the fresh air from behind.

"Are you Cuda?" AJ asked.

"Doubt it," the voice repeated.

"Suzy Soto suggested I speak with you," AJ said, pressing on and hoping Suzy's name would help. Most men who'd been around back in the day seemed to instantly warm to the mention of the pretty lady.

"'Bout what?"

"I found a picture of you. I think it's from the seventies. I had a few questions about that time."

There was no answer, but she heard movement, then shuffling feet across the hardwood floor. A thin, old man appeared in the doorway and swung the screen door open. Cuda squinted past the smoke wafting from the cigarette held between his lips and looked her up and down. Frowning as he caught her armoured textile trousers and leather boots. She handed him the picture.

"Curly," he said, taking it from her.

"Yes, we were chatting with him yesterday."

"He give you dis?"

AJ wondered quite what to say and how to approach their situation with the old Caymanian.

"It was his, yes," she finally said.

"What you wanna know?" he asked impatiently.

"Is there somewhere we could sit down and talk?" AJ asked. "In the shade outside perhaps," she quickly added, not wanting to set foot in the home for fear of destroying her lungs.

Cuda waved a hand at two plastic chairs under the window, and he started that way, letting the screen door crash closed behind him. His bandy legs moved him along faster than AJ had expected, but he paused before sitting down. He exhaled a stream of smoke and threw the butt into a bucket near the chairs.

"Start askin'," he said and had obviously decided his commitment to sitting would depend on the subject matter.

"Do you recall ever meeting the captain of the *Oro Verde*?" AJ asked, figuring she had to get to the point sooner or later.

His eyes narrowed, wrinkles gathering on his forehead like furrows in a ploughed field.

"Why?" he asked, his dark eyes searching her face.

"His grandson is here on the island and we're trying to find out any information about the man as Andy never met his grandad."

Cuda didn't sit. "Crew killed him. Threw him over da side. Dat da story I heard."

"We know that's not true, sir," AJ said, keeping a pleasant tone. "Curly met him. Raymond Butterworth was his name."

Cuda shook his head. "I don't know nuttin' about any of dat."

"I see. I guess Curly must have been mistaken then," AJ said, feeling a touch guilty for lying. "He said you knew everything that happened on the island back then."

The old man's brow tensed even more and he glared at AJ. "Damn right."

He finally let himself drop into the plastic chair, and foraged around in his trouser pocket, pulling out a pack of cigarettes. He shook one out and lit it with an old Bic. AJ scurried over and sat next to him, glad the wind was carrying the smoke up and over the house.

"So what can you tell me about the *Oro Verde* when it first arrived?"

Cuda softly shook his head and his jaw twitched. AJ waited while the old man decided what he was willing to share. *Or maybe he simply couldn't remember?*

"Dat captain guy, he were around for a bit, but a short bit, mind you." He took a long draw on his cigarette and eyed AJ as he let out a long stream of smoke through his nose. "You won't find nuttin' about him on dis island. Don't know where da man go, but he left. Never did see him no more."

"He was only here the once? When the *Oro Verde* was abandoned?"

"Didn't say dat," Cuda grunted, then went back to his cigarette.

AJ waited. She sensed he had plenty more to tell, just like Curly, but for some reason they were both reluctant to talk. Or scared.

"He here twice, best I know. When da ship left over da north side, den one more time. Dat were on anudder ship."

"Another ship?" AJ blurted, sitting forward in her chair. "What ship?"

Cuda shrugged his shoulders. "Don't recall da name. Stopped by here one, maybe two nights, den leave. Last I see da man."

At least he's admitting to meeting the captain, AJ thought, and wondered what to ask next. She wasn't sure where she could go to find out the name of a ship that dropped by the island sometime back in 1976. She doubted immigration or the harbour kept records from that far back.

"Did you speak with the captain? Was he a nice man?"

AJ thought she detected a slight grin on the old man's face, but if he did, it disappeared quickly, leaving her unsure.

"Never say a word to da man. But he seem nice enough. Best I recall."

"And you've no idea the name of the second ship he captained?"

Cuda shook his head. "Sure don't."

"What about the man he met here on the island?" AJ asked. "Do you remember who that was?"

Cuda's eyes narrowed once more. "Who you mean?"

"Well, we know he met with someone over at the old Seaview Hotel. You remember the hotel, right?"

"Course I do," he snapped back.

"Who was the man he met there?"

"I don't know what you talkin' 'bout," Cuda said, looking towards the road and taking a long draw on his cigarette.

"Does the name Rosewater mean anything to you, then?"

Cuda's jaw clenched and he threw the cigarette into the bucket. "I don't know anyting more to tell you, young lady. It's time you best be leavin'"

He stood and began walking towards the house.

"Who will I find down the road here at 2112 Rum Point Drive, Mr Crestwell?" AJ asked, following him.

Cuda turned and looked like he was about to yell at her, but stopped himself. He licked his lips and took a few breaths.

"You and your friend, da captain's grandson, oughta go looking elsewhere for your answers. Ain't nuttin' to be learned around here." He stepped inside the house, shoving the screen door open, then paused, turning his head. "Best I see you headin' dat way when you leave, girl," he added, nodding east, before letting the screen door slap closed behind him.

East was home. West was the address that had made the old man run for his house. AJ hurried to her motorcycle and geared up. Pulling out of the gravel car park, she turned left. Heading west.

35

AJ rode slowly along Rum Point Drive, taking her time covering the four miles to the house on the water at 2112. The name Rosewater hung in her mind and she couldn't shake the idea that Andy's grandfather was somehow involved. *Perhaps they were one and the same?* Curly had uttered the name with what he may well have thought was his dying breath, and Cuda Crestwell had abruptly ended their conversation at the mere mention of Rosewater. Raymond Butterworth had undoubtedly been involved in drug trafficking to some degree, so was it a stretch to imagine him involved with the CIA as well? Perhaps even Manuel Noriega? It all felt too far fetched to be true, but as she parked her motorcycle by the side of the road, AJ instinctively knew the home held answers.

A three-foot-high white wall lined the property with an ornate two-piece iron gate protecting the driveway. Stripping out of her helmet, jacket, and gloves, AJ shoved her mobile in her pocket, then checked the gate and found it latched but not locked. On the wall was an electronic buzzer or bell of some description, but she ignored it and opened the gate, slipped through, then latched it again behind her. Hoping a guard dog wasn't about to fly around the house and rip her to shreds, she boldly walked the concrete driveway and arrived at the old and slightly weathered front door.

The house appeared large, and was probably considered modern when it was built, which she guessed to be fifty years ago. It was stucco-covered concrete block with dark wood siding accents and hefty beams extending from the structure to create covered areas. Two vehicles were parked in front, a silver BMW and a white minivan with an odd-looking bodywork extension below the side. AJ rapped on the door, and waited.

Andy stood behind the one-way glass and stared at the five men before him. Detective Whittaker pressed a button and talked into a microphone.

"Starting with number one, I want each of you to say 'You're not welcome here'. One at a time, please. Go ahead, number one."

The man on the left of the line-up, holding a card with the number one written on it in large black print, spoke the words as instructed. Each man did the same in turn.

"Thank you," Whittaker said into the mic, then stepped back and turned to Andy. "No rush. Take your time."

Nora lingered in the back of the observation room. She hadn't got a good look at the man she'd chased after the assault on Andy and AJ, but she knew which one was the Haitian national they'd brought in. His name was Jeppe Etienne.

"Could they all speak again?" Andy asked.

Whittaker nodded and instructed the line-up to repeat the process, which they did.

"I believe it was number four," Andy said.

"Okay," Whittaker responded. "How confident would you say you are about that, Mr Butterworth?"

Andy sucked air between his teeth and looked at Nora, then back at the detective.

"I wouldn't say I'm certain," he admitted. "I was more certain until he spoke, to be honest. I remember his voice being higher pitched than he sounded here, but it was all a bit crazy as he was attacking me at the time."

"Sir," Nora said, stepping forward. "End the line-up and clear the room. I have an idea."

"We can't coerce or influence the identification, Constable Sommer," Whittaker responded.

"I understand that, sir," Nora replied. "Just give me a minute and listen to number four's voice."

Whittaker thought for a moment. "Okay. I think I understand what you're doing. But tread carefully."

"Yes, sir," she said, already bolting out the door.

Whittaker announced over the microphone that the men could hand their number card to the constable at the door, and thanked them for their time. Nora appeared and pulled number four and number five aside, keeping them in the room.

"What's happening?" number five asked her in heavily accented English.

"I'm not sure," Nora replied. "But the line-up is over. Looks like you're all free to go."

Number four's shoulders pulled back a little and he shifted his weight from one foot to the other. He handed Nora his number card, which she took.

"Give us just a minute," she said, looking past the two men to the door. "It's just procedure bullshit. They don't want all five of you passing by the desk and signing out at the same time. Won't be long."

The constable at the door looked at her like she was crazy, but she ignored him and the two suspects had their backs to the door so they didn't see his confusion.

"I got somewhere to be," number five said.

"Don't we all," Nora responded. "I'm sure he does too, right?" she added, nodding at number four.

"I'm in no rush," he said calmly, in his natural voice. "Happy dis mess over wit."

There was a brief pause, then Whittaker's voice came over the speakers, "Hold number four."

The man whipped around and looked at the glass, then back at Nora. "What the hell?"

"Dumb arse," she muttered, then pointed to the door. "You can go," she told number five who scurried out of the room."

Nora slipped her handcuffs on the right wrist of Jeppe Etienne, spun him around, and locked the other cuff to his left wrist. The man let out a stream of expletives in his native tongue. She pushed him through the door and down the hall to the lobby area, where she was about to steer him into another hallway when he stopped. An older couple were being led by a detective towards the hallway she was about to enter. The husband and wife both looked up and their faces showed their surprise in seeing the Haitian in handcuffs. The three all locked eyes as the couple were guided past.

Nora waited a beat then pushed her suspect down the same hallway, finding an empty interview room, one door beyond where the couple were being seated.

"I wanna make a deal," Etienne said as she sat him down at the table.

"I bet you do," Nora muttered.

"Get da detective in here, now. I know tings."

"You know you're being deported," she replied unsympathetically.

"I tell you tings," Etienne insisted. "But I get a deal, den I talk."

Nora continued acting uninterested, waiting on Detective Whittaker, who arrived after a few minutes. He closed the door, explained to the suspect that the interview would be recorded, and took a seat alongside Nora.

"Jeppe Etienne, you're under arrest for assault. We'll be adding multiple other charges to the list for dangerous driving, attempted murder with a vehicle, and breaking and entering and attempted murder," Whittaker began.

"You offer me a deal," Etienne interrupted. "I tell you tings. I know tings you want to know."

"Doesn't work that way," Mr Etienne. "If you have information which will assist us in a case, we will certainly take your cooperation into consideration. But we don't offer *deals* without knowing what you're giving us. So why don't we start with the old man who hired you to intimidate Andy Butterworth and attack Mr Roper?"

The Haitian shook his head. "I don't know 'bout dat."

"You've been IDed by two people as being one of the two men who attacked a local woman and a visitor in a car park near Rackam's yesterday evening. We're waiting for the forensics report which will tie you to the attempted murder of Curly Roper. Your accomplice is also in custody and has been quite helpful," Whittaker said.

Etienne sat back and appeared to be considering his options.

"If you have nothing for us, then Constable Sommer will see you to your cell. We have all we need to charge you, which we've done, so this is your opportunity to help your own case," Whittaker pressed, and began rising from his seat.

"Da people wit da boat," the man blurted. "I give you information on dem. Dis get me a deal."

Nora leaned over and whispered to the detective, who was doing a good job of not showing his confusion.

"An older couple just brought in for questioning, sir. We saw them in the reception area. He knew them."

Whittaker couldn't hide his surprise, and looked up at Etienne. "You can tell us something about the Pinks and their boat?"

The front door opened and a woman in her fifties or perhaps sixties glared at AJ, then looked past her down her driveway towards the gate.

"You're trespassing," she said in the scratchy tone of a long-time smoker.

"I apologise for intruding, but I was looking for someone," AJ replied with a smile.

"They're not here and you need to leave," the woman retorted.

AJ laughed, somewhat nervously. "I didn't tell you who."

"And I don't care. Leave, or I'm calling the police."

The woman began swinging the door closed but AJ looked beyond her into the house. She could see all the way to the Caribbean Sea through tall windows in the living room. Her hand shot out and stopped the door from closing. As she did, a wheelchair rolled into view for a moment, an old man staring at the intruder by his front door. He quickly wheeled himself backwards.

"Who lives here?" AJ asked, fighting to keep the door from being closed on her.

"None of your damned business," the woman gasped, putting all her effort into the door, but AJ was too strong for the older woman.

"Just tell me and I'll leave."

"I'm calling the police," the woman grunted.

"Go ahead," AJ retorted. "Or ask your husband in there to do it."

"Let her in!" came a man's voice from inside, but the woman didn't relent.

"I said, let her in!" he shouted again, and the woman finally stopped shoving.

"Damn it," she cursed. "Make up your mind already."

The woman stepped back and AJ went inside. The man was now in full view. He was probably in his 80s with thinning grey hair. His legs appeared thin beneath his trousers but his torso and upper body were in good shape for his age. The minivan out front made sense to her now – the odd bodywork was part of the wheelchair access system.

"Hello, sir," she said, moving closer and removing the old photograph from the pocket of her armoured motorcycle trousers. "This is what brought me here." She handed him the picture.

The man took a cursory glance and handed it back. "You're probably looking for the man who used to own the land. I bought it from him and built this house."

AJ felt stupid. *Of course. Why did she think the same person still lived there?*

"Do you recall his name?"

"Gould," he replied. "Sold it to me in the late 80s when he left the island."

AJ was deflated as well as embarrassed by her over-eagerness and assumptions.

"May I ask your name, sir?"

"Ford. Ford Redgrave. The door wrestler is my wife, Gloria."

AJ looked over at the woman, who glared back, her cheeks flushed.

"Do you know what happened to Mr Gould?" AJ asked, turning her attention back to the man.

He shook his head. "Not a clue. Never met him. I'm sorry you came all this way for nothing, miss, and I hope you understand we're private people, so when a stranger shows up unannounced, we're understandably cautious."

"I apologise, Mr Redgrave. And to you, Mrs Redgrave," AJ said, noting the woman's face still hadn't softened a bit. "I should have buzzed from the gate. Things have been going a little loopy lately, so I went all Scooby-Doo there for a moment."

The man laughed and wheeled himself towards the door. "I promise I'm not wearing a rubber mask," he joked.

AJ walked with him, but stopped in surprise when her mobile rang in her pocket. Retrieving it she saw it was Nora calling.

"Thank you for your time, and sorry again for disturbing your afternoon," she said to the Redgraves, and answered the call as she stepped outside. "Hey, Nora."

"That address we found," her friend said, getting straight to the point as usual. "We've found a connection."

"I'm here now," AJ replied. "What connection? It's a different owner from the bloke who originally had the land."

"Old man in a wheelchair?" Nora asked.

"Well, yeah. But he seems harmless enough. His missus is a bit nuts, mind you," AJ replied, dropping to a whisper.

"You need to leave," Nora urged. "We think that might be the guy who hired the thugs to attack you and Andy, and have Curly whacked."

"Bloody hell," AJ muttered, and turned around to look at the house she'd just left.

Standing four feet away was Gloria Redgrave. She held a gun in her hand, aimed at AJ.

"Give me the phone," she hissed, and AJ had no choice but to comply.

36

AJ had never met a gun she liked. This wasn't the first time she'd had one pointed at her, but it was just as jarring and unnerving as it had been on the previous occasions.

"Get inside," Gloria ordered. "Hurry up."

The woman scanned the road for passers-by and neighbours as AJ moved around her and pushed the front door open. Ford Redgrave was back in the living room and spun his chair around upon hearing the door close behind his wife. His face registered confusion before morphing slowly into anger.

"What on earth are you doing, Gloria? Is that my gun?"

Gloria shoved AJ towards him until they were in the sparsely furnished living room overlooking the turquoise ocean. AJ wished she was currently under the water in her happy place, doing what she did every day, instead of standing in a stranger's house with a gun trained on her. She berated herself for coming over here on a wild hunch, alone.

"Gloria?" Ford barked. "Have you gone mad?"

"Oh shut up, you senile old fool," she snapped back, waving the gun between AJ and her husband. "None of this would be happening if you hadn't got all worked up over nothing. Couldn't just let it be, could you?"

AJ guessed he wasn't used to her standing her ground, as his face registered shock once more.

"Stop waving the damn gun around," he managed, holding his hands in front of him as the barrel swung in his direction. "That's loaded! You're going to shoot someone if you're not careful."

"Damn right," she muttered, looking around the room as though she were searching for something. "Over here," Gloria ordered, tugging on AJ's arm until her captive stood about six feet from Ford. "Stay right there."

"What are you doing?" AJ asked, trying to judge whether she'd be able to knock the gun from the woman's hand.

She figured Nora would have disarmed Gloria and had the pair in handcuffs by now, but AJ wasn't as bold as her friend. Or reckless. There were a million ways a counter move could go wrong and bullets moved much faster than she could dodge. She was also confused by the situation. Ford and Gloria did not appear to be on the same page at all. Yet Nora had said the old man could be behind the assault and the attack on Curly.

"The police are on their way here," AJ added. "If you put the gun away they'll probably be lenient on you as I was trespassing after all."

If Gloria heard anything AJ had said, she gave no indication. The woman was completely absorbed in whatever was churning through her mind, and suddenly it all became clear to AJ... Just as Gloria raised her arm and pulled the trigger.

The report was both deafening and disorientating, causing AJ to step away from the noise, which she instantly realised was a mistake. She was now out of reach of the shooter and the weapon — which was waving around as the woman tried to aim it again.

"Gloria! Damn you, woman!" Ford raged, the first bullet having narrowly missed him and sent stuffing wafting through the air from the sofa.

AJ lunged at Gloria's outstretched arm, but the gun fired again a split second before AJ bashed the woman's arm to the side. Ford let out a fierce groan but AJ couldn't see him as she tumbled to the hard tiled floor, taking Gloria down with her. The gun skittered towards the tall windows and AJ felt Gloria scramble after it. Grabbing a fistful of blouse, AJ halted the woman's progress, then dragged her back and pinned her to the floor with a knee.

Gloria's eyes glared like a trapped animal and she swung her arm, smacking AJ across the side of the face with an open palm. Her cheek stung and AJ raised her elbow to deflect the second slap.

"Stop it, you bloody nutter!" AJ yelped, but the woman kept flailing both arms, scratching, clawing, and slapping at AJ's face.

"Get off me!" Gloria screamed almost incoherently. "You don't know what it's like living with that son-of-a-bitch!"

"Calm down, lady," AJ said, keeping the blows at bay with her arms.

"I can't take it anymore! He's lost his mind!" Gloria screeched.

"He has?" AJ gasped in amazement, then punched the woman square on the nose, feeling cartilage give way beneath her knuckles.

Blood shot from Gloria's nostrils and a red split appeared across the bridge of her nose. She instantly stopped fighting, her hands clutching her bleeding face. AJ couldn't believe she'd just punched a woman who was probably her own mother's age, but it had been a reflex in self-defence.

From near the window, AJ heard a noise and looked up. Ford was leaning out of the side of his wheelchair and for a moment AJ thought he was having a seizure. A blossom of blood covered his right shoulder and he leaned over the left side of his wheelchair, struggling and twitching.

"Sir, let me help…" AJ began, pushing herself up from the floor.

A step closer and she quickly realised what he was doing. AJ lunged again, this time slamming into the injured right shoulder of the old man, and ramming him and his chair into the tall glass. How it didn't break, she had no idea, as her momentum carried her into the window herself, where she bounced off and dropped to the floor. Ford quickly recovered and reached once more, so AJ grabbed the side of his wheelchair and pulled with all her might, toppling it towards her, spilling the crippled man out onto his living room tiles.

Landing hard on his wounded shoulder, Ford let out a scream of pain, and AJ kicked and shoved the chair from on top of her legs. A snarl from behind made her look up in time to see the enraged and bloodied face of Gloria wielding a statue of what appeared to be a mermaid. Unable to tell who the intended victim was, AJ rolled right as the bronze mermaid flew down, glancing off the side of her husband's head and smashing against the wheelchair.

"Gloria!" he screamed, clutching his scalp with one hand and defending himself with the other as she drew back for another attack.

"You selfish, evil bastard!" she babbled, her voice sounding nasal. "You've been an ass to live with since you fell off that stupid ladder and broke your back! I wish you'd smashed your head and got it over with!"

With blood covering the front of her blouse and spittle flying from her lips as she cursed the man, Gloria staggered around, struggling to balance the hefty weight of the now battered statue. AJ plucked a book from the end table by the sofa and launched it at Gloria, causing the woman to step backwards as the Tricia O'Malley hardback caught her on the left cheek.

AJ couldn't believe how her door-wrestling episode just a few minutes before had escalated into a gun-toting, club-wielding, all-out war zone, but she had to end it and end it now. While Gloria faltered, holding one hand to her face, her other dropping to her side under the mass of the mermaid, AJ grabbed Ford's shirt and dragged him and his wheelchair clear of the windows, revealing the gun he'd been trying to retrieve. She stumbled over him and picked up the weapon, hearing a banshee-like war cry from behind her.

The glass all around AJ shattered into a million pieces which hung in the air for a millisecond before dropping to the floor like raindrops in a tropical downpour. The mermaid statue bounced across the patio with Gloria falling out of the house through the opening once occupied by a floor-to-ceiling window.

"Everybody stop!" AJ yelled, and quiet descended over the house as the tinkling of glass pebbles died down.

"Bloody hell, people," she gasped, out of breath, holding the gun by her side.

"You saw!" Ford shouted. "That crazy woman tried to kill me!"

The old man was sprawled across the tile floor with blood covering his shirt and smearing the porcelain. His legs lay awkwardly wrapped over each other and he held a hand to his wound. His face looked deathly pale. Gloria groaned and rolled to her side, looking like she'd used her face to break the glass window. Tiny red marks dotted every piece of exposed skin where she'd landed on the pebbles of glass.

"I think we're both lucky she's a bloody awful aim," AJ said. "She couldn't shoot you properly, and she missed us both with your mermaid statue."

AJ found her mobile on the floor where Gloria had dropped it, the armoured knee of her motorcycle trousers clunking as she knelt to pick it up. She was glad she'd been wearing her gear as the protective inserts had helped break her fall to the hard floor in the struggle. She called Nora's phone and waited for her friend to answer.

"Hey AJ. Did you leave the house?"

"No, I was delayed a bit," she replied, surveying the bloody, moaning bodies amongst the carnage. "You'd better hurry up and get here. It all went a bit pear shaped."

"What happened?" Nora asked, and AJ could hear the wind and tyre noise from her Jeep in the background.

"I'll have to explain when you get here. But can you call for an ambulance, please? There are casualties."

AJ noticed Gloria crawling slowly closer to the mermaid statue on the patio. "Oi!" she shouted. "Stop that, Mrs Redgrave!"

The woman slumped in defeat and AJ heard Nora asking her something on the phone. "Hey, I gotta go. These two won't stay still. But get here as fast as you can, and don't forget the ambulance, okay?"

She didn't wait for her friend's reply and hung up. Stepping through the broken window, she picked up the mermaid statue.

"You wanker," she muttered, looking at Gloria. "You tried to bash me over the head with a scale version of Amphitrite by Simon Morris. He's a friend of mine! That would have been the headline of all headlines. *Mermaid Divers' AJ Bailey bludgeoned to death by mate's mermaid.*"

37

It took all afternoon to walk Whittaker through each step of the incident at the house, give her official statement, and drink too many cups of lousy police station coffee while she waited. When the detective finally told her she was free to go, AJ met Nora and Andy in the lobby, and they headed for the hospital to check on Curly.

"So, let me get this straight," AJ said after Nora had given her a typically brief version of the events. "The Haitian guy, Etienne, wouldn't tattle on whoever the 'old man' was, but he admitted to being the one who rigged the Pinks' yacht to sink?"

"*Ja*," Nora agreed.

"And Ford Redgrave was the guy who set the Pinks up with Etienne?"

"*Ja.*"

"And how did the Pinks know Redgrave?"

"They met him in the bar at Rum Point, but they didn't know his name," Nora explained impatiently.

"But they told you they saw him using the ramp thingy to get in his minivan, and you tracked it down through the Department of Vehicle and Drivers' Licensing records?"

"*Ja*. There was a modified for wheelchair ramp white minivan registered to Redgrave at 2112 Rum Point Drive."

"And that's when you called me?"

"*Ja*."

AJ thought it all over for a minute.

"But we're no closer to understanding why Etienne and his mate were harassing Andy, or why Redgrave would have put them up to it," AJ complained.

"Technically, we have nothing to say it was Redgrave who did," Andy said, leaning forward from the back seat. "The Jamaican guy said Etienne had been paid by an *old man*, but there's no evidence to prove that the *old man* he mentioned was Redgrave."

"So he's going to walk?" AJ blurted.

"Roll, actually," Nora pointed out.

"What about Gloria?" AJ asked. "She was spitting mad at her husband. I mean she was trying to kill the bloke and make it look like it was me. She rambled on about him overreacting. She hasn't spilled the beans on him?"

"She hasn't said a word," Nora replied. "I think she got scared when she realised her husband would live."

"Maybe she'll be more talkative when it hits home she's being charged with two counts of attempted murder," AJ said.

"One count," Nora corrected.

"Two bloody counts!" AJ quickly responded. "She planned to smack me over the noggin with the statue to make it look like she'd tried to stop me after I'd shot her old man."

"We can't charge her with what you think she was going to do," Nora said.

"I don't think it, I bloody well know it," AJ mumbled. "Well, bugger," she continued, cursing under her breath. "I really thought we were on to Rosewater. You should have seen how Cuda Crestwell took off when I mentioned that name."

"You and Reg were right about the *Tickled Pink* being an insurance job, though," Nora said. "We've solved that case."

"I suppose that's good, but not nearly as cool as tracking down a CIA drug ring from the 70s."

Nora parked the Jeep and the three walked into the emergency room of the hospital. AJ asked after Curly at the reception desk, then returned to the others.

"We should have called. They still have him sedated, and he's been moved to a regular hospital bed," she told them, and looked down the hallway. "I hope they've got Gloria Redgrave handcuffed to the bed. That woman's nutty as a fruit cake."

"I think she's already been patched up and is back at the station," Nora replied as AJ's mobile rang.

"Hey, Reg," she answered.

"Where are you?" Reg asked.

"The hospital. We came by to check on Curly, but they still have him knocked out. Why? What else has gone wrong?"

"Andy with you?"

"Yeah. Why, Reg? You're being all cloak and dagger."

"Stay where you are, all right?" Reg replied. "I'll be there in ten minutes."

AJ was about to complain, but the line went dead. She looked at the other two.

"That was a bit weird. Reg wants us to stay here. He's on his way."

They raided the snack machine, AJ checked her emails to see what she'd missed, and fifteen minutes after Reg had called, Detective Whittaker walked through the sliding doors into the emergency room reception area.

"Hello, everyone," he greeted them. "Any idea what this is about?"

AJ shook her head and Nora shrugged her shoulders.

"His Lordship told us wait here," AJ said. "Did he call you too?"

"If His Lordship is Reg," Whittaker replied with a grin, "then yes."

"Here he is," Andy said, pointing to the entryway, where the doors parted.

Reg casually strolled in alongside another man. His companion was older, but tall, lean and moving with a fitness belying his age. His skin was deeply tanned and his face weathered from years in the sun.

"I have someone you ought to meet," Reg said, looking at Andy. "He's a bloke I served with in the Royal Navy, back when I was a lad."

Andy looked at them both with a puzzled expression. "At the same time as my grandfather?" he asked.

"I think I might *be* your grandfather," the old man said, his eyes a mixture of joy and nervous anticipation.

"Blimey," AJ muttered, and stepped back to let Andy come forward.

Andy took a step and paused. "I'm not sure…" was all he managed to say.

"Yeah," the old man nodded. "I expect you have a few questions, mate."

Andy looked at Reg. "Are you sure it's him?"

Reg laughed. "Yeah, Andy. I'm sure. I recognised him, even after all these years, but I quizzed him pretty good about the old days too. It's him."

Andy looked at his grandfather in amazement and extended a hand. "It's very nice to meet you grandad."

Butty Butterworth shook his head and clasped Andy's hand. "You've no idea what this means to me, lad. I never got to spend a moment with your dad, so I never dreamed this would be possible."

"Where have you been?" AJ couldn't stop herself from asking. "Everyone believed you were… you know…"

"Dead?" Butty finished for her.

"Well, yeah."

"That was the idea, young lady," Butty replied. "But I don't think it matters anymore."

"Roy," Reg said, addressing Detective Whittaker. "We should take care of a little business, which won't be long, then we can let these two go somewhere to catch up."

"Certainly," Whittaker replied. "And what business is this we're taking care of?"

Reg led Butty and Whittaker down the hall until he found the room where Ford Redgrave lay in bed, tethered to an IV and wrapped in bandages around his shoulder. His weary eyes tried to focus as they entered the room, but the pain meds in his system left him staring at them in confusion.

"Hello, Gene," Butty said, and the man in the bed grunted.

"Who's that?" the patient mumbled barely loud enough to be heard.

"Butty Butterworth. James Lofton. Captain of the *Oro Verde*. Take your pick."

"Bullshit," the man muttered. "You're dead."

Butty scoffed. "Been mighty close more than a few times, but still ticking along, no thanks to you."

"You called him Gene?" Whittaker questioned. "This man is Ford Redgrave according to his identification."

Butty nodded. "I expect that's his real name, but he went by Gene Gould back when he worked for the CIA."

"That's who this guy said he bought the land from," AJ interjected from behind them. "He sold it to himself under a different name."

"Probably after the Iran-Contra nonsense when all the CIA spooks involved went scurrying away like cockroaches," Butty said, then thought for a moment, before laughing. "Ford Redgrave, you said?"

"That's right," Whittaker confirmed.

"Play on words, isn't it?" Butty said.

"I'm sorry, I don't follow," Whittaker admitted.

"Rosewater!" AJ blurted and Butty turned to her.

"How did you know that?"

"Red, rose, and ford, water," she said. "Play on words, like you said."

"But how do you even know the name Rosewater?"

"Crackin' good detective work," AJ replied with a grin.

"No..." Gould mumbled from the bed. "You can't know..."

"It was the radio call," Butty said, turning to the man in the bed. "You left the room when I spoke with Mr Rosewater. Came back afterwards. Always bothered me."

Gene Gould, whose real name was in fact Ford Redgrave, cursed incoherently and turned away.

AJ's mobile pinged and she finished setting up a BCD on a tank before pulling it from her pocket. Her heart skipped several beats and after a few moments she realised she was holding her breath. It was a text from Jackson. *What would it say?* Encouraging herself to breathe normally, she stared at the notification but didn't open the message. A string of expectations and dreads raced around her brain and made her feel nauseous.

"They're here," Thomas called down from the fly-bridge and AJ looked up to see Andy and his grandfather exiting the hire car.

She looked back at her mobile, opened the message with a shaky thumb, and slowly read the words.

'I feel half a person without you, but I was half myself not doing what I believed I should be doing. I truly wish we can find a way to make this work. I love you more than words could ever convey.'

AJ's eyes moved to the two men walking towards her down the pier. Andy was talking excitedly, and Butty had his hand on his grandson's shoulder, listening with a broad smile on his face. Two people who'd been held apart before they'd ever had a chance to be together, now united. *Was that the universe, or some higher power at work? Or simply the result of a billion tiny events, most unrelated, stacking in a way to bring them together? Who can know how every decision and action we take will affect what the future holds?*

Turning her attention back to her mobile, AJ let out a long, easy breath, exhausting the fear, anger, and pain, letting it drift into the breeze and be carried away. She typed one sentence, reread it three times to be sure, then hit send.

'I hope your path brings you the happiness you deserve.'

Hazel's Odyssey moved away from the dock in the soft morning light and glassy seas. Thomas steered the dive boat to deeper water before easing into the throttles and turning south. On the deck below, AJ leaned against the fly-bridge ladder and listened to Andy and his grandfather continue their conversation which had started over dinner the night before. The two men had much to catch up on.

"You worked for Manuel Noriega's lieutenant for how many years?" Andy asked, looking bleary eyed.

"Until Flores was arrested," Butty explained. "That was December 1989 when the Americans invaded Panama. They stormed Cárcel Modelo, the prison where Noriega kept anyone he didn't like, and freed Kurt Muse, an American spy who'd been caught. Flores ran but they caught up with him.

I'd been working for the lieutenant at the port ever since he faked my execution in exchange for me being his diver, captain, and anything else boat related he needed doing. All under the radar. Anyway, the Yanks invaded, but I kept working, waiting to see what would happen. Nothing really did. So I suppose I was free at that point, but it didn't feel like it."

"Did you think about returning to England?" Andy asked.

"Oh yes, I thought about it every day. Either England or Miami. The problem was, I'd been dead for fourteen years. They'd taken away my passports, and even if they hadn't, I was sure my name would flag the CIA and maybe Sal Herrera or Alfonso Pérez. I was stuck. In the mid-80s I discovered through a Miami newspaper that Lucia, my wife, had died and I assumed her family had taken in our child. There was no way they'd let me see the kid so I resigned myself to a life in Central America.

I married a Panamanian woman and eventually I managed to get a Panamanian passport under the name Butler Worth – that way I could still be Butty - but by then I had no reason to travel anywhere. Until now. And as I told you last night, it was my daughter who found you. She set up some internet notification thing that sent her anything which popped up related to my name. The news article in the paper here on the island triggered an alert, and I took the first flight I could get here."

The boat slowed, and AJ scrambled forward to tie them into the dive buoy. When she returned, Andy and Reg were helping Butty slip into a BCD.

"Everything feel okay?" Andy asked his grandfather.

"Feels light as a feather compared to the gear Reg and I used to put on," Butty joked.

AJ and Reg quickly put their own dive gear on and met the other two at the back of the Newton, where Thomas was keeping a steadying hand on Butty. AJ stepped into the water and then encouraged Butty to do the same. The seventy-five-year-old man didn't have to be asked twice, and after the group gathered on the surface at the mooring line, AJ gave the signal for them all to descend.

Just as his grandson had done a few days earlier, Butty's eyes got a little wider as he took his first look at the *Oro Verde*. A ship he'd last seen above the ocean, in 1976.

ACKNOWLEDGMENTS

My sincere thanks to:

My incredible wife Cheryl, for her unwavering support, love, and encouragement.

My family and friends for their patience and understanding.

The Cayman Crew:
My lovely friend of many years, Casey Keller.
My new friend, the incredibly talented photographer, Lisa Collins of Capture Cayman who provided the amazing cover shots for *The Oro Verde*.
Chris and Kate of Indigo Divers for sparking my curiosity about the ship and its story.
Suzy Soto for her wonderful input and help.
Ole Parker, Kent Eldermire, Peter Milburn, and Cathy Fox for their recollections of days gone by.

My editor Andrew Chapman at Prepare to Publish. I couldn't imagine placing AJ and Reg in anyone else's hands.
My advanced reader copy (ARC) group, whose input and feedback is invaluable. It is a pleasure working with all of you.

The Tropical Authors group for their magnificent support and collaboration. Check out the website for other great authors in the Sea Adventure genre.

Shearwater dive computers, whose products I proudly use. Reef Smart Guides whose maps and guidebooks I would be lost without – sometimes literally. My friends at Cayman Spirits for their amazing Seven Fathoms rum... which I'm convinced I could not live without!

Above all, I thank you, the readers: none of this happens without the choice you make to spend your precious time with AJ and her stories. I am truly in your debt.

LET'S STAY IN TOUCH!

To buy merchandise, find more info or join my Newsletter, visit my
website at
www.HarveyBooks.com

Visit Amazon.com for more books in the
AJ Bailey Adventure Series,
Nora Sommer Caribbean Suspense Series,
and collaborative works;
The Greene Wolfe Thriller Series
Tropical Authors Adventure Series

If you enjoyed this novel I'd be incredibly grateful if you'd consider
leaving a review on Amazon.com
Find eBook deals and follow me on BookBub.com

Catch my podcast, The Two Authors' Chat Show with co-host
Douglas Pratt.

Find more great authors in the genre at TropicalAuthors.com

ABOUT THE AUTHOR

A *USA Today* Bestselling author, Nicholas Harvey's life has been anything but ordinary. Race car driver, adventurer, divemaster, and since 2020, a full-time novelist. Raised in England, Nick has dual US and British citizenship and now lives wherever he and his amazing wife, Cheryl, park their motorhome, or an aeroplane takes them. Warm oceans and tall mountains are their favourite places.

For more information, visit his website at HarveyBooks.com.